CW01394489

FATAL
MOMENTS

FATAL
MOMENTS

A NOVEL BY
BRUCE HANNA

ANGUS
& ROBERTSON
PUBLISHERS

*Promotion of this title has been assisted
by the South Australian Government
through the Department for the Arts*

*All characters in this book are
entirely fictitious, and no reference
is intended to any living person.*

*Creative writing programme assisted by the
Literature Board of the Australia Council,
the Federal Government's arts funding
and advisory body.*

ANGUS & ROBERTSON PUBLISHERS

*Unit 4, Eden Park, 31 Waterloo Road,
North Ryde, NSW, Australia 2113, and
16 Golden Square, London W1R 4BN,
United Kingdom*

*First published in Australia
by Angus & Robertson Publishers in 1987*

Copyright © Bruce Hanna, 1987

*National Library of Australia
Cataloguing-in-publication data.*

*Hanna, Bruce, 1949–
  Fatal moments.*

  ISBN 0 207 15389 2.

  I. Title.

A823'.3

*Typeset in 11 pt English Times
Printed in Hong Kong*

Come to this fatal moment
when the veil of illusion is torn away,
only to leave deluded man
with the remorseful picture of his errors and vices,
do you not, my child, repent
of the many evils that human weakness
and frailty have led you to?

Marquis de Sade
Dialogue Between a Priest and a Dying Man

This secret ill which stalks the land
    Spreads death abroad on every hand.
The victim dies, a death unknown,
    From magic spear by magic thrown.

The Song of Evil
attrib. Djingali Tribe

CONTENTS

PROLOGUE

ONCE THERE WAS *a dreamtime. Then came the nightmare. The earth trembled with hoofbeats. There was only one black survivor, a boy who clung to a raft of slaughtered kinfolk floating down the creek among tangled streams of blood. A goanna with huge ancient eyes had stared at the human ark and the young voyager floating by.*

Once there had been many more goannas, but the farm dogs were ferocious. Once there were many eagles. Now the last eagle gazed down on the wrinkled landscape, the farm-infested foothills, and the higher hills where the cedar was hauled by enslaved bullocks along steep, rugged snigging trails. Among the ridges flowed the creek where the fighting had taken place.

The last eagle gazed down upon the rash of destruction eating away the land's green complexion. Gaunt ghosts of ring-barked trees marked the patchwork squares of shaved paddocks which had formed along with nests of settlement.

Kangaroos scooted, bounding across the wasted remains of the vanishing bushland. The scorching, blinding glare of the sun spread right across the sky, and the huge bird spread its wings and rose, a speck against the white brightness, its broadly fanned feather-tips flicking in the breeze. It peered under its wing down where unscathed, natural bush met the advancing wheel-ruts and fences. With each rain the soil decayed further, the running water flushed earth from the grasp of dead roots, the raw clay below was exposed. Now and again there would be a dry spell and then the bare earth would crack open. And in these wounds the seeds of alien plants took root, producing their strange thorns, fruits and flowers.

Stranger than all the animals and plants and tools of the

conquerors were their alien ways. They called the scene of the great slaughter Blood Gully. No other name fitted nearly as well, even though the blood had been washed away, the flesh had rotted and the bones had broken open. The township grew on its diet of sweat, cedar and scarred bushland.

After the massacre the lone survivor travelled far on his lonely feet. For months his belly was often empty and did not stop trembling, and for months his eyes were always wet. Only his voice dried up. As he grew, he grew ever deeper in mourning, and ever more filled with fermenting, poisonous hatred.

He grew on the scraps left by his own kind, a refugee among them, and they themselves refugees in their own land. In place after place he wandered disregarded, year after year, a fringe-dweller on the edge of pandemonium. The first of a new race of beggars.

Even among his own people he was a misfit. He could not speak, nor could he tolerate closeness. They gave him a name which was equivalent to "One of the Dead". He was unpredictable and violent. Everywhere he went there was trouble.

Then he was gone, just as he came, without warning. The old men said he had gone back to his country. And even if his people had all been killed as the white men said, then that was alright, they would still be there, waiting for him.

Soon after his return to the district of Blood Gully there occurred the first of the throat-slashings. But he was undisturbed by search parties, for he moved only at night. By day he slept in a burrow, like a wombat, with the entrance cleverly concealed. In his burrow he lived in the real world of his childhood. By night he became the master, and the conqueror became a monstrous child, sleeping with its belly exposed.

When the conqueror slept the world was safe. Then the survivor slunk out of his lair, creeping unseen, his very existence unobserved, to continue the war.

He would scan the skies, hoping to see the eagle.

Months passed. The eagle flew.

Now, back at the place of the massacre, he crouched for

hours, his face between his knees, buried in the dirt. He remembered it all. He remembered there had been more eagles. He felt the shooting bolts of fear in his body, heard the sound of loved voices pitched in every tone of terror and panic. He remembered the smell, and the stink as fresh as the earth in his mouth. He recalled clinging to the wet, slippery corpses of those who had loved him as a child. He remembered the goanna watching him from a tree. Now he could see the same tree in the shade. And the shadow of the same goanna was in the same place.

It was all the same. The stones were in place as they had always been. The running water made the same music it had always made. His blood ran with it and he entered another world.

He smiled for the first time in all the years since the massacre. Suddenly he felt his voice returning. He began to sing the children's song about the eagle.

In the far distance he could see the tiny mail coach moving along the thin, pale streak that wound through the bush into the hills. Behind the coach rose a plume of blinding dust.

The survivor settled into his underground lair, waiting for the night to bring him back to life. He dreamed feverishly. It was the season for vengeance. Now he could redeem the lost years of shame at having lived when all the others had died. The passion burning inside him, he was certain, was ripening.

Once there was a dreamtime. Then came the nightmare.

BOOK I

TORTURED HILLS

I

THE MAIL COACH tore along the track. At every turn it startled pink-and-grey waves of cockatoos, kangaroos, and even stray stock. The driver gave a lazy slash of the whip and drew the slender length of plaited leather round in an arc. As he did so he leaned instinctively with the lurching coach. Jangling chains and wrenching coachwork rang out. The driver let the whip fly; the crack as he flicked it echoed away. The wind cooled his faced and rasped at his lungs. His throat felt as dry as his leathery hands.

Beside the driver sat a wide-eyed man clinging to the coach with both hands, with his hat locked tightly between his knees and his grey hair flying. He was the Sydney hangman. There would be a big crowd in Blood Gully for his next performance.

Inside the coach sat the Blood Gully Police Inspector, Holman, beside his wife. Facing them sat a smiling stranger.

"Simple people, simple pleasures," the Inspector said. "The common folk love a good hanging."

"Really?" asked the stranger.

"Of course," explained Holman. "You couldn't get a bigger crowd than at a hanging in Blood Gully. And hangings are very much favoured as an entertainment."

"What is he to be hanged for?"

"He killed his own brother," replied the Inspector. "His own brother! You know, I really wonder about these people sometimes."

The coach trundled up and down the rises in the road. The woman passenger said nothing. The Inspector spoke of the Blood Gully murders, all alike in their gory execution. All the dead had been found with their throats slashed.

"At first no-one was unduly concerned," said the

3

Inspector. "One becomes accustomed to these occasional outbursts among the bush ruffians. But then the murderer struck for the third time in six months or so — right on the edge of town. This time he struck one of our chaps, a new constable. A promising chap too."

The male passenger raised both eyebrows.

"All killed the same way?" he asked.

"Ear to ear!" nodded the Inspector sombrely. He closed his eyes.

The other man began to stare at the woman. She had such a frail face. He imagined that if her voice could be tuned to match she would sound like a bird. She seemed so vulnerable and delicate that he felt an urge to reach out and comfort her.

From the mist of another world the Inspector's voice reached his ears.

"My wife amuses you, mister?"

The man turned his face dumbly.

"No," he said, after a prolonged pause. "She just doesn't look very well. That's all."

"My wife never looks very well, she's a sickly woman. But that is no concern for strangers," said the Inspector.

"No. Of course not," mumbled the man.

The whip cracked and dust rolled in through the window.

"Hyah!" shouted the driver and the whip cracked again.

Inspector Holman beat the dust from his knees, ignoring his wife. He smiled at the stranger opposite him. Holman's wife's head slumped and rolled, then it beat hard on the wall as the coach jostled. A group of wallaby heads appeared above the long grass of a paddock, then the trespassing marsupials scattered into a thicket.

"We're not far from Blood Gully now," said Holman, as though to himself. After checking his watch he added, "Perhaps half an hour to go."

Holman thought of his housemaid, with her sweet little body and her timid tip-toeing, and her powerlessness. He smiled. The men of the town called her the Goddess.

He glanced at his fellow passenger, wondering what

4

the man had to hide. Holman pursed his lips, nodding to himself. Everybody had something to hide.

"The coach is not usually this late," he said, arranging his clothing. "Everyone will be worried. Probably think some mishap has befallen us."

"No doubt," smiled the man, again glancing at the woman.

Holman lightened his grip on the leather strap as the coach slowed at the crest of a ridge. He peered through the window and through the clouds of dust. As the coach swerved over the crest, his wife's head thumped on the wood.

"You know, it is hard to believe that this was once all untouched wilderness," he said.

The man blinked, watching the landscape flash by — the tangled scrub and mangled areas of clearing. Slain trees lay in piles upon each other, dismembered and half burned away like carcasses after a battle. The dirt had been scarred by hoof and plough and the huge dragged logs leaked sap and water from their wounds. Their stumps remained, dying in the sun.

"It looks very nice," he hastened to agree, following the fenceline with his eyes. "You've got to admire the giant strides made by progress in so few years."

The post-and-rail fence ploughed straight through a tree, which had been used as a fence post even as it lived. Then the fence veered down into a gully as the coach roared and rattled across a filled-in culvert. The fence failed to come back up the other side.

"The land has been tamed, mister," said the Inspector. "And not by peaceful men. It was won by men prepared to take up arms to defend their womenfolk and children..."

"The spirit of an empire?" grinned the stranger.

"Men prepared to take up arms and win a land where they might prosper. That's the kind of man I understand," continued Holman. "Can you understand that, mister? That is strength — a strong society survives. You look at the natives, they're a weak society. Soon the only blacks you'll

5

find in this country will either be in the circus...or...like the black trackers..."

"Traitors?" the stranger asked.

Holman looked blankly at the man, caught, lost half-way between his own thoughts and whatever the stranger had said.

"Pardon?"

"It doesn't matter," the man replied, wiping the dust from his mouth with his bare hand. "I shouldn't have interrupted you."

"No. I insist," said Holman firmly.

The stranger smiled, showing strong, smoke-stained teeth. He shrugged. "I wondered if they are traitors...to their own people, I mean..."

Holman snickered. He tilted his head to one side. There was another thump as his wife's head hit the coach-work.

"Traitors?" Holman weighed the word in his mind. "That's interesting."

Sunlight slashed across the stranger's eyes and he grimaced. Holman just stared at him.

"Traitors, you say?"

The other man shrugged. The sunlight warmed his bare throat and slowly rose as the coach tilted with the camber of the roadway. Again, the glare blinded him. He heard the driver's whip lashing and cracking outside the coach, driving the horses on.

"Traitors to their own people?" Holman chuckled. "Surely you are not a missionary, mister?"

Holman's voice did not pause for an answer.

"I'll tell you something which will do you ample service if remembered. You cannot trust the black man. When the flag was raised on these shores, we set these people free of the Stone Age. Those who can make the transition will survive. These savages do not even have a people as we understand the term."

The stranger said naught. He glanced at the woman. She was slumped almost restfully in the corner, her lips all dried, cracked and flaky.

"Many people do not realise," said Holman, slowly impressing the words upon his fellow passenger, "that only a few of the natives have the ability to live in the British way. Those are the select few who will survive. That is Nature's decree, not mine. You see? Is the dog who protects the flock against the wolf a traitor to his own kind?"

Holman raised his hands, as if helpless in the face of his own logic. The smile on his face softened.

"I can see your reasoning. You've got a good point there," the stranger admitted.

Holman's wife's head continued to clunk on the woodwork.

II

"JUST REMEMBER," SAID old Tom Price, scratching at his pants and hitching the horse to the cart. "Call him Murphy. Don't *ever* call him MacGuire."

"That's if he ever gets here," said the blind man Danny Doyle, screwing up his face as if to squeeze back into his eyes the sight that was no longer in them.

"MacGuire will come. Don't you worry about that," said Price. "But don't call him MacGuire, whatever you do. Call him Murphy."

"Murphy, MacGuire or Kris Krankrindle, he didn't come before when he was supposed to," replied the blind man.

Price growled: "There were complications before. That's why he didn't come. Nothing mysterious."

"I know, I know," said Danny Doyle. "People die of complications."

He coughed sharply and rumbled phlegm up his throat and spat it like a comet through the air. The horse drooped her head and dragged her hoof through the dirt.

"It's too complicated for me," said the blind man.

AT MRS GILL'S place, overlooking the township, the two servant girls were talking, also of the coming coach.

Judith, the dreamer, was dozing as she scrubbed baking dishes in the outside tub. The sun gleamed through the halo of her unruly hair. Her own shadow darkened her sweating, plump face. The shadow of the gliding eagle passed over her.

"I hope someone interesting comes on the coach today," she said, partly to herself, as the other maid, Kathleen, humped a basket of unfresh linen outside to the lean-to.

Sticky steam streamed from the doorless doorway.

"Wouldn't it be a nice change?" said Kathleen.

Judith sighed, and with powerful strokes scrubbed a blackened dish in the grey foam of grease and soap. She spread her feet wide like a woodchopper, and let her mind drift.

"I'd love to go down and see them arrive. It's so different to see new people come off the coach. Much better than to just see them around town. I love to see their faces," she panted.

Kathleen had gone out of sight, into the lean-to laundry.

"Remember that man who came last year with two wives?" Judith yelled, as Kathleen swung through the door with an empty basket on her hip. "Weren't they the most beautiful..."

"They were alright," said Kathleen.

"Those beautiful dresses!"

The younger girl sneered. Judith stood still, up to her elbows in murky suds.

"They looked like fresh-baked tarts," said Kathleen.

"Don't be nasty," Judith replied, beginning again to scrub.

Kathleen grunted, "It's only nasty if it's not true."

LIKE A screaming siren in the wildest storm at sea, the howl of the sawmill rose above the town. Main Street outside the coach stop was in commotion. Mad Mick O'Reilly and three other men were making fun of the people going by.

One-eyed Albert Ross sat under the post office camphor laurel and pretended to be asleep. Between his quivering, barely parted eyelids he was watching the girls go by, just as he had done ever since he had been a young man with two eyes. He was hoping to get a glimpse of the Goddess.

A pregnant woman hobbled by painfully. She walked as if she was coming apart at the bones. One-eyed Albert couldn't understand his wife always wanting to be in that condition.

In the midst of the milling crowd, Sergeant Dirlsky stood, lost in thought. Once again, he went over the details of the Marker murder and the four throat-slashings. At last he had brought the case to a glorious close. But wondered why the bad dreams had not stopped. He wondered how many more murdered wretches he would find in his career.

"Where's that bloody coach?" chuckled one of the town's smart alecs, trying to sound important to the waiting crowd.

"She'll be here," said Jansen, the coach office over-seer, checking the time and scowling in the direction of the ear-splitting whine coming from the sawmill.

Freckle-faced Freddie Fairburn, the widower, pushed a wheelbarrow loaded with children down Main Street. The barrow was circled by a dog with its tongue hanging out. When Freddie stopped the barrow, the dog ran up and licked the children's snotty faces, while eluding their feeble punches.

The crowd outside the coach office and the Havelock Hotel watched as a dead horse was dragged along the road by two bullocks. Jansen shook his head and listened as a woman spoke to him. Her face was a carving of seriousness.

"They should have removed that carcass this morning. What if visitors arrive on the coach? What they would think of this town I dare not imagine," she said.

"They would think they were in Blood Gully, Mrs Gill," replied Jansen, looking at his bronze fob watch again. Then he scratched his head.

"What a name for a civilised town — Blood Gully!" Mrs Gill lamented. "It's not a name — it's a curse."

"I agree," said Jansen, clicking shut his watchcase. "I dare say people will change it some day. I once knew a *man* who changed his name."

"Preposterous!" said Mrs Gill. "A person should never change his rightful name."

Jansen turned away from the crowd.

"Anyway," he chuckled, "they still hanged him. New name and all."

"Mr Jansen! Please! Do not mention hangings!" the

woman exclaimed, holding a lace-edged silk handkerchief to her nose. Dust rose in the street. Sweat dribbled down her face.

"Don't worry, Mrs Gill," Jansen replied. "Some of the worst places in the empire have lovely names. No reason it can't work in reverse."

THE UNION JACK was flying over the post office. In the shade beneath it stood two men, one with teeth, one with none. The one without teeth, Bluey Miser, was picking at a wart on his hand. He spoke to his companion, who was cradling his aching jaw.

"I hope this coach gets here, don't you, Eight-toes?"

Eight-toes Marler remained hunched, continuing to cradle his jaw. He moaned.

Bluey Miser glanced at his companion, still picking at the wart. It was the size of a penny, and the same colour. He'd had it for years. The more he picked away at it the bigger it got, and the more it pained under the surface. But he figured that, from all accounts, a little pain never hurt anyone.

Bluey Miser spat into the middle of the road. The spit sizzled when it hit the dry dust. Mrs Gill scowled at him.

"Oh Bluey!" moaned Eight-toes as he clutched the ache. "The pain is dreadful. I've got a sawmill in my jaw."

Bluey Miser licked his gums. "Teeth are a blight. Get rid of them, that's my advice. I wish this coach would get here. If Holman doesn't come, they'll cancel the hanging."

He licked his wart and pressed the palm of his hand on his thigh to stop the burning pain.

The bright flag of the empire fluttered above them, and above the town rose the sawmill's roar.

III

WHILE THE TOWN waited, the hills swarmed with axe-men preying on giants. The huge, ancient cedars shuddered with every blow. The earth trembled under the hooves of straining bullocks churning the dirt as whips churned the air. The hills echoed with the blows, the chains and the bellows.

Several times a day there would be stillness and quiet, as the cutters let rest creep into their muscles. They would sit round their fires, filling themselves with black tea and smoke. They were darker of skin than the townsfolk. They would kick the dirt up over their shins as they trudged back to their labour, dwarfed under the towering eucalypts and figs and cedars.

The summer mists were all gone. Instead there was only heat. Even the ferns by the crystal creeks had begun to shrivel. The moss-covered sheltered rocks had already lost their green and turned brown.

The faces of the bush workers were deeply weathered. Their huge hands held the razor-sharp axes lightly. As they drove the blades right through the soft, light trunks, the giants waved their majestic branches a hundred feet above, their roots clinging tenaciously to their birthplace of a thousand years. Then they screamed and roared deafeningly as their trunks tore apart; and they plunged, knocking all before them. The crash as they landed lifted the bullocks off the ground.

Head and shoulders above the crowd in Main Street, Sergeant Dirlsky stared up the road. He belched and several heads turned toward him. Ignoring the stares, he stood watch over the crowd, sifting among the dumb faces for signs of guilt, guile, rebellion or mischief. And at the same time, he prayed for the coach to arrive.

Joe Marker was bound to die anyway. Maybe *that* would stop the murders.

A gang of ringbarkers came from one end of the street. They stopped to talk with Dancer Hughes. From the other end of town came old Tom Price the hermit, riding in his dilapidated cart pulled by his half-dead-looking horse. Beside Price sat his cousin, the old blind stonemason, Danny Doyle.

Dirlsky smiled. Killers were easy to catch. Didn't he already have one in the cell? Dirlsky found catching criminals as easy as picking rotten plums out of a barrel. If at first they might seem perfectly alright, one good squeeze would show how rotten they really were inside.

"Yes, he deserves to hang," Dirlsky muttered.

Cheers went up as the crowd heard the first sound of the coach echoing in over the hills.

Dancer Hughes let go a loud laugh and jingled the coins in his pocket. He had done well selling vegetables on the sly from Holman's garden. And the flowers were blooming on his Indian tobacco trees. Life could be good to an old man sometimes, he reckoned.

Dancer strode over to Tom Price and blind Danny Doyle where they sat in their rickety cart. The horse stood between the shafts with her eyes closed.

"Look at Dirlsky grinning now," said Dancer. "He's like a dog whose master is coming home."

"Who you waiting for?" asked Price.

"Me?" Dancer looked innocent. "I've been selling a few vegetables, that's all."

"Not waiting for your master by any chance?" quipped blind Danny.

"Thought I might as well wait for the Inspector while I'm down here," said Dancer. "What are you two up to?"

"We're meeting someone," Price replied quickly.

"Who?"

"Our cousin..."

"Not another cousin," said Dancer. "You must have more cousins than I've had birthdays."

"How old are you, Dancer?" asked Doyle, raising his

13

voice above the noise of the crowd as they now caught sight of the coach and its train of dust.

"I'm not bad kept, am I?" shouted Dancer, punching himself near the heart. His solid chest made a deep keg-like sound. "I don't look a day over fifty, and I'm at least a hundred and forty...I've lost count..."

"That's not all you've lost," muttered Doyle.

THE COACH crashed along the road into town and halted. The devil himself could not have arrived with more fuss, fury and cacophony. As the storm of dust swept all round the carriage, a mob of yapping, yelping dogs began to mill round the wheels.

"Step back," growled the driver as the crowd rushed down from the verandah of the hotel.

Dirlsky strode forward and swung open the coach door.

Inspector Holman appeared and barked with authority: "Get the doctor!"

Nobody moved, except to crane their heads over each other's shoulder, trying to look inside the coach. A change in the warm wind raised the coach dust again and blew it back through the crowd.

"Somebody's been shot!" yelled one of the young barefoot boys.

"Bushrangers!" yelled one of the others.

A murmur rumbled through the crowd.

"Dirlsky!" shouted Inspector Holman.

"Yes, Sir!" boomed the Sergeant's voice.

"The doctor!"

Dirlsky turned to the crowd. "Somebody get the doctor," he commanded.

The crowd crushed closer.

On the other side of the carriage, the stranger slowly climbed down from the step. He swung off stiffly and stood hunched for a moment, then limped toward the back of the coach, threading his way politely among the people. They stared at him as though he was about to fall over.

Off from the crowd, in an old cart, he could see two

men. One was wiping his face with a red rag. The stranger drew a red kerchief from his pocket and did the same, smiling aimlessly.

"He's come," hissed Price. "It's him alright. Don't act suspicious."

Suddenly Price froze as the street burst again into uproar.

"Here he is!" the crowd screamed with one voice.

Doctor Morrison sped toward the coach with one hand holding his satchel, the other his hat. He was a bubble-shaped man whose legs seemed to race to keep pace with his upper half. Jansen led the way. The barking dogs rushed toward them, then they dodged away at the last moment.

"Somebody's been shot," shouted Huley Colquoon, who had peeped through the blinds of the coach. A clatter of voices echoed Huley's announcement; it rose in a crescendo as the crowd made way for the doctor.

Inspector Holman raised his hand in a calming gesture.

"Friends!" His voice was appealing yet firm. He looked around.

"Nobody has been shot. My wife is ill."

Two dishevelled lads unstrapped the canvas flap at the back of the coach and the stranger grabbed his blanket roll. Price flicked the reins and the horse drew the cart in a big turn, through the thinning crowd, to the back of the coach. The man slung his roll into the back of the cart.

Price glanced at the man he had instructed Doyle to call Murphy. Murphy stared back at the coach with a sad look on his face, as the people pushed to get a glimpse inside the coach windows and the hangman fought his way out through the crowd.

"Did you leave something back there?" Price asked.

"Maybe," said Murphy. "Don't worry about it."

He turned back, away from the coach, and screwed up his face, listening.

"My God!" he said. "How do they live here with that noise?"

"That's Sam Sodge's music box," Danny Doyle chuckled.

"Bloody sawmill," Price muttered. "It's a pestilence."

15

Doctor Morrison leaned over in the cramped, dark carriage. The coach shook from people leaning against it, trying to peer around the sides of the screened-off windows. Morrison took his hand from the woman's brow and shook his head.

"You shouldn't have allowed Mrs Holman to travel in this condition, Inspector," he whispered.

IV

THE CONDEMNED MAN sat in his cell, ignoring the tiny stones that were thrown from the side lane against the wall of the lock-up. Sometimes a pebble would fly through the window, and Joe Marker could hear the stampede of tiny bare feet scurrying away.

Marker could also hear loud laughter coming from Main Street. It meant nothing. He didn't care.

The crowd in the street was jeering at Mrs Colquoon being pushed by her son in a wheelbarrow. Huley Colquoon's face was as bright as the Union Jack which drooped above the post office; he had gone all colours with shame. And the crowd loved it.

Mrs Colquoon was after Sam Sodge, who hurried across the street.

"You can't buy me off, Sodge! You insulting little turnip. I can see what you're trying to do. You're trying to bribe me 'cause my boy Huley saw you up to your tricks," screamed the woman.

She screamed louder to make up for the leeway Sodge was gaining, his coat-tails flapping, his face reddening, his hand holding the brim of his imported American beaver hat. She screamed louder to make up for the laughter of the crowd.

"Just because I've got no legs and my son's got no brains doesn't mean we're not as good as no-one else," she howled. "You bastard! We've got our pride! Faster, Huley! After him!"

Huley pushed the barrow about as slowly as he could. His legs were leaden with shame at the crowd's mockery. He even forgot there was soon going to be a hanging, and he felt as though he would be pushing that wheelbarrow

17

with his mother in it all the rest of his life, listening to the jeers of that crowd.

Faces peered over the edge of the Havelock Hotel balcony, and quickly looked away.

Sodge looked as much ashamed as Huley. Mrs Colquoon continued her tirade.

"You think my Huley's got nothing better to do than go round spreading news about you...you...Come back here, you coward!"

Sodge disappeared into the Havelock. After he had gone through the entrance, a short, strong man with clean hands, wearing a workman's serge shirt, stepped in the way. His arms, folded across his chest, were as thick as branches. He smiled.

Huley stopped the barrow. The old lady glared at the hotel guard. She scowled at his smile, and she swung her elbows with fury.

"Get going, Huley," she said, and Huley got going. He went faster than he had when chasing Sodge. Again he had to run the gauntlet of painful catcalls.

IT HAD BEEN great entertainment. Hours later the people of Blood Gully were still talking about it. They had gathered to see the hanging of Joe Marker, the killer of his own brother...and the fun had already started. Now they watched Mrs Gill's carriage as it drove her out of town. She had the tassel blinds closed against her fellow citizens.

To Mrs Gill they were not her fellow citizens. They were inferior — some more, some less. Her equals were elsewhere. Outside Blood Gully there was another world, but it was far away, and death was so close.... Every day she felt death closing in on her. Every day she felt older.

She could not turn back. When she was young she could choose. Not now. Her life had been lived, now dying was coming. Here in Blood Gully it was easy to be remote and aloof, in all ways an alien. In all ways she was exiled. She found her loneliness to be, after all, only the shadow of death.

She thought of young Mrs Holman, lying ill in a coma, dying, Doctor Morrison had said, of fever. Death was a brute — it preyed on the weak. She thought of her dead husband. The Big Man, they had called him. He too had died.

Deep inside the darkness of her polished black coach the old woman recalled the last summer of her childhood, far away where cobblestones paved the streets and where the city skies were thick with the smoke of industry. How she loved the mother country. If only she had been prettier as a child, she thought, she could have married a better man. Instead, she had accepted Gill — a man who had been making his way in the world. Little did she realise he would drag her to the farthest, hottest, dustiest corner of the empire, in the frenzied rush to gather up the spoils of conquest.

Once upon a time she had thought she loved him — even after he had dragged her all the way to Sydney Town. When she first saw Blood Gully, though, she no longer loved him. Nor could she love the land she lived in. Mrs Gill had found herself entrapped by squalor, the squalor of the common crowd. But as the major shareholder in her husband's cedar company and sawmill, she was answerable to no-one. Even the Inspector of Police shrank before her scowl. Even death baulked at her doorstep.

She did not need to look through the window to see the squalor. Clouds of dust filled the stuffy carriage. She raised the blind and a puff of cool breeze chilled the lines of sweat running down her face. She stared past the pedestrians turning their heads.

These people were mad. They could watch the brutal hanging of one of their own for fun. And they could plunder each other as easily as they could plunder an enemy. Only the brute force of the law and the power of wealth could prevent the rabble tearing at one another's throats for the slightest gain. If it had not been for the wealth brought by the sawmill and the cedar trade, the town of Blood Gully would surely have died, its citizens reduced to the level of the native tribes.

The carriage began to climb the long, winding road up the hill to her house and the surrounding estate. True, Blood Gully was just a speck among many others. Blood Gully in the larger scheme of things was very small. There were many other realms in the world and many far larger, but...every man, woman and child, every dog and horse, every bit of property, every deed, every punishment and every reward had its place, somewhere in the pecking order, somewhere in the hierarchy, according to its worth or value, or as it deserved...and here in Blood Gully they all looked up to the town's new big man, the only one who could even halfway fill old Gill's shoes. And who did Sam Sodge look up to? However reluctantly, Sam Sodge, the wealthiest, most powerful man in town, looked up to her; he looked up to the Cedar Queen.

The carriage stopped. Mrs Gill walked across the shady, close-cropped lawn below her bower. Two old gardeners raised their hats to her as she slowed down to watch a cat cross the lawn ahead of her.

It was a tough old hunting cat. Aloof and uncompromising, it sauntered by with a small, twitching bird in its jaws, blood dripping from the feathers.

Its sleek coat shone, showing its peculiar, reptile-like markings. Mrs Gill watched it thoughtfully. At a word from her the cat would be banished — forever, if she chose. She need only command the gardeners. Mrs Gill smiled.

As they hacked away at the lawn edges with hoes, the two gardeners discussed their mistress.

"Don't tell me she's finally gone soft on that inbred old flea-bag," muttered one of them.

The other one smashed a big clod of garden dirt to bits with the back of his hoe.

"Nah. Don't be simple," he said. "She only likes it 'cause it kills the birds."

Mrs Gill watched the cat play with its half-dead victim before licking the blood and carrying it off. Inside the kitchen, and in the dining room, the two young servant girls, Judith and Kathleen, hurried about their chores.

THE CONDEMNED MAN sat in the tin-lined sweat-box. Only when the police guards prodded him with a broom-handle did he fly into a rage: two bits of the broken handle now lay in the corner of the cell. He did not care if the whole town burned around him or if he burned himself. He just sat there.

Another pebble flew through the tiny barred window. It meant nothing to Joe Marker. Nothing happened. The town was frozen still — as it would be at the moment of his death. But he was already dead. He was as dead as the cedars falling through the air. The rope was already round his neck. They just had to cut him down.

He did not know how many spectators had come to see him die. Senior Constable Hedges had told him how many had been counted, but the news had fallen on deaf ears. Senior Constable Hedges had talked of the paddocks around town — especially on the less dusty side — being alive with campfires. Main Street was like a parade, he had said. Now Hedges leaned on the cell bars once more.

"Hey, Joe," the Senior Constable whispered. "I reckon you aren't a bad bloke. How about giving me a break? It wasn't right what Dirlsky done to you."

Hedges glanced furtively over his shoulder and drew a piece of paper from his tunic. The paper was smothered with ink-writing. Hedges poked it through the bars.

"Sign this, Joe. It'll get Dirlsky for you. I'll make sure of that. You can trust me, Joe. You know that. I treated you square. Put your mark here."

Hedges looked over his shoulder. No-one was coming. He turned to Joe Marker. Marker stared at the floor.

"Come on, Joe. Joe? Give me a go, Joe. What have I done to you? Come and take this. I'll grab the pen and ink. And some rum. How about it, Joe? Like a nice drink? Help you sleep. Joe? Joe?"

But the condemned man was as deaf as he had been at his trial.

Hedges glanced again at the door. Sweat ran into his eyes. He blinked. When he looked back Joe Marker was staring at him. Hedges held out the paper and smiled weakly, with his eyebrows raised.

"Okay, Joe?"

"Piss off," said Marker, barely moving his lips.

Hedges quickly put the paper away.

"No hard feelings, Joe," Hedges said, gripping the bars. "You think about it. Alright? I've got some rum over there in the drawer. Let me know when you want to do business."

Joe Marker stared at the floor.

V

MRS GILL HAD seen the display by Sodge and Mrs Colquoon in the street; but her opinion of Sodge was not damaged. Such outrages of public decency could occur before her very eyes without affecting her. They merely reinforced her general disgust.

Sodge, however, was now standing in the dark stairway of the Havelock Hotel recovering from his ordeal. Cursing under his breath at his crippled persecutor, he listened lest someone should catch him there and gain the mistaken impression that he was hiding in shame; then, having regained his composure, he climbed the broad stairs, puffing and wiping his face, only to be met at the top of the stairs by the hotel owner, the Austrian, Major Stumic. Major Stumic was deeply disturbed.

"That Colquoon woman is a disgrace...an outrage," he said.

Mr Stewart, one of the government men, came from the parlour. He was dressed in a freshly starched shirt and a wine-coloured vest on which Mrs Gill had once complimented him publicly.

"There needs to be a place where we can put people like that," he declared, ushering Major Stumic and Sam Sodge into the parlour.

Sodge exchanged greetings with the two other gentlemen sitting there.

"You're right," said Father Mitchell to Stewart as he gave Sodge a consoling pat on the shoulder. "It should never have been allowed to happen. In Sam's position I myself would have been much flustered."

"Yes!" exclaimed Major Stumic. "But if you get rid of the old cripple, who is going to keep that imbecile son of hers in check? I had a touch of Delhi belly and was most indisposed one day...and I looked up. And there was Huley Colquoon, spying on me from up at the window. He is a menace."

Stewart muttered, "He came spying on me too. I dare not say more."

The priest laughed and punched Stewart's shoulder.

"Ho! You old devil, you!" he guffawed.

The other gentleman, Young Mr Callow, Stewart's assistant, began to giggle as he left the room.

DESPITE the almost unbearable heat, kitchen fires were beginning to puff smoke. Down the road, in a stringybark and slab-sided hut, Mrs Ross, One-eyed Albert's wife, tossed a pinch of salt into the fire before making butter.

She was thinking, how is it some people get all the luck and others get all the misfortune? How does one woman have ten children, and another none?

FRECKLE-FACED Freddie Fairburn kept pushing his children down Main Street in the wheelbarrow, lost in thought. He was handsome enough to attract any woman who wasn't scared off by a widower with three children. He could catch a woman's eye, but when it came to catching the rest of her, that was a different story. All of a sudden he would find he had said something wrong, or he would let his attentions stray for too long at the wrong moment, or the lady of his affections would get allergic to children, or he would become too busy being a father and trying to be a mother at the same time, and some rival would win her away.

But he never gave up.

That was why he had begun courting Ten-cow Miller's pretty daughter. Felicity Miller was twenty-five years old and a virgin, but she dressed like a widow.

After Bartholomew the blacksmith-farrier had been kicked by a horse and had his leg broken in six places and had to be carried to Sydney, screaming all the way, Freddie had got a head-start in the race for Miller's daughter.

One day, before Jack Marker had got killed, Freddie had told Tom Price and Dancer Hughes and old Rooster Gorman all about it.

"I'm in love," he said. "Can you believe it?"

"What? With Miller's daughter?" laughed Dancer Hughes.

Freddie blushed like a bushfire.

"Who said?" He wanted to know.

"No-one had to say anything," said Dancer. "The way you followed her around last week I thought she owed you money."

"Nah!" said Price. "It'd never work out. You're too old. You'll be forty in a couple of years. You ought to be like me, be independent. No-one tells me where to go or when to stay. You get married to one of them young girls, she'll have you in your grave before you satisfy her."

"No," said Dancer. "I have to disagree with you there, Price. A young-blooded woman is good for an old man. Makes him appreciate what he's leaving behind, so he dies slow. Look at me . . ."

"Dancer! You've got no woman," said Rooster Gorman.

"I did once," said Dancer. "And it did me no harm."

The scrawny little gardener and black-market merchant in vegetables stood his ground proudly.

"Yeah, well you listen," Price said. "Remember what I say. If a man don't act his age he ends in trouble. Remember Shannon's father. The old bastard ran around like a young man and blew his heart up chasing women. At his age! He wouldn't have known what to do if he'd caught one."

"I bet *I* would," said Dancer with an expression on his face as if he had just eaten something nice.

Freddie looked at Dancer sympathetically. He nodded.

"Me too," Freddie said.

The other three went on to talk about Shannon's father, who had placed a row of clean human skulls over his mantelpiece. This, of course, led to a discussion about the massacre.

Price wanted to call Tom Shannon over to prove how many skulls there were on old Shannon's mantelpiece. Freddie thought he should leave before Shannon found out that he was in love with Miller's daughter. Tom Shannon had the loudest laugh in Blood Gully.

Freddie wasn't getting a great deal of help. He left when the other three started arguing about whether white men were smarter than black men.

Later that week everyone forgot Freddie's problem, in the excitement of the murder of big Jack Marker. Dancer said that it was just like the story of Adam and Eve in the Bible. Eve slew his brother Adam in a fight. They were both cedar-cutters in Palestine.

"Rubbish," snarled Rooster. "That was the story of Cain and Abel..."

"Don't argue with me," sneered Dancer. "You should know better than to argue with me, Rooster. I was there, wasn't I Freddie? I was there when Joe Marker came out of the lock-up, after he locked up the traps. I said, 'Hey Joe, where are you going with that gun?' But I knew where he was going. He didn't have to say nothing."

"What did he say?" asked Rooster.

"What would you say if you were just going to kill your brother?" Dancer answered. "He didn't say a word."

Freddie didn't bother to ask them about his problem again. When they parted company, he followed Gorman. Then suddenly, without planning to say anything, he heard himself speak.

"What should I do, Rooster?"

Rooster Gorman smiled. He started to pull up his pants and lick his lips, as if he was going to pay for something, wasn't sure what he was getting, and had to guess the price anyway.

"That's a mighty hard question to answer, Freddie."

"You're my last chance, Rooster," said Freddie. "I thought Price could help me — he's a man of the world — but he's hopeless once he takes to an opinion."

"Well, alright," Rooster mumbled.

"I'll think about it and if I come up with something I'll let you know."

Freddie stopped and grabbed Rooster by the arm.

"I'm serious, Rooster. Bugger you. You've got kids. Can you imagine? It's no picnic on your own. Do you think it could drive you mad? Well?"

Rooster Gorman just looked at Freddie. His face was twisted as if with pain. He panted. Then he looked down and began tucking his shirt in even further.

"Right. Let's look at your choices. That way..." he began, stretching his fingers and grabbing the small one to begin counting.

Freddie closed his eyes and shook his head.

"I know what the choices are," he said. "I've looked at them till that's all I can see...all day, all night, whether my eyes are open or closed. I've got to know the answer. Now!"

Rooster Gorman licked his lips and grabbed Freddie. Very slowly and calmly he spoke, looking deeply into Freddie's eyes.

"There's only one thing you can do. And you know it. Ask her to marry you," he said, as Freddie nodded his head. "You haven't been drinking, have you?"

Freddie shook his head.

"Good," said Rooster. "That way you can't come back at yourself later...not if you made an honest mistake. And you can't come back at me, because it's your decision."

"There's no come back at you, Rooster," Freddie sniffed. "You're only doing what any friend should. I appreciate that."

"I appreciate you appreciating that," grinned Rooster, slapping Freddie's long, muscular arm. "I've got to go..."

FREDDIE'S CHILDREN looked at each other as he stopped the wheelbarrow. He started to whistle while he began to check their heads for ticks. He found two of the blood-suckers. He had once seen a child that had been killed by a tick bite. It had been a terrible sight.

There was no doubt Felicity was a handsome, strong woman, he thought. In fact, only those whom she had rejected ever criticised her looks. Freddie thought she was pretty most of the time. But when he held her in his arms she began to glow like Aladdin's lamp in the tales of the Arabian Nights; and she radiated such loveliness that his legs trembled. Could he ask such a beauty to be his?

After his talk with Rooster Gorman he had resolved to ask her first if it would be alright if he did ask her.

The same night, when the three children were asleep, Freddie had sneaked out of his hut as if he was going on a robbery. At the rope-hinged door, he turned and stared at the walls around him. Could he ask a young woman to share this? Even with the packed-clay floor swept clean, and with all in tidy and clean order, he had to confess the place remained a bit of a hovel. He shut the door softly, making no sound. If the children woke up and began to play while he was gone the place would look as if a cannon-ball had hit it.

He scurried off into the dark, to keep his rendezvous with Felicity.

When he held her in his arms he felt the blood rush through his body. His face prickled, his hands tingled, he felt his skin tighten. Ask her now, he told himself. In a moment, he replied. The dialogue went on inside his head. The little he did say aloud revolved around how beautiful he found her.

Felicity Miller became agitated.

"No man owns me till he puts a ring on my finger and changes my name," she told him.

Freddie guiltily moved his hand away from her breast. It was a big decision; there was much to consider. He began to worry that Rooster Gorman might have given him bad advice. He moved his mouth but no sound came out. He kissed her hair, sucking sweet-smelling strands into his mouth and pulling them out wet. Somehow he found it hard to picture Felicity Miller with her sleeves rolled up cleaning his shack. She did not like Freddie's children a lot, but sometimes he didn't blame her. A man on his own can't do wonders. But she even refused to go with him when he wheeled them around town. Felicity even sneered at his dog. Yes, indeed. It was a very big decision. But think for the kids too, he told himself silently, staring into Felicity's hair perfumed by her own sweetness; they need a mother. Poor Felicity had so much to think about, and how could he tell her? Where could he start?

Before Freddie Fairburn could answer his own questions, Ten-cow Miller's daughter got up without a word. She rubbed her hands together. Flakes of skin fell away from the milk rash which was rotting her skin. She boldly thrust her breast to the dark, taking a deep breath which made her shudder. She folded her arms and began to walk.

At first Freddie thought, she's going to pee or something. But she didn't turn off the track. She just kept going. Felicity, he thought, come back! But she didn't. She kept going, and then she was gone. Freddie stared at the hills, thinking only with the surface of his brain. Everything was hopeless. His head ached from the split in his brain and the hills shimmered in the starlight as if his mind was on fire.

Then he thought of the children alone in the shack. He thought of childlike innocence and mischief. A coldness ran down his spine. Up he jumped and ran as if he was ten years younger, to make sure his children were safe. To make sure the shack was not burning down...but it was silent and dark, and safe.

Freddie Fairburn shook the memory of that sad night from his mind. He picked up the wheelbarrow once more and started to push it. The children began to hoot with delight. The dog's tail started to swing frantically as the animal began again to run round and round.

SENIOR CONSTABLE HEDGES sat at his dark. He had just about given up trying to talk to Joe Marker. Bloody Joe Marker, he thought, sign this paper and die. He was keeping the paper in his tunic for the moment when the condemned man might see reason. He stood up and walked over to the cell. Joe Marker was still staring at the floor.

Hedges glanced at Constable Jones, who sat at his desk with his eyes closed and his head slumped.

"You thought about my offer, Joe?" Hedges hissed to the prisoner. "You know it isn't right for Dirlsky to stick all those cut-throat murders on you, Joe. That isn't right."

Hedges glanced at Jones, who hadn't moved.

"Take my word for it, Joe, justice will be done. If it takes me two years, I'll make him pay for this."

"What are you talking about?" asked Constable Jones, without opening his eyes. "He's going to be dead in a few hours. What does he care?"

Joe Marker's hands were clasped, his head bowed, his eyes blinking.

"It might relax him," snarled Hedges. "How would you like it, getting hanged for five murders when you only did one?"

Constable Jones opened his eyes and shook his head contemptuously, "You're just keen on knifing Dirlsky in the back. You always have been. Don't think he doesn't know."

"You told him, you bastard?" growled Hedges.

"Of course I didn't tell him. I didn't have to," laughed Constable Jones. "Anyway, what's it matter to me? You or him; him or you; Holman...or poor bloody Joe in there. It doesn't matter a shit to me who's over me or under me. Just so long as I'm alright. Dirlsky treats me alright."

With these words the Constable leaned back again and closed his eyes.

Hedges stared at the condemned man. He found it hard to remember that such a short time before Joe Marker had been a free man with a clear name.

"What's it like to know you're going to hang, Joe? What did it feel like when you first knew you would? Made you shit yourself, I'll bet, didn't it? Eh?"

VI

THE LAST WEEK of Jack Marker's life had not been remarkable in Blood Gully, except that the sawmill had just paid out on a lot of its contracts. The fun-starved men had gone crazy. Drink by drink they had drunk themselves out of their dull existence into a temporary glow, slowly to burn out. One of them had danced the length of Main Street three times, and had sworn that after ten more drinks he could do it again. He staggered away to piss after seven drinks and didn't come back.

"Well that's one that the throat-slasher didn't get," Dirlsky had said, when the corpse was found drowned in its own vomit.

That was the morning after the night of the Markers' first great battle. All the men of Blood Gully were frightened to walk on the same side of the street as the two brothers. But all the cedar-cutters were the same — their huge, brown-muscled arms and their labour-stiffened shuffle, their bearded, ogre faces, their gruff, grumbly voices, their ant-like swarm instinct, their menace and unpredictability.

The most harm the wild axe-men of the bush did, however, was among themselves. They liked to fight, and they liked to poison themselves with alcohol and tobacco and to dance until sunrise. They needed no piano and wood flooring, they needed no bullock-dung floor and accordion — the street would do.

The night of the Markers' first great battle, dancing cedar-cutters had kept Major Stumic awake for hours. He looked down from the balcony in the morning, and they were still dancing, with their own stamping and yelling for music.

"God almighty," he had gasped, turning to the other

gentlemen on the Havelock balcony, "It looks like a pagan war dance."

"Don't worry about the dancing," Stewart had said, "they'll be at each other's throats any minute. It's a war dance, have no fear."

For the cedar-cutters used the street for fighting too. They were the roughest of rough fellows, like bullockies and bullocks rolled into one and cut out in the shape of men. They were as muscly and hairy as Malayan ape-men, observed Stumic. They fought as ferociously as rats, said Sodge.

And when the Marker boys locked horns, it was the worst of all. No-one else would fight them; and as they were both peaceful men unless provoked, there was no need for anyone to tangle with them.

Unfortunately the brothers had the habit of provoking each other, as brothers often do.

The Marker boys, big Joe and even bigger Jack, had been fighting like animals during the night. There was already blood in the dust. So that morning the people of Blood Gully were waiting, and making bets on the outcome. The brothers' faces looked crazed — from the heat, the drink, the sleepless nights and the excitement of blood. The blood was dark, deep and bright.

Sam Sodge had hurriedly laid out pounds in favour of the big fellow. Father Mitchell did not bet; he said he too preferred the larger fellow but that the two brothers were both brutes. Major Stumic had then obliged by covering the wagers.

As the civic leaders watched the brawl from the Havelock balcony, neither Marker had given his brother any quarter. It was great sport. Sodge squealed with delight when the big one sent the smaller one sprawling with a dirty kick.

But the kick had only half done its work. Joe Marker crouched to his feet as big Jack rushed forward for the kill. Joe lunged and the instant before their hands gripped together with bone-crushing clutches, their heads collided, brow to brow in mid-lunge.

The collision had sounded like an axe-blow against a dead, hollow tree. The roar of the crowd was cut silent as if with a knife. One of the brothers, Joe, lay unconscious. The spectators thought that with his pulped face and the trickle of blood from his ear, he would die.

THEY EXPECTED the rest of the day to be quiet. But just in case, groups of people still hung about the street on look-out. And just when it seemed they would be disappointed, word passed along that Joe Marker had regained consciousness. His camp was empty, and someone had seen him bathing his face in Rooster Gorman's dam.

When they told big Jack, drinking in the Bushman's Arms, he laughed and then winced painfully. "I told you he'd get over that headache. Now there'll be trouble."

Jack Marker drained his glass, then he drained the little bit left in the bottle beside it. Then he started pawing and kissing Marianna, the dark-eyed, dark-skinned bar girl. His kisses left all the side of her face glistening.

Dancer Hughes saw the crowd following Joe Marker for the third time down the street as if he was a drowning man. Dancer could hear them asking Joe where he was going, but they didn't have to. They knew where he was going.

Dancer hadn't seen anything like it in a long time. He looked at the faces of the crowd. They didn't look any more warm-blooded than reptiles. Then he looked at Joe Marker.

Joe was huge, but of course his brother was bigger. Joe's face was carved up like Main Street in the rain on a busy day. The lacerations that Jack had chopped into his face were still tender, bloodied, bruised, puckered and part-open. Joe squinted and nursed his brow and one eye, but he kept walking. Now and then he spat out blood, and one of his ears looked as if it had been painted with it.

Dancer hadn't seen the first two fights. He began to welcome seeing this one. He was ashamed of himself, but things moved too fast for him to change his mind. Suddenly

33

Joe Marker and his blood-thirsty entourage were outside the Bushman's Arms. And Joe Marker had begun shouting in the street, calling his brother to come out.

Sam Sodge looked down from the Havelock balcony — and he almost choked with glee on his brandy.

"Major! Major!" he cried. "It's on again. Here is your man. Where is your money?"

Joe Marker, battered and sluggish on his feet, continued to yell out, calling his brother Jack everything that moved, stank or had hair on it.

Jack Marker came out of the Bushman's Arms smiling. As soon as Dancer Hughes saw the smile on Jack's face he was sorry for Joe. From what Dancer could see, nearly all the bloodshed he had heard about must have come from Joe's face.

Joe Marker stood in the dust, stripping his shirt off; he looked like a knot of hairy muscle, all glistening with sweat and blood. Jack Marker watched his brother with an amused grin, rolling up his sleeves clumsily. Joe was more than six foot tall. Jack Marker looked eight foot easy, standing on the steps.

"You're going to beat me one day, you little bugger," said Jack, as though they were alone. "I may as well get mine in now."

He jumped down to the street and the two men circled each other, pawing the air and taunting each other. It looked like a childhood game gone mad. Huley Colquoon ran up the street yelling, "Fight! Fight! Fight!"

The first punch landed with a whack and the crowd roared with encouragement. The noise reminded Huley that he was running in the wrong direction. He realised he might miss the fight. He heard a woman scream, and he turned.

Dancer Hughes had grabbed the woman and was trying to drag her away. She was drunk and trying to join in the scuffle. Huley was afraid to go back, and as he walked slowly he saw the woman punch Dancer Hughes in the guts. The old man buckled over.

From a distance Huley saw the two brothers rush like

bulls into each other's arms. Their hands held each other like eagles' talons. Huley didn't like it. He heard the punches as if they were hitting his own face. Each smack made Huley shake.

The brothers' knees smashed together as they went for the groin, and their heads smashed together with vicious butts. Inevitably, they toppled into the dust and had a wrestle. That made Huley feel safer, so he hurried on back to watch.

"You wouldn't believe they live out in the hills and work as peacefully as babies, would you?" said Sam Sodge, leaning on the balcony without taking his eyes off the brawl below.

"How do you keep them under control?" asked Stewart.

"By authority, Mr Stewart," said the Major. "The brutes would make wonderful soldiers."

The gentlemen grinned, looking down on the Marker brothers tearing each other to bits like gladiators below.

The crowd wheeled and broke backwards as Joe swung Jack over and butted him in the face, splitting open his own forehead. Jack's face by then had been battered and was bleeding. His nose was flattened to one side. But Joe looked as if he had gone face-first through a glass window.

Huley got there just in time for a good look. He squirmed. It was awful. Torn pieces of skin swung like shreds of wet, red rubber, and blood splattered from their mouths and noses.

"Right! That's enough!" a voice boomed from the crowd. Everybody recognised it as Suggestible Humphrey's. Humphrey always tried to be friends with everybody — especially with Mrs Donaldson, his boss.

Humphrey stepped into the thrashing space. Suddenly all eyes were on him. Even the Marker brothers turned his way. There was an angry shout from Sodge up on the balcony of the Havelock.

"Now that's enough," repeated Humphrey, putting his hands between the two men and pushing them away from each other.

The two heavily panting and bleeding giants did not

35

move their feet. The mangled bodies just swayed like trees, towering over the peace-maker.

Huley saw Mrs Donaldson smiling proudly at Humphrey. Humphrey couldn't see her, but Huley bet if Humphrey saw her looking like that, he'd drop everything and go over and ask her what was wrong — just as he always did. That was Humphrey all over.

"Now we've all had a good show." Humphrey kept reasoning with the Marker brothers, ignoring the jeering taunts of those onlookers who wanted more. "Youse have done enough. We don't want to see you get hurt..."

One or two men raised their voices to agree.

"Who is that?" snarled Sam Sodge. Then he yelled out loud, "Get out of it there, you fool!"

Major Stumic put his hand on Sodge's shoulder. He shook his head when Sodge looked at him. Angrily, Sodge shrugged loose. He went over to the hotel guard who was standing in the shadows of the doorway, his arms folded. The hotel guard nodded and went on downstairs.

"This won't last long," Sodge chuckled.

In the lull Huley Colquoon was watching the pretty ladies who went with the men in the Bushman's Arms — those girls his mother had warned him about. They were watching the fight, even though it wasn't a fight any more. He felt proud that they were all looking at something he was involved in. Huley was proud of his friend Suggestible Humphrey too. Huley heard someone laugh, then he heard an almighty whack as the hotel guard's hand reached out of the crowd and smashed into Humphrey's head. Then disaster.

Two sounds rose above the pandemonium. One was Mrs Donaldson's scream. The other was Sodge's hysterical laughter from the balcony of the hotel.

Humphrey never knew what hit him. Huley heard Mad Mick O'Reilly yell out, "You mongrel!" as he grabbed the guard. Then someone grabbed O'Reilly.

Huley felt a hand trying to grab him too. He ducked straight down before the fingers could close on his shoulder, and he ran on his hands and toes, like a rabbit, out of sight.

36

Two men smacked each other in the face with their knuckles; at the same time they both fell down.

"Did you see that?" squealed Sodge. "It's better than a bullfight."

The more timid members of the crowd broke to a safe distance. A number of small scuffles developed. Suggestible Humphrey lay among several sprawled-out bodies. Nearby, Jack Marker was pounding Joe Marker's face on the ground just as he had the night before.

"Someone should stop this," said Mrs Donaldson. "It's not a fight, it's murder."

She looked at the wide-eyed faces, she looked at old man Donaldson grinning like a dog, and she looked at brave Humphrey — knocked down in his moment of real greatness. Then she looked up at the balcony of the Havelock Hotel, and saw more grinning heads.

Old Donaldson even pushed a couple of people out of the way so he could have a better look. He stood with one hand behind Sarah, one of the tavern girls. Occasionally, as he yelled at the fight, Sarah would wiggle as if she had been pinched. Then she would look up at him with a devilish smile.

Joe Marker was blind with blood now. He swung wild punches that hit nothing. With a cunning lunge he clung to his brother. The two men went down, the smaller one giving from underneath as good as he was getting from above. Joe had big Jack by the beard; he hung on like grim death, smashing his punches into Jack's cheekbone; and as Jack drove his fist into Joe's flaming-red face, his neck muscles bulged. Bit by bit big Jack pulled his beard free.

The smaller fights were now being broken up by three of the constables, Hedges, Taylor and Fraser, who had just arrived. They would have been on the scene faster except that first they had gone looking for Constable Jones, who couldn't be found anywhere. The three police officers hurled the drunken brawlers in all directions, booting and punching them for good measure. Hedges thumped at them with a long, weighted truncheon.

Jack Marker, his own beard jerked free, had Joe's

37

head in his two hands. A furious scuffle ensued, resulting in the two being tangled like Siamese twins in a circus. Joe had Jack trapped in a backward scissors-lock. Jack rolled over, trapping Joe underneath. Joe hung on with his legs and grabbed Jack round the waist, bending him backwards from behind. Jack couldn't throw a punch. He was helpless.

The spectators started snickering either at big, helpless Jack Marker, or at the police, bashing up the last of the small-time brawlers. They couldn't see Joe Marker's face, hidden under Jack's body.

Jack Marker's face began to bulge. His neck swelled and veins stood out on his forehead. Jack trembled all over with the strain; then he began to rise, against all the force that Joe could exert to hold him down.

He sat upright and wrenched Joe's legs loose. His backside was in Joe's face...and he farted.

The smell was immediate and potent, like something dead, they said.

Bucking furiously, Joe wrenched loose. Jack landed with a thud in the dust. There wasn't one patch of skin visible through the blood on Joe's face. Constables Fraser and Taylor leapt on Joe's back. He shook them off. Then as Joe Marker sprang at his battered brother, Senior Constable Hedges lunged from the crowd, swinging his truncheon down from over his head and sending Joe Marker sprawling at his brother's feet with one blow.

"Go on, leave him alone, you mongrels," said Mad Mick O'Reilly, wiping blood from his lips with his hand. "Four to one it took before you beat him."

"You'll do, O'Reilly," said Hedges. "You're under arrest."

O'Reilly shrugged. "Anything for a laugh," he mumbled.

"You two carry him," Hedges said to Fraser and Taylor, pointing to the body of pulpy-faced Joe Marker. "You grab a leg, O'Reilly."

Taylor and Fraser could not lift Joe Marker. And O'Reilly did not try. Hedges had to help and all four had to rest halfway to the lock-up, with a small crowd following at a respectful distance all the way.

"What about him?" O'Reilly said, pointing to Jack Marker.

Jack the giant grinned from the midst of an admiring crowd.

"I'll take care of him later," muttered Hedges.

Before the two prisoners could be taken to the cell, Joe Marker slowly rose to his feet. He didn't have to struggle very much to make the constables put him down. Hedges was first to let go. He pulled the truncheon from under his armpit and stood at the ready.

Joe Marker got up and shook his head, and as he did blood sprayed off him like water from a shaking dog. He blinked and looked at the surrounding police. They remained silent, ready to spring or run — it was not clear which. Joe looked back and saw his brother smiling.

"Come on, Joe," said O'Reilly. "The bastards have arrested us."

Joe Marker was panting. His belly rolled, shook and quivered. He coughed and spat up bloody lumps of gizzard. Then he walked on with O'Reilly, the police all looking at each other with relief.

The hot weatherboard office, with a low tin ceiling and a tin-lined cell, was filled with stale air. Joe and O'Reilly stood by the large desk. Taylor and Fraser slumped in chairs at the desk and pulled their tunics open.

"You two watch them while I get Dirlsky," said Hedges as he went out again.

Mick O'Reilly waited for something to happen. He was happy to stand there like a fool rather than be locked up in the kennel like a dog. Joe Marker looked between the two constables at the wall behind the half-open back door. Like a man staring between bars at an open field, he saw the rifle.

Fraser stood up.

"Sit down, you," he snarled to O'Reilly, pushing him toward a bench.

Fraser suddenly felt his feet leave the floor as Joe Marker tossed him against Taylor. Together the policemen crashed to the floor. Joe Marker jumped to the back door.

The rifle was in his hand. His fingers closed around it.

"For Christ's sake, Joe!" yelled O'Reilly. "No, mate!"

Joe Marker shut him up by pointing the rifle at him. Then he pointed the rifle at Taylor and Fraser, down on their hands and knees.

"Careful, mate," cried Constable Taylor, holding up his white, shaky hand as if to fend off a bullet. "That's loaded. It could go off any minute. Take it easy."

"That's right. We're just doing our job. We've got nothing against you," said Fraser. Then he smiled and rose to his knees.

"In the cell," said Joe Marker, no sign of emotion showing through the blood on his face.

"No, Joe," said O'Reilly as the police obeyed. "It's not worth it."

"It's too late," said Marker. "This is between me and that..."

He said nothing for a while. O'Reilly walked into the cell behind the police and closed the door. Marker looked at his prisoners through the bars. He had nothing to say. Words had caused all this trouble. Words and hatred, rotting inside a man till they tainted everything and built up a callus on his soul, till only pain, violence and the fires of drink and tobacco could break through...

For an instant he felt everything at once, as his life unwound inside him. In that instant he realised why he and his brother fought. It was because of this wordless sadness, finally too great for one man, or even for two men, to contain. The realisation passed through him like a tide of emotion, all in a mere instant — a shattering, crushing instant of such sadness his eyes flickered and tears formed. The tears did not run down his bloody face. They ran down inside.

O'Reilly waited for Joe Marker's words, expecting to hear a torrent of abuse aimed at big Jack. But no abuse came. Joe Marker said nothing. He felt the rush of core-twisting sadness gripping his insides, and he knew that beyond this there was no sadness, no joy and no life. And he felt all at once that this was his brother's sadness too.

All things were as they would always be.

The front door opened. Joe Marker swung round and pointed the rifle at Sergeant Dirlsky's belly as he came through the doorway. Senior Constable Hedges closed the door behind Dirlsky and turned, rushing into the back of his frozen, speechless sergeant. Dirlsky hadn't moved since he had seen Marker with the rifle. They had no escape.

"Over here. With them," said Marker, motioning with the rifle barrel toward the cell. "Drop that thing, you!"

Hedges let the truncheon fall to the floor.

"It's a trick, Hedges. You half-wit!" hissed Dirlsky over his shoulder. Then he turned to Joe Marker. "Put that weapon down, man, before you have something serious to answer for."

"Get in that cell, Sergeant, and save your life. You too, Constable. Now!"

Joe Marker locked up his five prisoners. O'Reilly looked at Marker's hands. They were as bloody as skinned beef. O'Reilly looked at his own knuckles. They were bruised and bleeding. He marvelled that Marker could even move his fingers as the big man fiddled with the lock and turned the key.

Marker ransacked the desk drawers. He found a ring of keys and unlocked the chain on the weapons cabinet.

Dirlsky glared at Hedges.

"I didn't put them there," whispered Hedges. "It must have been Jones."

Fraser and Taylor looked at each other and glared at Hedges.

"What I want to know is where he got that rifle," hissed Hedges; then both he and Dirlsky glared at Taylor and Fraser.

Joe Marker loaded a double-barrelled shotgun and threw the rifle down as though it had been emptied. He swooned for a moment and held his head, blinking his eyes.

"Turn it in, Joe," yelled O'Reilly.

"Shut up," growled Hedges under his breath.

O'Reilly ignored him.

"Turn it in, Joe. It's a losing hand. Turn it in now,

we'll only get five days. Your head's hurt. You're not thinking right. Five days or a month..."

"They're not caging me up for five days, a month or five bloody minutes," screamed Marker. "If they want me they can have me — in one lump!"

Marker walked calmly out the door into the street, his red face darkening as the blood began to dry.

Two of the brawlers, still sitting on the ground, watched Joe Marker walk past. He didn't even look at them. They could not take their eyes off him. One of them got up as Marker went past. He started to walk in the opposite direction.

"Where you going?" his companion yelled. "Don't you want to see what happens?"

Without looking behind, the other man yelled back, "When that thing goes off I don't even want to be in town."

Inside the station, locked in the cell, the police began to argue.

"Where's Jones?" snarled Hedges to Constable Taylor who sat dejectedly in the corner of the cell.

"Don't worry," said Dirlsky, assuming command. "I have the other key in my pocket. You take these two and bring him back.

Dirlsky searched through two pockets and found the spare cell key in the third.

"You want us to bring back Constable Jones, Sergeant?" asked Taylor.

Hedges looked at Taylor blankly.

Dirlsky snarled at Hedges, "Senior Constable, take these two men, get out and arrest that barbarian while this town is still standing."

Hedges tapped his nose for a moment. Then he smiled as though he had had a thought. He opened his mouth...

"Now!" screamed Dirlsky.

HULEY COLQUOON was looking up into the hot, sunlit sky. It was the sort of day when nothing ever happened. But something had happened alright — there'd been blood every-where. Huley thought about poor old Joe Marker and Mad Mick O'Reilly locked up in the hot cell. Huley knew how hot it could get in there.

He rubbed his eyes and looked again when he saw Joe Marker walking down the street with a shotgun in his hands. Joe Marker looked bigger than ever. One moment his face looked as black with blood as a black man's, the next moment it seemed to turn to fire as the blood was lit up by the radiant sunlight. Wait till big Jack sees Joe with that shotgun, Huley thought.

"Get home, Huley," Joe Marker yelled.

Huley ran. He crossed paths with Dancer Hughes.

"Hey Joe!" Dancer yelled. "Where are you going with that gun in your hand?"

Joe Marker stepped into the Bushman's Arms. He saw the tavern crowd cringe from the gun. Blood oozed down his neck. The room became dead silent. No-one moved. All were frozen, sitting and standing...all sweating.

Sarah stepped forward and thrust out her tiny breast and smiled at Marker. She squinted her little eyes.

"You looking for me, Sugar?" she said before some-one grabbed her arm and pulled her backwards out of the way.

"Where's Jack?" Joe Marker asked Mrs Donaldson, clearing the frog in his throat as he pronounced his brother's name.

"He's not here," Mrs Donaldson replied. "You can see that."

Marker looked round the room. The still faces looked dead. It was over for them, too, Joe felt. But let them find their own way off the treadmill. None of them met his eyes. Dancer Hughes stood in the doorway. Humphrey sat in a corner holding a filthy rag to his face.

Joe Marker watched the faces carefully. Eyes shifted. Most looked downwards. Some glanced expectantly to the back. Old man Donaldson turned his head.

Slowly, Marker began to walk. Mrs Donaldson fol-lowed him. She stepped in front of him and stood in front of the back-room door as he reached for the latch. Old man Donaldson rubbed the sweat off his squarish bald head and turned away sheepishly, as Sarah the tavern girl glared at him with scornful eyes and shook her head. Humphrey rose from his seat, one hand on the backrest, one hand on the table, clutching the filthy rag. He stood, leaning forward, poised, all one side of his face swollen and bruised.

"Marianna is in there," said Mrs Donaldson to Joe Marker.

"I won't hurt her," Joe replied.

Mrs Donaldson rubbed her hands together and stepped aside. She looked away, saying, "Aren't you going to knock?"

Joe Marker walked straight into the room and closed the door behind him. He slipped the latch. Marianna screamed and big Jack Marker sprang from the bed. His head almost hit the roof of the dim little room. He was naked except for a torn and bloody shirt. Marianna had blood on her face but it wasn't hers.

Big Jack crouched ready to pounce, but Joe pointed the twin barrels of death at him. Jack looked.

"Turn around and put your hands on the wall."

"Don't, Joe," said big Jack. "You'll just make me madder."

"Don't, Joe!" screamed Marianna.

In the bar of the Bushman's Arms no-one moved. The tavern-keeper, Mrs Donaldson, had turned away from the back room. She stood alone, biting her knuckles and staring down into a corner. The heat seemed to rise as if there was a fire under the floor. Sweat poured. Breaths were held. Ears strained listening for whispers. They heard Marianna scream. Then nothing.

"You never fart in a man's face," whispered Humphrey.

In the silence of the back room Joe Marker raised the gun to his shoulder and spread his legs. Marianna looked at Jack Marker's face. He smiled at her...and winked.

Joe Marker leaned against the butt of the gun and fired. Both barrels spat flames of burning vengeance, with a roar of sudden death.

FATHER MITCHELL was reaching toward a tray of drinks on the Havelock balcony. When the shotgun went off, the priest knocked the drinks off the tray and clutched his gold cross to his chest. Sam Sodge spun around so fast on his heel that he fell over. The maid just stood there with an empty tray, staring at Sodge lying on the floor. She screamed.

"Good Lord!" gasped Stewart as he came onto the balcony from the parlour; he rushed back into the parlour.

Father Mitchell clutched at the ache in his fluttering heart, gasping for air like a fish. He could hear Stewart's voice booming in the parlour, and he could hear shouts below in the street.

"Callow! Stumic! Come here quick! They've shot Sam!" Stewart yelled. Major Stumic's mouth dropped open.

The shotgun blast had shaken the whole tavern and filled the back room of the Bushman's Arms with smoke. Jack Marker's howl made Marianna's scream seem like a whisper. Big Jack was cut in two, and the double-barrel blast had blown a hole in the back wall.

Big Jack lay twisted where he had crashed, broken beside his legs on the floor, howling, the tail of his shirt slashed to bloody shreds.

"Don't, Joe. Don't, Joe. Please don't," big Jack Marker howled on the floor where he lay, gushing a slippery swamp of blood and insides. The door broke open as Joe let the smoking shotgun fall to the floor. He just stood there as old man Donaldson, Bluey Miser, Humphrey and Eight-toes Marler entered. They too stood there, looking at him. Miser's toothless mouth gaped. Humphrey began to heave and rushed from the room.

Mrs Donaldson pushed between the gape-mouthed men and stood still at the sight of Jack Marker moaning and bleeding like a half-slaughtered steer.

Marianna knelt naked on the bedding. She bit the back of her wrist and the other arm covered her breasts. She stared at Joe Marker. He just stood there, looking at nothing.

"Sarah! Sarah!" Mrs Donaldson screamed. She began

to push the men backwards out the door. Sarah was pushing from the other side to get through. The young girl's head popped up between Bluey Miser and Eight-toes Marler. She looked at big Jack shivering all over and moaning on the slimy floor. Then she looked at Mrs Donaldson.

"What?" asked the young girl.

"Get everyone out of the bar and keep them out," ordered the tavern-keeper. "Quick, get Morrison, Bluey!" she continued, treading into the puddle oozing out of Jack Marker.

She shook her head, biting her lip.

"Oh God, no!" she mumbled, then raised her head. "You go with Bluey, Eight-toes. And you, Joe. Get out of here and don't come back."

Jack Marker howled and sobbed, cursing his mother for ever letting him breathe.

Joe Marker shuffled to the door. He was blubbering like a baby.

"I didn't think it would be like this. I didn't think it would be slow like this," he said.

Old man Donaldson wiped the sweat off his head with the bar cloth in his hand and patted Joe Marker on the shoulder.

"You had to do it," he said.

"You piss off too," Mrs Donaldson said to her husband, kneeling down in the slime to lift Jack Marker's shivering head in her hands and resting it on her thighs.

As she lifted him the blood ran faster from the ragged end of his body. She shrugged and shook her head.

"Marianna. Get some clothes on," she hissed. And as Donaldson followed Joe Marker out of the dark room she yelled, "You're all the same! Close the door."

The door slapped shut.

Marianna dropped a crumpled dress over her head and wiggled her arms into the sleeves. She glanced from Jack Marker to the shotgun lying in the middle of the floor in a pool of gore. Then she turned her eyes to Mrs Donaldson.

"Oh, Jack Marker," Mrs Donaldson crooned, resting

her hand across his lacerated brow. "You're all the same."

The tavern-keeper looked up to Marianna and nodded at Jack Marker's trousers. The girl put her hand in the pockets and drew out paper money. She put one note back and handed the rest to her mistress. Then she pulled out a coin pouch. She took out two half crowns and handed them to Mrs Donaldson.

VII

JOE MARKER GOT as fair a trial as most people do, a fairer trial than many. Sergeant Dirlsky testified that he had suspected the defendant all along, but said he had had to wait for the villain to show his hand.

"Unfortunately that meant there would be one more victim," said Dirlsky, gripping the rail of the witness dock.

The trial was held in the church in a paddock of dust on the edge of town.

The judge, brought in from Sydney Town for the occasion, nodded. His worship had a face like a spectacled mouse. He was buried in hot robes and a wig. He sucked a pencil thoughtfully.

Evidence was produced. The weapon was a large Canadian hunting knife suitable for skinning beaver or kangaroos.

"Or..." suggested the judge, "for cutting men's throats."

"Precisely," said Dirlsky.

Also endorsed as evidence were many items of clothing, a multitude of documents and diagrams, and a surveyor's map of Blood Gully. The judge found it all intriguing.

When the shotgun was carried forward, the judge removed his glasses.

"And this?" asked His Worship. "This, I presume, is the weapon which dispatched the victim..."

The judge flipped through the sheaf of documents on his elevated bench. In despair he flapped his hands down hard and thought. The court waited. Then the judge saw a name on a piece of paper. He put his glasses back on and peered at the writing.

"...which dispatched the victim...Joe Marker?"

There was a bureaucratic delay as the judge's misin-
formation was corrected. Joe Marker sat staring at the
floor, his hands in chains and one ankle shackled to the
cedar rail of the courthouse.

"So," the judge said, upon the advice of his assistant.
"The deceased is *Jack* Marker. The *prisoner* is Joe Marker!"

The prisoner was called. But he did not answer. Doctor
Morrison was called to examine him. Morrison declared the
man fit to stand trial.

Under cross-examination by the judge, Dirlsky sat back
with his arms folded.

"You have shown us the evidence, Sergeant," said the
judge, waving his hand in a swirl. "A large amount of
evidence has been presented...but what of a motive?"

Dirlsky's adam's apple rose and fell in his throat.

"I am not a medical man," he said. "But in my opinion
it is a case of criminal derangement of the mind. As op-
posed to mental derangement of the mind."

The judge nodded.

The only confusion in evidence arose from the police
accounts of the events. Sergeant Dirlsky and Senior Constable Hedges differed on many insignificant details.

It seemed that once the police had secured their own
release from the lock-up they had spent a remarkably long
time organising their pursuit of the accused. Had they been
more prompt they might have intercepted Joe Marker and
saved his brother's life. The judge said he thought the
constables might have spent a little too long checking their
weapons and planning a course of action. He dismissed
suggestions by Senior Constable Hedges that Sergeant Dirlsky
had shown misjudgement by not leading the search party
himself. At the same time the judge praised Hedges' role
in the apprehension of the perpetrator subsequent to the
dreadful crime.

The judge noted the evidence of civilian witnesses and
lamented that he detected fear and suspicion among them
which were unfounded.

"The law is for the protection of all, regardless of

wealth or social worth — it is applied equally and without favour to high-born and low. There is no need for fear!" he said. "Far too many witnesses have failed to exert their memories."

The judge stared at the sea of sweating faces gathered beneath him. He read from a note.

"In particular I refer to the evidence of the tavern-keeper, Mrs Donaldson, the man O'Reilly, even the Inspector's own gardener, Hughes..."

The judge looked quizzically at Inspector Holman. Holman glared at Dancer Hughes. Mrs Donaldson was looking up at the ceiling. Mad Mick O'Reilly glared at the pink, old judge. Then he spoke up.

"I served my five days. What more do you want?" he said, his voice rising among the murmurs of the court crowd. Dancer Hughes turned and gave him a scolding frown. The improvised courthouse fell eerily silent. The constables looked at each other. The judge looked away from the Inspector and toward the crowd, where heads began to turn to each other questioningly.

The judge blinked his eyes. He glanced down at his note.

"While on the subject of restrained effort in recalling or revealing evidence — which, I might remind you, is an offence punishable by law — I must note the absolute reluctance of the accused to co-operate with this court. I may assure you, Mr Marker, that your refusal has done your case no good. No good at all. Be certain of that. In fact, I must warn you, I believe in all honesty that these silent tactics of yours have only done you harm."

The judge removed his glasses and stared down the length of his nose at Joe Marker. Marker stared at the floor.

"I have met such tactics before," said the judge. "Believe me, Marker, men tend not to live very long to regret the mistake."

He put his glasses on and referred to his note with his finger. Joe Marker did not move as the verdict was passed down. A murmur rose in the court...

SENIOR CONSTABLE HEDGES did not hear a single word of it all. He was reliving the capture of Joe Marker. The memory was etched deep in the tissues of his brain. As the judge's voice droned on, Hedges cursed Dirlsky under his breath for sending his men out alone to possible death, and not sharing their fate. Dirlsky had not even tagged along to help.

Hedges recalled how when Constables Taylor and Fraser and himself finally got out in the street he had suggested they split up.

That should never have come out in court, Hedges thought. And it never would have, except Taylor had wanted to brag about how he had been the first to guess where Joe Marker had gone.

"He's probably at the Bushman's Arms to shoot mad Jack," Taylor had said.

"Don't be stupid," Hedges had replied. "Where would you go? He's probably bolted for the hills."

Everybody laughed when it all came out in court.

"You two go to the Bushman's Arms and check if he's there," Hedges had told constables Fraser and Taylor. "I'll check the rest of town and see if I can find Jones while I'm at it."

Then, he told the court, he had said, "If Joe Marker is there, don't do anything. Come and get me."

But neither Fraser nor Taylor could remember such a remark being made by Hedges at the time. Hedges had accused them of withholding evidence.

At the time, however, there had been no time to make sure everyone had heard what he said. There had been no time for mincing words. Joe Marker was at large with a loaded shotgun. Hedges felt a ripple of the huge fear he had felt when he had hunted for Joe Marker.

"Pig's arse we will! We're not splitting up," Fraser had said. "Either we all search the rest of town, or we all go to the Bushman's Arms."

"Come on, you two gutless bastards," Hedges had snapped, losing patience with them. "Marker is probably miles away by now."

Then they heard the blast of both barrels. They heard the shockwave resonate throughout the Bushman's Arms and echo down the street. They heard the howl and scream from the tavern. They heard the screaming and shouting from the Havelock Hotel.

Hedges remembered Eight-toes Marler stumbling along behind Bluey Miser, he remembered Young Mr Callow and the hotel guard rushing out of the Havelock. His strongest memory, though, was the memory of fear — the fear of death. So overpowering was it that his stomach had clenched like a fist, as if it was falling out of his insides.

Then, like a gift from heaven and a joy to behold, Joe Marker had walked out of the Bushman's Arms unarmed.

The relief was immense. Hedges recalled the wide smiles on Taylor's and Fraser's faces, he remembered the feeling. Even after the arrest, in the dead of night, he had woken up trembling all over and laughing.

Suddenly he felt a tug at his shoulder. It was the judge's assistant. The court was empty. Hedges was alone.

"The session has risen," said the assistant. "Everyone else has gone. You may care to go yourself."

"I must have fallen asleep," mumbled Hedges.

The assistant smiled, bowing a little with his hands clasped behind his back.

"I sometimes do that myself," he said.

HEDGES trudged out, fatigued with heat, and as he stepped into the open, the still afternoon air hit him hard. Rooster Gorman, Dancer Hughes and Eight-toes Marler watched him walking alone up the long, dusty street. As he passed a group of cedar cutters, each one turned and spat into the middle of the road in his path.

Hedges' step did not falter. He stared straight ahead and walked. A lump of spit hit his boot. He felt the hit on his toe through the leather. He ignored it and kept walking.

"Look at that, will you?" said Rooster Gorman.

"I don't remember seeing anything," said Dancer Hughes, repeating what he had told the judge.

The three men roared laughing as Hedges strode by.

He stared straight ahead, sweat pouring down his red face.

"Bushmen can't live by town and city rules," snarled Gorman. "It's different forms of madness..."

"That may be true," said Eight-toes Marler. "But if you'd seen Jack Marker lying there blowed in two, you wouldn't be so sure of what was true any more."

"They should have just left those Marker boys to settle their grudge. Probably been building up for years. If the traps had kept their beaks out of it there would have been no gun, no murder and there'd be no hanging."

Gorman spat into the street, but Hedges was gone.

"They would have killed each other anyway," Marler said.

"Be buggered. They would have had their fun and gone back up in the hills to cut timber like they always do," replied Gorman.

They began talking about Nancy Ogilvy, whose husband had been killed in the sawmill. She had stabbed old man Gill, the sawmill owner, to death in broad daylight as the Big Man came out of the Havelock Hotel. Before the hotel guard had had time to unfold his arms, Gill was kneeling on the verandah with an iron skewer through his heart.

Nancy Ogilvy had stood on the back of the wagon on her hanging day, with the rope round her neck as they tried to pull the black bag over her twisting head.

"You can all go to hell!" she had screamed. "I hope your town burns to the ground."

"That was the worst," said Dancer Hughes. "That and Tobacco Williams. He wasn't no bushranger. You couldn't trust him, true, but that was all...poor bugger."

"They couldn't have hung a *hat* on the evidence they hung him on," muttered Gorman.

The three men suddenly looked upwards over their shoulders, squinting from the glare of the sun, as they heard three cheers ring out from the Havelock Hotel.

"I WOULD have expected to see you dancing in the street, Sergeant," Major Stumic said, raising his glass. "It is a marvellous feather in your cap."

53

"Our future city!" declared Sam Sodge, raising his glass and grinning.

"The sergeant merely did what he is paid to do," said Inspector Holman. "Sergeant?"

"Hear, hear," said Sodge, waving his glass.

Dirlsky clicked his heels and bowed slightly.

"To the best of my ability, sir."

"Well, this time you have excelled yourself, Sergeant," said Stumic.

"I say," Stewart broke in. "Tell me, Doctor Morrison, did that Jack Marker wretch feel much pain once he had been shot?"

"He was in shock without doubt," replied Morrison, clearly not taking much pleasure in the subject. "But I dare say shock alone would not have erased the agony completely."

"I must say that I found certain references by the judge to your part in the whole affair rather uncharitable, Doctor Morrison," said McCartney, one of the bank managers.

Morrison shrugged.

"Perhaps he had a bill from his doctor," Morrison quipped amiably.

"I honestly thought Sam had been shot..." sputtered Stewart. "I saw him lying there. The girl screamed."

"I can vouch for that," interjected Father Mitchell. "I myself was stricken by a heart seizure. How I survived it I'll never know."

"I can understand how the judge was concerned," said Young Mr Callow with a smile on his face, which he twisted as if he was trying to suppress it. "It does look strange on face value — prima facie, so to speak — that the good doctor was treating a man for a sprained ankle in one part of the town, while in another part a man was dying unattended of shotgun wounds."

"You're not suggesting..." said Morrison.

"I'm not suggesting anything," said Young Mr Callow. "I know what happened. It's understandable. But I can also understand people being concerned about it."

Sam Sodge stepped back into the crowd on the balcony.

He glared with slit eyes at Young Mr Callow.

THAT NIGHT, after the trial and the celebrations, the heat rose from the ground in waves. The smoke of cooking fires snaked into the darkening blue sky above town. Two patrolling policemen admired the broadest, strongest limb of the hanging tree.

"That's a good average," chuckled Dirlsky to his wife over dinner. "One hanging a year since I've been here."

He had just been telling her of the celebrations in the Havelock parlour, how the travelling judge had declared that his preparation of the case was the finest he had seen. That was Dirlsky's proudest moment. All eyes had been upon him. They had raised their glasses.

Mrs Dirlsky stood stiffly behind her husband. She held a long, saw-toothed bread-knife in her hand. She glared at the Sergeant as he sang his own praises and lived again his moment of glory.

"I was the man of the hour," he said.

Mrs Dirlsky sneered, twisting her face and glaring at the back of her husband's skull. She threw the bread-knife flat onto the draining board beside the cast-iron sink.

The hot night air crept slowly among the houses, where panting dogs lay in the humid grass and trees drooped sluggishly. Women groaned and rolled exhaustedly away from hands too heat-weary to pursue them. Babies sucked for fresh air in dingy rooms, too tired to cry, with little eyes too weak to stay closed.

Full-grown horses in stalls fretted and ached for open spaces. Men camped in the wild enjoyed the luxury of every slight zephyr, as each short-lived breeze licked at their sweaty, bearded, sleeping faces bared to the stars. Their hairy necks and faces attracted swarms of savage mosquitoes. The whispy insects feasted on bare hands clutching blankets closed; and under the blankets the bushmen roasted in their own itching sweat. By means of one torment or another, time drained its vengeance from every being.

SERGEANT DIRLSKY rolled over in the worst nightmare of all, a nightmare clutching him remorselessly, irretrievably. He was doomed. He stared crazily into all corners of the room. His wife stirred.

"Don't move, Hedges," Dirlsky whispered. "They're here alright. I can smell their eyes."

"Go to sleep," groaned Mrs Dirlsky, nudging the upright Sergeant with her elbow. She rolled over and pulled the pillow over her face.

"He wouldn't even let me tell him. What am I supposed to do? What would you do?"

"Go to sleep," she said, lifting her face from the pillow.

Dirlsky turned toward her in the dark.

"How can I sleep? My mind is full of murders and my commanding officer won't take responsibility. They're all here," he cried, shaking his hands turned like claws in the dark toward his face. "Here in my brain, with their throats cut!"

Mrs Dirlsky sat up.

"For God's sake, not this again!"

She flung the sheet off, bounded out of bed, trod into her slippers and walked around the bed. She stood in front of Dirlsky's face. He grabbed her by the wrists.

"Hedges! Hedges!" Dirlsky yelled as excitedly as a child. "I've got one. Quick."

Mrs Dirlsky tried to wriggle free, but the Sergeant held on tighter. She grunted and gasped as she struggled more and more strenuously. Dirlsky began to shout and to twist her arms in different directions.

"Hedges! Where are you? He's trying to get away," Dirlsky yelled out.

She screamed. It had no effect. She wrenched one arm free and slammed the palm of her hand across his face.

He blinked once and saw her. He let her arm go.

"I couldn't see you in the dark," he muttered, shaking his head. "What happened?"

He wiped his face on the bedsheet and blew his nose on it before tossing it in a heap in the middle of the bed.

Mrs Dirlsky slumped on the corner of the bed, rubbing her wrists.

"This is the last time I sleep in this room," she said. "I mean it."

Dirlsky rubbed his face with his hands.

"You're as mad as the poor fool you're going to hang," Mrs Dirlsky said. "My God, I feel as if the whole world has gone mad. Half the town knows he didn't do it."

She stood up.

"I'll sleep in the other room and move my things out tomorrow. You can sleep with your friends."

"What friends?" he snarled.

"That's your business," she said, going to the door.

"You can't blame me for what happens in a court of law," he yelled.

"Court of law? Huh. That's a good one," she sneered. "More like a circus of fools."

"Where do you think you're going anyway?"

"I told you," she said. "I'm not putting up with all your carry on."

With that she disappeared through the pitch-dark doorway.

"Don't be a fool," Dirlsky called after her. "It was only a dream."

He lay back with a sigh. He snatched her pillow up and hurled it in the direction of the door. He could hear her fussing about in the kitchen.

"Go on," he snarled. "I never get anything out of you anyway."

The steamy, crushing calm hung heavy, heavy, heavy... like the footsteps of an invisible giant come out of some unseen dimension to trudge on the living ruins of souls... as if the world was roasting from the heat bursting within it...as if heat walked like a curse among those too weak to do more than breathe it...trudging among the tiny shacks, sheds, huts and humpies propped up with poles...trudging among the few cottages with gardens, and the mansionlike houses on their Blood Gully estates.

VIII

JOE MARKER, the convicted mass murderer, glanced aside at his guard, then looked back at the floor.

"Five men. That must have took guts. And your own brother!" said Constable Jones. "Real guts! Unless you've got mice in the roof. Heh-heh...you're not really mad are you, Joe?"

Constable Jones wondered aloud as he got up from the desk. Senior Constable Hedges quickly took his chair.

"Hey Joe," Constable Jones continued. "Why you never killed no women?"

He grinned at the condemned man in his silent cell.

"You're not a gentleman deep down are you, Joe?"

Constable Jones whistled awhile, listening to the sound of nothing. Then he smiled.

"Are you mad, Joe? I don't think you're mad. Just because you don't talk don't mean much. You wouldn't have a lot to say, I don't suppose.... I suppose you'll have a lot of explaining to do...later...up there...in the big courthouse in the sky. You might not get off so easy up there," chattered Jones. "I bet that's what you're thinking, eh, Joe? I can tell you're thinking something."

The door opened behind Jones. Senior Constable Hedges leapt up from the desk. The hangman who had come into town on the coach entered, with three ropes over his shoulder, like a rope juggler's helper in a travelling show.

"This is Gartney, the hangman from Sydney Town," explained Hedges.

Jones and Gartney smiled at each other without warmth. The hangman had no teeth. His coat was scuffed and frayed.

His handshake was soft, limp and greasy. Jones wiped his hand on his tunic.

Joe Marker glanced up sideways and looked back down.

"This is Constable Jones," said Hedges.

The door remained open. A bunch of dishevelled children in bare feet clung to the awning-post, staring into the lock-up.

Constable Taylor strode from the street.

"Go on. Clear off," he growled.

Taylor walked into the office. Hedges grinned and waved his hand in Taylor's direction.

"And this...is Constable Taylor. He helped me and Constable Fraser capture the prisoner. It was no easy game I can tell you," said Hedges. "No easy game at all, which you will appreciate when you see the fellow. He is a giant."

Taylor's chest expanded proudly, and Jones looked a little glum.

"And here he is," said Hedges, stepping over toward the cell, which sometimes contained up to ten men. Now it seemed crowded with the bulk of Joe Marker alone.

"Mad Joe Marker!" Hedges declared, as though naming a new country. "Joe Marker the throat-cutter — the shotgun murderer of his own brother."

Gartney raised his eyebrows.

"Say hello to Mr Gartney," Hedges told Joe.

Joe Marker stared at the floor. Hedges laughed. Jones joined in the laugh and Gartney smiled. Joe Marker stared at the floor.

"See. I told you. It's a waste of time hanging him. You could bury him just like that. He don't even eat no more," Hedges chuckled to the hangman.

Gartney looked Joe Marker up and down and placed two ropes on the low bench. He tested the third for strength, jerking a couple of feet of it between his hands like a silk merchant showing off a length of his cloth. Then he kissed it.

Hedges and Jones looked at each other in amazement. Taylor just looked through the bars. He wondered if Gartney's thick, tough rope would be enough to break Joe Marker's neck.

THE ROPE was attached round the branch of the tree while the neck-snapper supervised. Gartney was starting to make enemies in town already.

"Further along, further along," he yelled to the man up the ladder in the tree.

The man lost his temper and began to climb down.

"Look," said the sweating rope-fixer. "You want it here...there and back again...a little bit further...back and forwards. Do the bloody thing yourself."

Gartney stared at the man. He wiped his bristly jaw. He looked up at the rope and made a loud thinking sound as he nodded deeply.

"No, that will do," said Gartney. "That's fine."

The crowd started to assemble in the vicinity of the tree. Overhead, the eagle flew; and in his cell, Joe Marker watched his guards of honour preparing themselves for their duty.

Constable Taylor was polishing his boots for the third time. Constable Jones had brushed his hair and was patting it down flat, so flat and hard it looked as if it had been painted on his scalp. American hair-oil ran down the back of his neck.

Marker sat on the cell cot, his elbows on his knees and his hands clasped together. There was nothing else for him to do. He had lived his life and he had ended his brother's. His lips twitched as he recalled his brother begging for death with his eyes, as he lay chopped to bits. His mind tossed around and raced away from the memory, fading away and rolling like mist among the unthinking cedars — among the feeling giants like himself who would be cut down...cut down.

Joe Marker would never see the forests again, with their broad branches arrayed in a design as marvellous as that of any city building or cathedral. He was as dead now, he knew, as he would ever be...dead to the bright, glossy, pointed leaves of the cedar greenery...and the lilac spring flowers in showy sprays. Marker knew he would never swing an axe again. He could feel the bulk of his arms withering. He felt himself shrivelling up inside.

He had seen men so sickened by the slaughter that their hands had become too weak to hold the axe. He had heard the many excuses they thought up to hide their weakening. He too had felt his own hands grow weak, but no-one had ever seen it — except his brother, Jack. And Jack Marker himself would have been the last man ever to show such a weakness. His taunts had been deep. Joe had felt them deeply, as deep as only your own blood could cut, driving in the shafts of ridicule. Jack's taunts had been unbearable.

What Joe Marker felt inside, as he slumped leaning on his knees in the death cell, he fled from thinking. He fled from thought to feeling, and then from feeling to feeling. He lunged through his jumbled soul for the sweet feeling of being among the gentle giants, with their smooth leaves and massive wood. He felt among the darknesses inside him for the footsteps that he had once stolen among the cedars, when their round, gold clusters of bead-like fruit had formed a carpet of baubles. Marker felt the muscles in his hands now turning into meat. They would never again touch an axe, not even with a fingertip; they would never again lean against a tree with its bark all grey and slightly furrowed. He would no longer look up to the huge glossy canopy of leaves above him, and he would no longer crush the dryness of the bark to dusty fibre between his fingers, sprinkling the soft, blood-like cedar dust all over him like powder....

In the street the crowd was staring at the tree and at the Sydney hangman. They had started to discuss Tobacco Williams and the way he had smiled and winked when the black bag was drawn over his head. They discussed Nancy Ogilvy too, up there screaming blue murder at the town that had killed her husband, until her face was covered.

The hangman shuffled up, his hands almost hidden by

the sleeves of his coat. He lifted his hat and brushed his hand through his greasy, grey hair, then he clamped the hat down to hold the hair in place.

The crowd stirred as Senior Constable Hedges marched briskly from behind the buildings. Behind him followed constables Jones and Taylor, with rifles sloped against their shoulders. In their midst, stumbling to keep up, with his hands tied and his legs hobbled at the ankle, was Joe Marker. A deep, audible hush rose from the crowd.

For the first time the crowd saw Joe Marker look up. Hands were raised and heads were nodded to great him. The crowd was stretching right across Main Street. To gain a better view the people of Blood Gully had installed themselves on horses; some stood on the backs of wagons, carts and drays; and they held onto each other for balance.

Joe Marker looked up at the rope. He felt himself drawn to it, as if this was the purpose of his whole life. The hangman tapped him on the shoulder with the black bag and jerked a dirty yellow thumbnail toward the makeshift gallows.

Gartney removed his hat and his matted grey hair fell free in tangles round his face. He clambered up the wooden steps onto the back of the funeral wagon. Then he slipped, almost tumbling over the side. Hushed murmurs of delight arose from the crowd. Gartney's hat slipped out of his hand.

"Good Lord, I thought so," hissed Holman as the crowd began to laugh. "The fool is drunk."

The hangman grabbed at his hat three times before it fell to the ground. He nearly followed it, but clutched the wagon-side and saved himself. Then he stood up, bare-headed, puffing and red-faced, staring at the crowd.

Marker mounted the steps. He shrugged off Taylor's offer of a helping hand. But the chain on his ankles prevented him from raising his foot far enough to reach the next step, and he fell forward with a clunk against the hardwood. Like a trained animal, he crawled up on his elbows and knees, dragging his shackled legs behind him and clutching the wagon tray with his manacled hands.

Broad smiles spread across the faces of the crowd. Joe Marker stood on the back of the funeral wagon. His head bumped the noose and the rope began to swing. Again he looked down at the crowd.

Suddenly the street was silent.

As the noose was looped over his head, Joe Marker saw the blur of rope pass between·his eyes and the deep, faraway hills. He felt the comforting cool of the hanging tree, all of its leaves breathing and cooling the hot air of the long, merciless afternoon. The dry, white oval cedar fruit was dead forever. The flamboyant wands of baubles, lilac and pale pink, were dead. The cedar cutters were all dead. The voices of the axe-men were dead, and so were their axes, along with their grunting and growling as they tore at the giant trees. Dead was the hatred which makes killing easy. Dead was the longing which makes dying hard. Dead was the rain of sweat falling to the ground from platforms high on the tree-trunks...

Joe Marker took one deep breath. He did not fear to leave it all behind.

He stood still. The noose lay round his thick neck, his smooth throat glistening with sweat. Not a muscle in his face or throat moved.

A leaf fell down and balanced delicately upon his unbrushed, messy hair. Joe Marker raised his chin and looked at the rope. The cedar cutters knew the gesture. Marker had looked at the rope in the casual way an axe-man might check the build and probable twist and fall of an easy tree.

Marker closed his eyes and waited. If the rope was strong enough, he did not have a care in the world.

The crowd simmered with whispers. The people of Blood Gully could not remember what Joe Marker really looked like, underneath all his bruises, his slowly healing cuts and battering-marks.

Joe Marker's eyes were dry as he stared in the darkness of the hood placed over his head. His lungs strained for fresh air. With the crack of a whip and a jerk of chains, the funeral wagon shifted forward. Inspector Holman still held his signalling hand in the air.

Mouths opened with horror and excitement all over Main Street. The priest turned his face away in prayer as Joe Marker's hobbled feet did a little shuffle. Then, with a shake of the chain, they half stepped, and half slid, into the air.

With a vicious shock, the rope snapped out its length. The bones cracked so loud with the whack that the whole crowd, as one body, flinched. The street stirred with murmurs of "Shame," and "Animals," and "Worse than murder", and there was a loud vomiting noise, and in several places the crumpling sound of collapsing bodies as people fainted.

Then the crowd started to break up like a decaying carcass. Three men self-consciously backed up the funeral wagon under the dangling dead man, dragging legs and chain along the tray.

Behind them, small boys stared upward, at the giant being cut down. The three helpers took the strain, clutching Joe Marker's last shirt as the hangman cut the rope. With one solid chop of the knife the rope frayed a little.

Gartney gripped the rope with one hand and began to saw laboriously. It seemed forever before anything happened. Then, with a ping, the rope was cut through. Marker's body slipped out of one man's grasp. The other two stood there holding the rags of Joe's shirt as the body bashed down onto the wagon tray.

"Dirty rats . . ." Huley Colquoon cried.

IX

EACH DAY BRINGS worries, but each day's hope is that the night will give relief. This day passed like the day before it, as all days do and the denizens of Blood Gully sought rest as the night came. But first there were many who needed strong drink inside them — to stupefy their minds which had long lost the power of restful sleep. As if in some giant ritual the stars overhead turned across the unblue sky and the water in the creek shone back reflections.

The creek gurgled far across the hills like a gigantic whisper, and in the small town two dogs barked and then snuffled down to sleep away the hot day's weariness. The heat of the night was no more than the usual fare in time's treacherous feast.

Dancer Hughes was reclining in the natural sofa of a bowed tree. The fork in its main branches was perfect for relaxation. He was puffing on a pipe loaded with the shaggy, dried flowers of his Indian smoking medicine. In the background he could hear the voices of the Donaldsons, the husband and wife carrying on the tradition of untold centuries.

They were screaming at each other. Old man Donaldson was telling her what she could do with her head if she wasn't careful; and Mrs Donaldson was telling him that if he wasn't careful she would cut his throat in his sleep.

Dancer Hughes closed his eyes, his hands folded across his belly. He could hear Donaldson's laugh.

"Don't tempt your luck," Mrs Donaldson laughed back harshly. "If you put my mind to it far enough I'll find a way. How do you like dog bait in your onions?"

Dancer Hughes looked up. He saw old man Donaldson answer his wife without a word, flinging out his arm to punch her with the back of his hand. He clipped her cheek as he lost balance and staggered backwards into the long grass. She stood there, the noise of the tavern behind her, her mouth hanging open and a welt across her cheek, as Donaldson staggered to his feet. He shook his finger at her as he swayed, shifting his feet to keep balance.

"Mind your own business and I'll mind mine," he ordered her. "If you don't like it...bugger off. I don't need you to run this place."

Donaldson staggered away, his eyes aflame. His wife nursed her face in one hand till a voice from inside the Bushman's Arms called her. Resolutely she wiped her cheek, turned and went back in.

Donaldson in turn forgot her...and all else, as he burst with love for his own soul, much satisfied with the path that he had carved through life.

It had been a very weaving path, just like the faltering steps he was taking now. He burst into song.

> *Hurrah for Australia the golden*
> *Where men of all nations toil*
> *To no-one will we ever be beholden*
> *While we've got strength*
> *To turn up the soil*

As he sang he waved his arm and swung his huge body as if conducting some great unseen orchestra. Then he staggered down the lane where it was dark, and he vomited.

IN HER SOFT dark bed in her big dark room, Mrs Holman heaved with the fever. Inspector Holman puffed on his pipe in the next room, listening to his wife stir, thinking that at least as long as she was moaning she was not dead.

Holman heard the door click as the maid entered the sickroom. Rebecca, the one they called the Goddess, was shuffling on the rug. The sound came to Holman through the wall. He smiled and rose with his pipe gritted between his teeth, then he tip-toed to the door.

He listened with his ear to the timber, waiting for the girl's footsteps to come out into the hall.

ON THE OTHER side of town, Jansen, the coach office over-
seer, lay asleep, snoring and dreaming of Mrs Gill screeching
at him like a demon with flapping wings...

"What parcel?" Jansen moaned groggily as he rolled
over, sweating in his tortured sleep; then he rolled back
and snored and dreamed of his dead wife, a hard-working,
kind woman who had been cut down with a cramp in her
broken heart long before he had even tired of her.

Jansen woke and wished Mrs Gill to hell with her
parcel. Anyway, she herself had come down to the coach
for it in the end. What right does she have to disturb my
sleep, he thought, does she think she owns the whole town?

OVER THE HILLS, through the decimated forest, through the
paddocks, the heat trudged...through inaccessible gullies,
where the last eagle had sheltered in the tallest, toughest
tree, and down below, where the remnant colonies of wildlife had sought refuge. Hot air moved slowly among the
fallen giant corpses, over pools of red left by saws and axes.
Ridges that by day rang with the echoes of the savage axe
were wrung now by the merciless heat as the curse trudged
in, marking the sleeping faces with sweaty scowls and
smearing their sleep with restlessness.

A gang of marauding kangaroos crept across a miserable paddock of eaten-out, trampled-down stubble, nibbling
at dust.

"I'm not patrolling anywhere in this heat," moaned
Senior Constable Hedges, rolling over on a blanket in the
open cell. Outside, the night was a turgid darkness. Hedges
rolled his head from side to side and moaned. Constable
Taylor wiped his nose on his hand and wiped his hand on
his trousers. He stared at the shadow formed by Hedges'
hairy body, which lay naked except for his long pants.
Taylor flopped into the chair, exhaling heavily.

"I can't go out patrolling on my own," he said. "Fair
go, Hedges. I'm new at this."

"Do what you like," groaned Hedges. "Just don't
breathe."

AS REBECCA wiped the caked cack off the bedding, sweat dripped from her face and soaked into her clothing. Strands of hair stuck across her eyes and mouth as she rinsed the large rag out in a bucket of putrid water. The girl clamped her mouth shut so no disease could enter her. She held her breath as she fluttered her eyelids to work tears into her eyes, which had become dry with tiredness.

Inspector Holman's ear burned against the cedar door of his room. He listened with his heart beating like a young Romeo for the sound of Rebecca's delicate movements. Soon she would again be in the hall.

Holman's hand sweated as he squeezed the decorative enamel doorknob. Rebecca squeezed out the wet rag. She put her hand under Mrs Holman's nightdress and pressed her fingers down between the sleeping woman's breasts. The heartbeat was so soft. Rebecca felt outside Mrs Holman's clothes and put her hand over the woman's heart. There was nothing. It was only with her hand to the bare skin that Rebecca could feel any life in the heart at all. How close to death is this? she wondered.

A LONE OWL, the eagle of the night, glided across Main Street. It cooled itself with its own flight and landed out of sight, to deliver its message of death to some wretched little nocturnal rodent. The coach driver heard the swoosh it made. He looked when he heard it, but it had gone.

Blood Gully was the end of the line. The coach driver never slept much. The wheels took so long to stop rolling around in his head. He leaned forward where he was sitting on the chopping block, by the driver's sleep-out outside the coach office back door. He turned his wizened face to stare at the stars and started talking to himself again. Tomorrow would bring another journey, more faces, more dust, more sufferings to witness, more blessings. . . .

This was a bad season. So far he had seen three funerals for babies in three towns on the last leg of the trip. All of them had been killed by the heat. Waterholes along the way had all disappeared. The journey was taking longer and longer each time, as the horses flung their heads back gasping for air, as he chopped the air to bits with the whip over their faces.

"Ah," the scrawny driver snarled to himself. "That's just how it goes."

Towns, he thought, are all the same — half of them burning themselves out in twenty or thirty years, no doubt, some sooner. The folks get thrown together too hard. They get hurt. Simple science. Like the coach passengers, stay-put folks, who get sucked up by the road and hurtled along at speeds they can't even think at...and they end up all over the place...and all over each other. They too sometimes get hurt, he ruminated. He had seen healthy people begin a rough coach ride only to be dragged out dead at the end. Or near dead, like Mrs Holman.

"Poor young bitch," he muttered, then reached for the clay bottle of rot-gut rum nearby.

His eyes sparkled, as if they had absorbed some of the bright stars he was staring at. No sweat glistened on his skin, except where his beard itched. It was as though his body was too old and thin and leathery-dry to yield any moisture. He swallowed an odious taste of rank tobacco and mused, yet somewhere, something remained outside his grasp. It griped him. Some secret...of how it all hung together.

He tried to work it out, just for interest. He figured he had something in his idea of the coach passengers all jumbled up. Sure enough, that was how it was, with the whole world full of people all jumbled together as they were in this little town, squashing each other, treading on each other, bumping heads and getting hurt. Killed even.

He grabbed the bottle and gulped like a man afraid. What was this bowl into whose shape life was bent? This force to which whole nations bent themselves with ferocious conformity?

Who knows? he thought. He had seen towns born and towns die. He had seen them growing fast and slow. He had seen more towns than the average man could dream existed...and yet...and yet...

He stood up and his clothes hung from him, creased as if he was still sitting. The bottle hung from his fingers. He spat into the dark and shook his head and muttered, "And still a man knows shit all, damn it."

THE MAN WHO called himself Murphy woke from his dream and gripped the sapling frame of the hessian cot. He opened his eyes warily. The dull bush light started to give shape to the hut's insides. At first the room seemed filled with hunched men holding themselves still. But slowly they shrank away into the vague shapes of lifeless objects.

Murphy could hear Price's peaceful snoring. He smiled. It was true, let the mind dream what it will, he was free. Sweat dribbled from him.

The strong smell of eucalyptus cleared the drunken fuzz from his head, and he fell back into sleep, only to be swept along through the calm waters of sleep into dreams. First you jump...you fly...then you fall. He felt the sting of a wound, the claws of the law seizing him, hurling him down stairs all over again into the deep, damp, stinking earth. A swirl of abysmal images swept him along, knocking him to his dreaming knees. He wriggled in bed as they buckled. He bled again. The sweat dribbling all over his face and body was the blood in the dream...Murphy felt the foul breath of a kiss on his lips, a furry kiss...then he felt a fingernail or a hairpin piercing his skin.

Murphy tossed in bed. He flailed his arms weakly and moaned. He bled again into the dungeon slime, too defeated to cry, too defeated to feel. He woke again, into a dream of something beyond his reach. It was a rose, just beyond his fingers. He could stretch and almost touch it. There were a few others near it, but he could not reach further and they were surrounded by briars so he could not step any nearer. The scratches of the briars burned. Then he felt the rose prick at his cheek. The prick became a bite. He grabbed at the thing on his face, but it bit his hand as he seized it. It leaped from his hand as he half threw it at the wall. He rolled through another door, to the feel of clammy, sweat-soaked clothes, and the taste of eucalyptus everywhere.

He breathed and flicked his eyelids in the dark, and then lay there, lathered with sweat, thinking of the woman in the mail coach. He licked his lips, imagining her softness. His fingers twitched. He pictured to himself her peeling, dry lips, then her eyes...surrounded by pools of discolouration as dark as bruises. And he heard distant echoes of her head beating against the wall of the coach...far off...far off...in the bush...

SOME OF THE people of Blood Gully were having less rest than Murphy. A frazzled mother bowed over the burning brow of her only child. The candle burned low and then it burned out, and still she sat there, falling asleep, feeling the hot little forehead under her fingers. She closed her eyes and whispered.

"Thank God," she said.

The child's temperature began to fall, just as the night reached the peak of its deadly calmness. It seemed, for that short moment, that all life had left the world.

The mother cried and cried. Her tired eyes became swollen with streaming tears, her head dangled, and as she cried she dreamed a dream that the devil came. The devil walked like a man, and dressed like a man. She had seen him before. Everywhere. He spoke to her. She did not hear the words, but he told her he would trade her soul for the happiness of her child. He began to drag her soul out of her. It was tearing away at her insides. She swore and kicked her shin against the bed. With a jerk of her body she woke, as the pre-dawn glow sparked birds into song and the big saw in the mill began to whine. She reached out and touched the child's cold face. And she shrieked.

The thin, strong woman with bedraggled hair and sunken eyes shook all over. Then she calmed to a tremble. A smile flickered on her mouth then faded instantaneously as she reached to the child's face, and touched it. She felt the coldness. She screamed and tore at her blouse — for it dared to touch the breast which belonged to her child. She stood and rushed into the street, with her stiffening, cold little child in her arms.

The sawmill howled like a demon in panic as the first log of the day hit the big blade.

X

TWO DOGS LAY sleeping in the middle of Main Street as the two policemen strode in step along the rickety wood boards, then stepped down into the dust.

Constable Fraser chuckled as Sergeant Dirlsky muttered under his breath.

"When I heard all the screaming this morning I thought there'd been another murder," said Dirlsky.

"What did the little one die of, Sergeant?" Fraser asked as they walked along.

"How would I know?" mumbled Dirlsky, turning his head to investigate a display of clothing on the tailor's counter. The tailor grinned at the Sergeant and waved with a dustpan in his hand. Dirlsky twitched his head and winked. He had a good look at the blucher boots and blue shirts and tall yankee hats on display, but what had really caught his eye was a shilling piece on the floor near the door.

"Maybe it was pneumonia. Maybe..."

"Pneumonia in this weather?" exclaimed Fraser.

"Well it was dead and it never had its throat cut; that's all that matters."

Dirlsky shuddered to recall the feel of that little corpse in his arms as the woman lay bawling in the dirt at his feet.

"Wait here," he told Fraser.

He walked nonchalantly to the tailor's doorway, craned his neck and looked in. Then he looked up and down the street, ignoring Fraser. He did not notice Jansen coming over behind him as he bent down and reached into the tailor's store.

Jansen walked between the two sleeping dogs. They both half growled at him. Jansen hesitated, as though he

73

was going to give them a kick each for their trouble. He didn't take his eyes off Dirlsky, shaking his head.

Dirlsky rose and turned as he put the coin quickly in his pocket. He saw Jansen and blushed.

"Good morning, Sergeant," grunted Jansen, without a smile. "Doing a bit of cleaning up around town, I see."

"Oh, that?" Dirlsky said, slapping the side of his pants pocket. "I dropped that as I went along. I just came back to pick it up."

"Oh?" said Jansen. Fraser was grinning from ear to ear. Dirlsky started walking. Jansen turned and glared at the mangy dogs lying flat on the dust under the sun.

"Go on, you mongrels," he snarled, swinging his boot at them.

The dogs didn't move. Jansen stomped in the dust and yelled right near them. One stretched its four legs and shivered in disturbed sleep. The other raised its head and looked with one eye at Jansen and then lay back down with a lazy growl.

Jansen walked on. Dirlsky looked over his shoulder from a distance.

"Do you think he believed me?" he asked Fraser. Then both policemen stopped and turned in the direction of the sawmill as it let loose a murderously piercing whine.

MRS GILL sat at her study window, on her throne above the town, the signs of the restless night clearly marked on her softly crinkled face. She opened the neat parcel, which had been wrapped and unwrapped many times. Outside the window crept the hunting cat with the reptilian markings. The hair on its shoulders was prickling as it stalked through the garden.

The sawmill screeched and shrieked as it squealed and ground to a wailing standstill on the other side of town. Eerie silence sank across the whole valley.

The huge house was piled about Mrs Gill like the magnificent shell of some uncrushable creature. She removed the dark bottles from the grey package and placed them in two neat rows. Pills to the left and ointments to the right.

Well-being radiated from the old woman. This was her health. The pills were so powerful they worked even before being taken.

Mrs Gill read the labels and tittered gleefully as she dipped her finger into the largest bottle. Then she began to rub the ointment into her face.

THE DAY had begun late, with the weight of the night before upon it. News of the dead baby was travelling from kitchen to kitchen as the doors slowly opened. The two dogs just lay where they lay, impervious to insult and injury. A third dog soon lay dead with its head squashed in Main Street, where a wagon had driven over it.

When Mrs Ross heard of the child's death she wrung her hands in her apron and sat down. Soon she dried her tears and stood to knead the dough again.

"No use crying though," she said to herself, wiping her eyes. "The saddest thing is it was her only one. Even then she was lucky enough...though, who knows?"

She shook her head sadly and new tears welled in her eyes.

BACK IN THE HILLS where the axes sang, the bush-rats and ruffians had now found their circumscribed place. With sapling levers they shifted tons of log, grunting and groaning. They missed the strength and reach of the two giant brothers. The smell of dryness spoiled their every breath and dehydrated their lungs. Their mouths were still bitter from the taste of the hanging.

The same dry air was feeding the lungs of all. Those standing on their Snob's Hill estates or on the Havelock balcony, the traps and thumpers and shopkeepers of the town, the hungry-gutted dirt-scratchers and the thousands of worse-off poor bastards who dreamed only of a slightly more salubrious form of poverty, and all the thieving, land-gobbling squatters who thought they were kings on a couple

75

of hundred acres you could walk around in a single day.

The landless bush men drank their scorching black tea and looked down on the rest of the world. Some even dreamed of saving enough money to buy a little place of their own. They could not swing axes all of their lives, except for the likes of the Markers — men who blaze through life like comets and never grow old.

BREATHING the hot, dry air on Snob's Hill as he hoed over the dirt and the rich pig-shit in the Holmans' garden, Dancer Hughes thought of his harvest of the Indian smoking medicine flowers, with their long, shaggy purple heads and oily beads of elixir nectar. He remembered the day they hanged Tobacco Williams. As the black bag was being put over his head, at the last moment, they saw Tobacco Williams's lips move into a grin.

"Who's next?" Tobacco Williams had yelled out with the noose round his neck and his head in the bag.

The whole crowd had turned to where a loud voice behind them had called out "Me!" Jack Marker stood there, grinning; and beside him, Joe Marker looked sour as can be, glaring at the fate of Tobacco Williams, the funny man. Dancer wondered if it had really been Jack Marker who had yelled out. It could have been Joe. The story was strange enough to go in the Bible, he thought.

He preferred to remember the potato harvests, and the women's beautiful backsides, solid and warm in the foggy, silver mornings. . .a long way away from the hot day around him. He thought of the backs bent in full swing in the fields, and the spurts of mist from the red, wet lips in the cold, colourless faces. As he chopped into the dirt at his feet he could smell the sparkling women of those silver mornings, with their hands dirty to the elbow and their sacks filling with spuds.

Dancer wiped his face and began to slow his work. He felt like stopping soon, he told the garden.

"WHAT was all that hoo-dah last night in aid of?" grunted Price. "Aren't you happy with your blanket or something?"

"Nah," Murphy said, sipping a mug of resurrected tea and chewing bread. "I had a bad dream."

Price grumbled incoherently.

"What are you doing when you leave here?" Doyle asked Murphy, looking blindly in the direction of Price's voice. "What would bloody Holman and Dirlsky think if they found out we had MacGuire here?"

Striking the table with his hand, Murphy stood up. The bang sounded like a gun going off. Doyle jumped.

Murphy sat down. He looked at no-one. He stared at the crumbs on the plank table. In the midst of speaking, he flicked his eyes to Price. Price flinched.

"What's with this MacGuire bit then?" he said.

Price stood silently, hanging his head. Doyle smiled toward the voice. Murphy picked up a pointed carving knife and began to dig at the table as Doyle began to speak. Price nudged the blind man.

"Leave him be," Murphy told Price icily.

"You're MacGuire, aren't you?" said Doyle.

"We put two and two..." said Price.

"Shut up. Go on, Doyle," ordered Murphy.

"That's all."

"What do you mean, that's all? Nothing's all. How did you find out?"

Doyle sat without speaking. His head shrank down between his shoulders.

"How did you find out?" barked the hunted man.

Doyle's lips pressed shut. His shoulders hunched till he looked as if he had none.

"I told him," said Price, swallowing as soon as he had spoken.

"Who else knows?" Murphy asked. He shook the knife and then flipped it in the air. It spun so fast it looked like a plate.

Murphy let it fall into his hand with a slashing slap. He closed his hand round the handle, then pointed the blade at his own throat.

"See this?" he said, pressing the point of the blade up under his chin, stretching the soft skin till it looked ready to tear. "This is how MacGuire lives. He is very nervous. Now tell me. Who else knows?"

"No-one," whispered Price.

"Honest," said Doyle, "we wouldn't tell anybody. We're not like that."

"Everybody is like that," said Murphy. "If they weren't so stupid we'd still be living like bloody blackfellows in the garden of Eden. More men been sent to hell by a loose tongue than ever got there by a straight-out gunfight."

Doyle nodded.

"I didn't mean nothing."

"Well," Murphy smiled. "I suppose I've got no choice. I either trust you or cut your throats."

"You can trust us, M...Murphy," said Doyle.

Murphy flicked the knife again.

"I don't owe anybody anything. I'm Murphy. MacGuire's the bad one. I don't want to hear that name again so long as I'm here. That clear?"

Price and Doyle grinned gratefully and nodded. Price sat down alongside Doyle on the bench.

"You know," Murphy said, "When I first came here I spent a lot of time wondering if I could rely on you two. Now I feel much more relaxed," he laughed.

For half an hour Murphy sat there, sometimes resting his hands behind his head, staring at the crumbs on the table. Then he stood up and without a word trudged outside.

Outside the hut Murphy tried to figure out what was lying in store for him. And what lay behind him.

He felt the weight of all possibilities descend on him. Every branch felt like a tap on the shoulder. Every sound of the bush fired an impulse in him to run or dive out of sight. Every unexpected rustle made him jump inside.

He thought about what he wanted next, and then laughed at the thought. It would make a good play for the Melbourne Theatre or some toff place like that — *MacGuire the Murderer and the Police Inspector's Wife.*

He had known many women in his life. There was much about women he could teach women themselves. He

could tell from the smallest clue — the tilt of the face, a
scrap of conversation, the meeting of eyes across a room, a
way of standing — the "Yes" that is really "No", and the
"No" that is really "Yes", just like the black people could
read signs in the surviving bush.

He smiled, certain that he would reach her, somehow...on some level.

PRICE SAT BROODING, muttering monosyllables in answer to
Doyle's questions, and flinching to the sound of Murphy's
woodchopping. Thunk, the sharpened, pitted head struck
with a whack, splitting the dried timber, to be followed by
one or two more thuds as lumps of wood fell to the ground.

Price went out once or twice to offer advice, but each
time the old farmer returned shaking his head. The barrage
of flying wood continued outside.

"The know-it-all won't take no advice if you give it to
him with a spoon," said Price.

After each blow of the axe Murphy would take another
small piece of wood and place it across yet another piece,
and then he would raise the axe far over his head and
swing...

"The fool won't be satisfied till he's knocked himself
unconscious," said Price.

"He pays his way," said Danny Doyle.

Price looked across. Doyle faced toward him. Bits of
food speckled his beard.

"You know what I'd do if I was a rich man?" Doyle
mused."I'd pay someone to walk around with me everywhere. They could tell me what was around me. They
could tell me how they looked when folks spoke to me, so I
would know whose friendly voice masked a sneer...you
know what I mean?"

"You've got all shit in your beard," grunted Price.

Doyle brushed his beard, hitting his chin without concern.

"They could read to me and everything," he pined. "I
tell you what...she'd be beautiful — even if I couldn't see
her..."

Price made a disparaging grunt and looked down at his block-like hands. He turned them over to stare at the scars in their callus plating.

"Then everyone would say, 'Look at Danny Doyle's beautiful eyes. Ain't she sweet?' they'd say."

"Well, that's you," grunted Price, dragging himself upright and walking to the doorway. He pulled back his hair and looked out into the silent yard. Dogs lay in the open dirt, the shade they lay down in having wandered away, leaving the snoring hounds to baste in the sun.

"Not me," said Price looking around the yard to see where Murphy was. "No matter how rich I was, I'd do exactly the same as I'm doing now — just what I'm doing now. Nothing different..."

"Exactly the same?"

"Exactly the same. That's my idea of satisfaction. And let the world go to hell."

"You must be pretty happy."

"Happy? Be damned!" coughed Price. "What's happy about it? Too late for that now."

Nothing changed the unhappy look on Price's face. Murphy strolled from behind the fence of the vegetable garden with a spade in his hand. He lay the tool against the brush-and-branch fence and looked up under the sun's bright butchery.

"Back later," Murphy yelled. "I'm going for a walk."

Price spat into the yard and waved back. He retreated into the darkness of his hut, shaking his head.

"You should see the fart-arse little bit of wood he's cut up out here," he said to Doyle.

He took a big, black kettle off the fire-hook and swore at himself as tea leaves spilled from the metal canister. He tossed the old tea leaves through the rough hole which he called the window.

"Walks around like he owns the place," he muttered to himself. "He hardly does a thing, and even then he does it wrong."

Price pushed his pelvis forward from behind with his hands and tried to straighten himself.

"Can't you understand him not talking about who he is and what he's done?" said Doyle. "It's not just himself he's got to worry about."

Price stared into the dark, hot brew. The steam rose from the tea and licked out at his face. He shook his head, sounding wounded.

"He doesn't trust us."

MACGUIRE AND MURPHY had gone soul in soul for a long hike through the hills. He felt as if he had trudged thirty miles through a blizzard of his own sweat by the time he saw smoke again from Price's chimney. His feet ached, but he smiled as he hobbled. The walk had been worth it just to get away from Price's grumbling.

Murphy had met a sawyer along the way. They had had a smoke together.

"Cranky old piece of goods, old Price is," the sawyer had said. "But he wouldn't willingly do no harm. And that's a rare enough item these days."

The sawyer had smiled, baring his gleaming pink, toothless gums. "He's not a bad old jaw-fixer neither. Cheap too."

Just then, a man and his daughter had driven by in a rickety old sulky that had at one time been a showpiece.

"They think their shit don't stink," the sawyer had said, after giving the travellers a smile, a wave and a friendly remark. "That's the Dransfieldses. Squatter bastards."

"Where they from?" Murphy had asked idly.

"Where?" the sawyer had shrugged. "Up the road like everyone else. He's an ambitious bastard. He'd cut your quoit out if he thought his pigs would eat it."

Murphy had snorted contemptuously at the thought.

"He comes from Sydney someplace," the sawyer had explained. "From a family of toffs. I wouldn't mind chasing that young daughter round the paddock awhile though."

"Not bad," Murphy had said, looking down the road, watching the travelling dust settle before he spoke again.

"Know anything about that police inspector?" he had inquired.

"Police is police," the sawyer had replied.

Murphy had nodded as though it meant a lot.

"What about his missus?"

The sawyer had thought a moment, straightening out a bit of grimy rag twined round a trembling finger. The rag was soaked with dirty blood.

"Forget the missus," the sawyer had said. "Wait till you see their maid, the Goddess. She lives with them in town, but you'll never get near her. None of us will, ever. One of those gentlemen bastards will grab her up. You mark my words..."

As he walked Murphy could now see two splitters by the road, driving solid hardwood and iron wedges along the grain of a long log, whipping their mallets down in a rhythm of grunts and thumps, followed by the slow tearing apart of the compressed fibres. Then without another blow being struck the log began to groan inside. The splitters stood back as the last holding fibres tore apart and the log broke with loud complaint, falling into rough, splintery halves.

He suddenly came upon an abandoned slab and shingle hut with black charcoal on the door, reading "Pox". The hut was a faithfully enough built structure and it seemed a waste for it to be deserted. For a silly moment, Murphy imagined himself as master of the humble place, but he did not venture in. He poked the door open with a stick. The inside of the hut was clean and tidy, as if the occupant had walked out...and taken nothing.

Murphy felt the presence of death and disease. All round him he could hear echoes of axe-blows ringing across the hilltops and down the gullies, just like a plague of frogs at night. Behind the deserted hut, Murphy found a basket of shrivelled and petrified parsnips.

"Who are you?" a voice said.

Murphy spun round.

"I don't know what you want," said a grubby, decrepit man, pointing his gun at Murphy's navel, "but it isn't around here. Piss off!"

"Look..." said Murphy.

"You got bad eyes or something, mister?" asked the man. He raised the butt of his hand-held muzzle-loader to his shoulder.

A rusty bent nail and a number of small red pebbles slid out of the barrel. Murphy looked down where they had fallen.

"Plenty more in there. Don't you worry," said the man. "If you don't believe me just stand where you are for another few breaths. They'll be your last."

Murphy backed away. On the roadway he took a number of deep breaths and smiled into the bush, seeing only the roof of the strange place above the low, tangled brush. He thought of ways he could even the score with the cheeky hermit. There had to be some way of doing it without touching the poxy old goat.

Murphy wondered if the man really had the pox. He didn't seem any more sick than anyone else. Then he heard a voice behind him.

It was the same voice. Murphy turned. And there was the same man, in different clothes, but the same dirt.

The man was pointing a rifle, not the muzzle-loader as before, at his belly.

"You one of them government fellers?" said the man.

"He's just going, isn't that right, mister?" said the same voice. It was suddenly behind Murphy now, on the other side of the road.

Murphy turned his head again. The same man was speaking but now he had the muzzle-loader again. Murphy turned his head from one side of the road to the other. The two men were identical except for their weapons, both aimed at him.

"Yes. That's right," said Murphy, walking as he spoke, and stumbling as he walked, looking over his shoulder.

"I ought to go back and piss in their well," he muttered to himself. "That's if they ever use water."

The hills were dying slowly under the heat of summer. Murphy heard a gun go off, and there was an outburst from the scrub immediately behind him. As instantly as he spun, a family of kangaroos or wallabies rushed past him on the road, bobbing their heads and tails up and down in time. He could have reached out and touched them. They thumped the hard, stony road, skidding on the loose pebbles.

Murphy followed the road back to Price's, warily keeping an eye on the bush, and often turning round to look behind him.

XI

"MURDER! MURDER!" screamed Huley Colquoon as though he had discovered gold.

Huley ran right down Main Street with his shirt out and his braces flapping.

Sergeant Dirlsky and his constables were sitting under the camphor laurel tree, relaxing and smoking tobacco in the shade.

"Huley, come here and shut up!" yelled Dirlsky as the barefoot boy raced past the post office. The post office flag dangled like a lifeless mess of colour.

Heads craned from doorways. Putting his helmet on and rising to his full height, Dirlsky towered over Huley. The police grinned at the boy. His luck had turned against him before he was born, when his pregnant mother had been kicked by a horse in the spine and had almost died. Instead, Huley was retarded in the brain, and his mother's legs were useless. She talked about them now as if they were not there.

"What the hell are you screaming about?"

"Murder, Sergeant," puffed Huley. "Another one. Old Donaldson! He's got his throat cut...I found him."

Dirlsky's shoulders slumped, his face sagged and went pale.

"Damn!" said Constable Fraser, while Taylor's eyes darted from Hedges' face to Dirlsky's. The Sergeant glared at Huley Colquoon with malevolence. Hedges stood up with a little laugh.

"Where is he?" asked Hedges.

"You want me to show you where?" panted Huley.

"As long as you don't run along screaming out murder all the way," said Hedges.

Huley ran along Main Street, leading the squadron of marching police, their boots drumming on the dusty surface, their metal decorations bright against their dark tunics.

"Go and inform the Inspector, Constable Hedges," snapped Dirlsky. "And take Taylor with you."

Huley doubled back down the street so the police could catch up with him, as Taylor left the main body of men and followed Hedges.

Hedges began to complain.

"What's up with you?" Taylor asked.

"Dirlsky just wants me out of the way because I know more than he does about what to do," Hedges replied.

"The Sergeant is a clever fellow," said Taylor.

"Huh?"

"Well, he is. Even the judge said so," Taylor said.

Hedges' eyes looked polluted with disgust and hatred. He could hear the bootsteps of his colleagues receding behind him.

Taylor saw Hedges' anger and swallowed.

"But you're a clever fellow too, Hedges."

"Don't bullshit me, Taylor. I'm not clever. I'm intelligent. There's a difference...and an important difference. You know why?"

"No..."

"Right!" said Hedges as they strode along in time with each other's footsteps and approached a gang of small, wiry axe-men. Ringbarkers.

"At least you're honest," continued Hedges. "You don't know nothing, but at least you admit it. You're like Dirlsky. You wouldn't know if a horse fell on you. Neither of you."

"I don't know about that, so much," Taylor said, defending himself.

"That's what I said. You wouldn't know nothing," repeated Hedges. "Go and tell Holman! If anyone wants me I'll be manning the office."

DUST-COLOURED, deserted cobwebs hung from unmilled poles which formed the structure of the hut. The ceiling seemed pressed down by the long summer heat. Mrs Ross stirred the hogget stew, straining her face away from the sizzling steam. She thought of her sister who had married a top-hatted gent who sold top hats to toffs at highly inflated prices. He was a Cornishman who had rapidly amassed himself a small fortune under suspicious circumstances.

Perhaps her sister's luck had changed. She hadn't heard from her in ten years. Mrs Ross thought of her own luck and of One-eyed Albert. He might not have been such a great catch when compared to a top-hatted man, but he was pleasant enough to have around. She bit her lips, and wondered why she had been cursed with never having any children. She felt for her womb through the wall of her abdomen.

She heard a voice screaming and recognised it as Huley Colquoon's. She wiped her hands on her hand-marked apron and went out the front. The top of her head brushed the top of the doorway. A house cat watched her from a home-made chair by the cold, clean tin fireplace. The heat of the open air made her squint. She leaned out from the door into her treeless, withering garden devoid of flowers, and looked down her dusty road to Main Street. She saw nothing.

INSPECTOR HOLMAN folded his arms over his heart and at-tended to the piece of meat stuck between his teeth as he stared at the body. He rubbed at the trapped particle with his tongue, and he sucked the dangling strands to and fro like the weed in the bottom of the creek washed by water, trying to dislodge it. Old Donaldson had interrupted his breakfast. He wrinkled his face and glared at the slaughtered man as though the body was still alive.

"It's Donaldson. . ." began Dirlsky, but as he spoke so did Holman.

"What happened?"

Sergeant Dirlsky shrugged and shook his head; then he rubbed his jaw. Constable Taylor's face had gone ashen the moment he had seen the gaping gash in Donaldson's throat. Constable Fraser waved a switch of dead weeds over the wound to keep away the flies.

"It couldn't be suicide, I don't suppose?" muttered the Sergeant, shooting a furtive glance at his superior officer.

Constable Taylor swayed without taking his gaze from the huge swathe of bloody gore under Donaldson's peaceful face.

"Look at that," grimaced Fraser. "That's how they die with their throats cut. The pain must drain out of them with their blood."

"Who's that?" Inspector Holman asked briskly, looking up toward the long grass.

Huley Colquoon squashed down low as he heard Constable Taylor say solemnly, "It's Mr Donaldson."

"Yes, Constable. I can see," said Holman patiently, stroking his side-whiskers one at a time. "Begin your investigation. I want a full report by this evening."

"Yes, sir," said Dirlsky begrudgingly.

The ring of police stared down at the corpse huddled softly in the open.

"Looks like he's been hit in the throat with an axe," muttered Fraser as he stood, stiff at the knees.

"How is Mrs Holman, sir?" asked Dirlsky, lowering his voice.

"Don't you worry about Mrs Holman, Sergeant. Concern yourself with your responsibilities."

"Yes, sir," Dirlsky said slowly. "Taylor! Where the hell is Hedges all this time?"

"Sergeant!" pleaded Holman. "Don't worry about Hedges. I'll speak to him. You speak to Mrs Donaldson... anybody. Just bring me a murderer."

"Yes, sir. I will have a preliminary report ready for you this afternoon, perhaps..."

Huley Colquoon sat hidden in the long grass, listening to the police conduct their case. He sat breathing through his gaping mouth, and holding in his hand a tuft of hair. That was all he had found in Donaldson's dead clenched hand.

Huley had tried to tell Sergeant Dirlsky. Huley tried four or five times, but always the Sergeant refused to listen, and just told him to go to hell. But Huley only got as far as the long grass. There he hid, twiddling his unwanted evidence between his fingers.

Strange hair it was. He twirled the stuff and he sniffed it. Poo, it wasn't no ordinary hair. It smelled like dirt. Deep dirt out of a wombat hole. Huley had never seen hair like it anywhere, except on a black fellow once in the next nearest town two days' walk away. Huley had gone there once, when his mother had told him to go to hell. That was the last time she ever told him to go anywhere.

The next town had some black people who lived in the town except when the townsfolk chased them away. Huley remembered them very well. He had touched an old man to get the feel of his skin. The old man had looked at Huley and Huley had looked at him. Huley had never seen anyone look at him like that before. But no black people came to Blood Gully — except Marianna, and she wasn't really black. She was half white, they said.

When Huley returned to Blood Gully he could not believe his eyes. He was welcomed like a hero, or an important government man. His mother was seated on a chair at the coach office and Jansen was waiting on her as if she was a toff. She cried and begged him never to leave her again. People sure were hard to work out. One of them says, Go to hell, and they mean go away. Others say, Go to hell, and they mean go nowhere.

Huley shook his head, twirling the hair, breathing through his open mouth, sweating and feeling the grass dust itching his skin.

But no black ever came to Blood Gully. The old black man had told Huley why. He said it was because of the big massacre. Blood Gully was a terrible place of deep mourning. The old man had shaken his head and told Huley many things. Huley was amazed at the scars on all the black people's bodies. Huley showed them the belt buckle scars on his back, and they all gathered round and said he was a good white man.

Huley had tramped about half-naked and half-starved among his emaciated minders, bothering nobody. He felt so happy. Nobody had laughed at him, except in a friendly way. The old man had warned Huley he should hide because the white manhunters were coming. When Huley had laughed, the old man had poked him in the back scars to remind him that life was not funny. The old man had said his people must go away and hide, but Huley convinced them they would be alright, because he knew the police. When the police arrived, Huley did not know even one of them. He remembered the screaming.

Now, he could hear Sergeant Dirlsky talking behind him; as he turned around he could see no-one for the long grass. The police were tired of waiting, and Huley heard the raised voices. He could hear Sergeant Dirlsky talking with his men about old Donaldson, and then about Inspector Holman. They were waiting. That was good enough for Huley.

Huley thought of old man Donaldson's deep, blood-filled neck, and then he recalled how the old black man had said a great serpent would rise from the bush and swallow the people of Blood Gully.

"All of them?" Huley had asked.

The old black man with grey hair and beard had nodded sadly and said maybe. Sometimes the spirits are hungry, sometimes they are lazy, sometimes they are angry, sometimes they are merciful, he had added.

"I better go back there..." Huley had said.

The old man had smiled as if he had been trying to tell Huley that all along.

"There's nobody there to look after my mother. I have to save her," Huley had explained.

The old man had nodded again and picked his handsome, gleaming teeth with a slice of torn-off toenail. Huley grinned at the old man. The few teeth Huley had left were as dull as unclean gold.

"My mother is crippled," Huley had said proudly.

"Go back there. Take your mother away from that place," the old man had replied. "Big bad spirit there. Bad thing come one day. Too many people die. All the blood in the ground...deep in the ground...all soaked up. Bad thing must happen. True! It must happen."

When Huley first heard Inspector Holman's voice, he was thinking maybe the hair he had found in Donaldson's hand was off some big spaniel hound. But there was no big spaniel dog. Not in Blood Gully. No spaniel dog, no black folks. And old Donaldson didn't have any hair to speak of. Hmmm...Huley wondered...unless it was some woman's fanny hair!

Huley cast the stuff from his hand and moved slowly away. He sucked air in and out of his open mouth and a fly flew in. One suck of air and the fly was lodged in a tube somewhere deep in Huley's chest cavity. He could feel it buzzing its wings and trying to escape. He made a coughing, grunting and groaning noise as he crawled about the grass, trying to splutter the insect out of his gizzards.

"Wild pig!" shouted Constable Fraser.

Unclipping his pistol pouch he drew his police issue handgun out and aimed low into the area of the disturbed grass.

The grass stopped moving and the grunting fell silent. Then they heard spitting noises, like a pig snorting.

"Who is there?" yelled Dirlsky. "Anybody there?"

The grass moved. Up popped Huley. Then he bobbed straight down, so the police could only see his messy hair and frightened eyes.

"Huley!" barked Dirlsky. "Get out of there and go home before you get your brains blown out."

"If you've got any," Fraser muttered as he resheathed his pistol.

"Sergeant," Inspector Holman hissed, "have you questioned that imbecile?"

"Yes, sir. He knows nothing," said Sergeant Dirlsky.

HOARDING their precious sweat desperately, the older cedar cutters paced themselves deliberately as the afternoon began. They kept themselves apart and talked of yesterdays when sweat flowed with less pain. What about that woman in Tenterfield who built her own house and it never fell down. And in Grafton that time they shot those four blackfellas trying to kill a bloke beside the river, and he recovered and told them the blackfellas had saved him from drowning. Yeah, well when we got to Port Macquarie and I saw him for the first time...don't lie to me, in Morpeth the way we...and in Illawarra...and...episodes which interrupted only the hours of jarring with their bones, the straining with their muscles.

As the sweat shook from them after the shock of each pounding blow, they longed for cooler times, spare-chaining logs to rivers — rivers in flood, so-called dry rivers where men drowned.... Through the grinding hours they grunted and mumbled of days rafting down to Ballina, riding endless tons and superfeet to the mills. They talked of Dorrigo Dave, the king of the head-butt, and of Brick-face Keeling who split Dorrigo's skull so bad it punctured his brain and the fluid ran out of his nose and ears and he almost drowned in it...and of how Dorrigo stayed demented, while Keeling turned religious and never fought again. They remembered the swagman who drowned in the flooded Bellinger River when he tried to save the life of a cocky's wife who had jumped into the river when her husband had caught her on the riverbank kissing the swagman.

"Good riddance," the cocky's famous words had been when the bodies were swept away. "I was going to shoot the mongrels anyway."

In the smoke of pipes they revived their taste for life. They talked of how the tall timbers lie, and how they fall...dogging them onto chains...tightening them... foggling them, so they didn't spread or rock when you walked along them. But the huge, dead giants always spread and rocked anyway, sometimes extracting most grievous vengeance. A man could lose a leg as easily as a foot.

And they talked of how men lie, and how they fall. They talked of old camps, deep in the bush, high on ridges overlooking glorious miles of lush rainforest. They spoke of places ruled by the mosquito, as though the mosquito were a single, mighty demon. They recalled floating camps on big planks set in the middle of long rafts of cedar...

92

They played four-handed euchre with an audience of advisers.

"And what about old Horst the Bavarian."

"He landed in Sydney without a shilling in his pocket."

"Did he end up buying a pub on the inland road?"

"Then he got killed in another man's pub."

"They reckoned the other publican couldn't believe his eyes when he pulled down the robber's mask and saw Horst's face."

"He didn't know how to rob a pub but he sure could play cards."

"Nobody could stack a deck of cards better than Horst did."

They dealt out the cards for one last quick game to shorten the day.

"Bad luck about those Markers."

"This heat would drive anyone mad."

"I'd rather be hanged than shot in the arse with a shotgun."

"Any day!"

"I'll miss the poor bastard, you know."

"I'll miss both of them, in their way."

The words faded away with the tea and the tobacco like steam and smoke, and while the mighty, shattering axe-blows ticked away the day, the tavern-keeper Donaldson was carried from one part of town to another, dead.

XII

SENIOR CONSTABLE HEDGES came out of the little wooden dunny behind the police office. He was chewing a piece of bread and rubbing his hands together. He gulped as he saw Inspector Holman strutting up Main Street towards the lock-up.

Hedges hurriedly did up his pants and slipped back into the building. Inspector Holman found him hard at work polishing his boots.

Later, however, Dirlsky found Hedges snoring without a care in the world, his feet up on the desk.

"Hedges!" he yelled. "Wake up! You're on duty."

Hedges sputtered and began to snore again, only to be interrupted by Dirlsky's booming roar.

"Hedges!"

Dirlsky stuck his helmet on a hook and undid his tunic as Hedges answered without opening his eyes.

"What?"

Dirlsky wiped sweat from his chest.

"Can't you snore less loud?"

"Of course, but it gives me less pleasure..."

The Sergeant narrowed his eyes and put his hands on his hips.

"Do you want to end up on a report?" he barked, glaring at Hedges' insubordinate grin.

THE NEWS travelled slowly. The coach rolled out of town late, and with it the driver took the details of the latest Blood Gully butchery. When the driver started to urge the horses to exert themselves he muttered.

"This place *is* cursed, after all."

As the coach faded out of hearing, Jansen strode out
of the coach office with a paper in one hand and his hat in
the other, fanning his face.

He smiled at an old man shuffling by.

"It's nice and peaceful now the mill has shut down,"
said the old man. "Did you hear about Mr Donaldson?"

"Two murders in one month, eh? This town is turning
into a real modern city," Jansen replied.

Jansen looked at his watch. He shook it and glared at
it. He stretched the chain attaching the watch to his trousers
and put the timepiece to his ear.

"Damn," he swore. "Even watches won't work in this
heat."

He put his hat on, but as he did his paper blew away.

"Hey, boy," he called to one of the barefoot coach
hands. "Get that paper."

The boy looked at the paper, then looked at Jansen
without shifting.

"Eh?" he said.

"Go and get it!"

"Oh! Yes, sir, Mr Jansen..."

The body strolled toward the centre of the road, following the paper, with Jansen closing the gap fast, unseen
behind. By the time the boy caught up to the paper, Jansen
was almost upon him. As the boy bent over Jansen put his
foot on the boy's backside and shoved, sending the lad
sprawling. Jansen picked up the paper himself and turned
away.

IN ONE OF the cool gullies, where the shade came from all
angles at all times of the day and where the mosses were
evergreen, two boys played in the deep sawpits.

Nearby lay the carcass of a wallaby torn to bits by farm
dogs, along with two empty and rusty rabbit traps and a
snare of rope and wire.

"We can tell them we hunted it down and killed it with
our bare hands," said the younger one, suddenly pulling
the knife from his belt. "No! With our knives."

"They'll never believe it," said the older one. "What about that chewed-up leg?"

"I know, say we ate it," suggested the young one, squatting down and starting to hack the leg off at the hip.

"Ah," he yelled as he jumped back and a cascade of maggots spilled from the torn-open joint.

Without their wallaby carcass the two boys wandered among the shadows lengthening toward the east and argued.

"Kookaburras don't kill snakes, you fool. They might bloody pick up a dead one."

"I seen it killing it with my own two bloody eyes."

"Rubbish."

"I did, you bastard. Do you want to have a rock fight to find out if I can see?"

"It couldn't have been a snake — or it couldn't have been alive. That's all."

"It was a snake."

"It could have been a legless lizard and you wouldn't have known the difference at a distance..."

The two boys argued like rivals in a life-long contest for prizes they would never receive, standing in the ruins of an arena where giants had been slain...

"NO SENSE making a fuss over a dead man," cried Mrs Donaldson. "If he wasn't worth crying over when he was alive, it won't do any good now..."

"True, Missus," said Suggestible Humphrey, who was never known to disagree with anyone, especially not Mrs Donaldson.

Humphrey looked round the other faces gathered in the dingy, crowded den of the Bushman's Arms. The girls nodded sombrely and the men grumbled into their beards. Over to the side, Huley Colquoon sipped at his horehound root beer and watched with ravenous eyes.

"I always thought old man Donaldson would be too tough to die," One-eyed Albert said, shaking his head.

"Pity he got murdered," said Sarah the tavern girl, daughter of convicts. Then she whispered to Marianna,

"Getting murdered was too good for him. He was cruel."

Humphrey looked at Sarah with a tight mouth. He said nothing. He drummed his fingernails on the benchtop. Each nail was tipped with a thick, dark crescent of muck.

Huley Colquoon picked his nose and stared in the tavern's darkness.

"Why? That's what I can't understand. Why? You just never know what's going to happen next in this place..." Mrs Donaldson sobbed and burst into tears, and then fled to the back rooms.

Humphrey looked helplessly behind her, toward the empty door.

Suddenly Huley stood up and raised his one and only clean finger to the dim light. Every eye turned to him.

"I found him," Huley declared. "His throat was cut from here to here...and his tongue was poked out like this."

Huley swelled his chest and held his breath. He poked his tongue out and widened his eyes. Everyone just stared at first. Then one of the men started laughing, and everyone joined in except One-eyed Albert, who raised his eye to the ceiling and slapped his face.

Huley tried to look away, but each time he looked back only to find them still looking and laughing at him. He looked one way, then the other. He wiggled his head as though it was loose on his neck and he sat down, rubbing his eye as though it had something in it. The laughter grew louder, and for a moment Huley thought he heard old Donaldson's voice there too, laughing cruelly like the others around him in the bar.

DOCTOR MORRISON hurried along Main Street, trailing the Goddess, the Holmans' maid Rebecca.

"I feel as if we're part of some children's tableau," he said, puffing to keep up with her. "I'm the Beast and you are the Beauty."

Rebecca gave him a suspicious glance and walked on, her lips clamped bitterly. They passed a man opening his mouth so wide he rose high on his tip-toes. It was Eight-toes Marler, showing Bluey Miser his craters of bleeding gum.

"It was the best idea I ever had, getting those aching bastards yanked out," said Marler. "They were driving me crazy. I never knew in the morning when I woke up if they'd be aching or not. It was..."

"That's a good job," said Miser, holding Eight-toes Marler's mouth wide open with his thumbs and lowering his head to look in deep. "Price doesn't do a bad job. And he's quick."

"And cheap," said Eight-toes Marler, working the stiffness out of his jaw. "He only charged me a deener and..."

"That's good," said Miser. "Real good. A toff dentist would have charged you twice that much for the two of them. Heaven's got no mercy on pain, I can tell you. I went to one once, and he charged me ten shillings for three teeth. It's broad daylight robbery. I had to take a bit of a stupid chance to get the money, but it was worth it."

As Doctor Morrison and Rebecca clomped by the Bushman's Arms, they heard loud laughter. Morrison looked into the dark doorway.

"Sounds like the widow is deep in mourning," he said. "How touching."

The doctor still had Donaldson's bloodstains on his mind. And now he was rushing to the bed of the Sleeping Beauty who breathed without fogging a mirror and whose blood pumped without her heart beating. He swallowed the bile trying to erupt from his throat.

He swirled in the waters of suffering, stumbling and bumbling from mysterious cures to even more mysterious failures. The dead ones like Donaldson were child's play. It was the deep ones and the young ones who gave him sleepless nights. He slaked the thirst for oblivion in lonely, late drinking hours and in the chemicals of his trade.

He rubbed his red eyes as he walked and yawned. How would he find Mrs Holman, he wondered. The girl had said the patient was worsening. To Morrison that could mean the poor woman was already dead — or even worse, it could mean she was recovering. He hated the sick. They slipped through his fingers as he tried to juggle their last chances.

Yes, the young ones are the worst, Morrison thought, they are so weak and innocent. They cried out as he touched them with his dull, clumsy hands and they screamed as he felt for the source of the pain or the sickness. It seemed sometimes the pain had colonised their entire bodies. They tossed and resisted every invasion of their person. Whenever they saw the scalpel blade, Morrison knew his cause was lost. The children did not trust him. They had no faith.

He wiped the sweat from his eyes. Rebecca listened to the warmth and vitality of the laughter fading away behind her. The noise radiating from the ramshackle wooden tavern sparked something inside her, as she led the doctor briskly toward the dark, stale, silent house of sickness she had come from.

"There it is," he said, pointing across to his sulky. It was tied to the wrought-iron post of the Havelock Hotel, which shone like a huge pink rock in the flaring glow of the early afternoon.

IN THE PARLOUR of the Havelock, Sam Sodge was haranguing the bank managers Mr Jones and Mr McCartney about the glorious future of Blood Gully.

"We're not talking about a town," Sodge said. "We have the possibility before of us of the first inland metropolis. There is a continent at our doorstep..."

He stretched his arm and ashed his cigar in the monkey-skull ashtray.

"You wait and see. When the railway gets here!" he continued. He made a severe tunnelling action with his hand.

"We'll bore straight through those mountains."

He brushed the cigar ash from his trousers and smiled at the two men. McCartney and Jones smiled at each other in return.

"Time will reveal all," said Jones.

"With time and art, gentlemen, the leaf of the mulberry tree becomes satin," said Sodge. "And I swear, with the railway, Blood Gully will become a city."

He leaned back into the chair and breathed smoke out through his nose.

"We have the trees, for God's sake. After we clean out the cedar, we'll still have trees coming out of our ears. We have forests, literally forests, to run our trains on."

"Modern trains run on coal, Sam," said McCartney, leaning forward.

"Coal?" Sodge cried impatiently, looking at McCartney patronisingly. "For God's sake...I'm talking about sleepers."

McCartney and Jones looked at each other. Sodge stared into space.

"You know, you may have a point there," he said. "Yes, sir, you just may have a point..."

He leaned his elbow on his knee and poked a finger at the air.

"I bet those hills are full of it."

He slapped his hands together, stamped his foot and cackled.

Jones and McCartney looked at each other again, then they blinked at Sodge stupidly. Sodge stared back at them.

"Well, they might be," Sodge said with an expression of defiance.

"What on earth may be what, Sam? For heaven's sake, we're bookkeepers, not mind-readers."

Sodge blinked a few times.

"Let's put it this way," he said. "It's as though we are at the front of a stampede. We are the first wave. Out there, there's nothing...but opportunity. First in first served. There's a tidal wave behind us. You see what goes on here in the street at night. It's the law of the jungle. There is nothing, nothing. Nothing can stop us..."

He opened his palms to the two bank managers and shrugged his shoulders.

"Those that get in the way...well!"

McCartney looked at Jones, and Jones rose.

"What on earth do you mean by that?" he asked.

Sodge crossed his legs, leaning further back and waving his cigar in the air as he turned to McCartney.

"Time reveals all," he said.

AMONG THE SWARM of huts in town many were sunk in drowsy silence. One-eyed Albert sat at a table of split slabs which had been adzed smooth. The table stood on four stakes driven into the dirt floor. He sat there eating cold doughboy and plain suet pudding. A plate of crumbling sugar cakes sat nearby, surrounded by squashed ants. Mrs Ross sat with him, eating a piece of bread dipped in gravy.

"I would give my left leg for a feed of mutton pie and fat cakes," she said. "When does the work for Gorman begin?"

The dog licking its paws on the floor looked up at the woman as if there could be trouble.

"You going to take it?" she asked, not taking her eyes from One-eyed Albert as she pushed bread into her mouth.

When he finished chewing to his satisfaction, he swallowed. Then he answered her questions, one by one, as if it took great effort.

"The work starts after the heat dies down. Gorman'll send his girl Anna into town to tell me when he feels like getting round to it. That's if he doesn't see me himself first. I said for him or her to come here and to tell you if I'm elsewhere," he said victoriously, yet begrudgingly all the same. "And as for your second question, if I haven't answered it good enough already, the answer is yes."

"Good," Mrs Ross replied.

One-eyed Albert put his hand on her knee and gently rubbed it.

"Now I'd like to ask you a question," he said.

She didn't take her eyes from his. She chewed and she looked, without showing emotion, unmoved. He winked at her and hunched his shoulders mischievously, then he

101

squeezed her knee. She put her hand down quickly with a weakening, one-sided smile and dug her fingernails into the palm of his hand, staring at his one seeing eye.

FREDDIE FAIRBURN had gone to the back of the Bushman's Arms and now he sat nonchalantly in the afternoon shade. Even though it was daylight he sat with his back to the wall for two reasons — first, for something to lean on; second, so he didn't get his throat cut without seeing who did it. He tried to think of any other possible reason while he waited.

When Mrs Donaldson came out he meant to ask her in a roundabout way if she could entertain the thought of extending to him a small amount of credit, for he had to spend all his drinking money on food for his children. And a mother's work is never done, leaving little time for the odd paying job which may or may not come along.

He sagged in the heat. Nobody would pay for odd job work in such heat. It would be throwing money away. He wiped his face. He licked dried sweat-salt off his lips. He wondered when Bartholomew would come back, and maybe take Felicity Miller away from him. But still, it was only right to give Bartholomew a fair chance.

Freddie felt cruel even to think of stealing Felicity Miller out from under Bartholomew's nose when the poor blacksmith lay days and days away an invalid. Besides, the times weren't the easiest. A wife had to be fed too. And a hungry woman is an angry woman.

He started talking in a whisper, talking to himself, and gradually he got louder.

"Price is a modern man. He's got a farm, he can fix sore teeth, he's got a plank floor in his place, he understands politics, he's got a horse and a cart. One day, I'll be a modern man too, by Jesus I will. I'll make those kids proud of me."

"What kids?" said a voice out of nowhere.

Freddie Fairburn raised his eyes, looking up on the iron roof of Mrs Donaldson's lean-to.

For one cold moment he thought it was the ghost of old man Donaldson.

"Huley?" Freddie hissed. "Huley, where are you?"

"Over here, in the grass," said the voice out of nowhere.

Above the grass-tops a waving hand briefly appeared.

"Huley. I want my kids to be proud of me."

"They're proud of you, Freddie," said Huley. "I'm proud of you too."

Freddie slapped his knees.

"Bloody hell, Huley. You wouldn't know what day of the week it was..."

"I do too," said Huley, getting up on his knees to see Freddie sitting there forlornly. "It's today!"

Freddie looked at Huley and Huley disappeared, leaving only the rising haze of heat above the grass, shimmering. He turned back just as Mrs Donaldson came through with Suggestible Humphrey.

Freddie smiled. Now was his big chance. Humphrey would give him a kindly reference.

Then Freddie saw them let go of each other's hand. Humphrey put his hand in his pocket, turned back to the door and was gone. Mrs Donaldson put her two hands together, tilted her head back and straightened her hair.

"And what are you doing here, may I ask, Mr Fairburn? Skulking around my back door?"

Something made Freddie gulp.

"I was just talking to Huley..."

"Huley Colquoon?" she asked with disbelief.

"Yes," he said with relief.

"Water finds its own level, I suppose."

She turned and walked back inside. Freddie's lungs deflated with one long, downhearted gasp as he recognised that life was just like that and would continue to be like that — a stream of opportunities slipping through his fingers.

"Phew, that was close wasn't it, Freddie?" said the voice out of nowhere, when the danger had passed.

Freddie looked up and saw Huley smiling at him, standing in the long, dead grass.

THE PEOPLE OF BLOOD GULLY ate in fear that evening, as the afternoon light receded — in fear that the curse would strike them again that night with unbearable heat and calm. Even before the dinner was over in the houses, and before the teas were finished in the shacks, the wind stirred up their hopes. The leaves flew from the trees as it became dark.

Mrs Gill's servants wearily cleared her dining table by candlelight. Then they closed the tall cedar doors behind them and retired to the cluttered kitchen.

With the whole mess cleaned and the kitchen in order they sat down to eat their own meal.

They ate without speaking. They huddled round the corner of the table, with their backs to the doorway where Mrs Gill stood concealed. She had come from the dark, and so she cast no shadow into the room. And she made no noise.

Mrs Gill listened like a cat, holding her breath, her fingers clutching and clenching and straightening.

Huddled over their plates, leaning on their elbows, too tired to even cross their legs, the girls sat in silence.

Kathleen looked at her round-shouldered partner. Their eyes met. They chewed. Judith sniffed and rested her fist against her temple. She stared at the table as her jaws pounded nourishment from the washtub of her mouth.

Mrs Gill stealthily paced backwards. Rationing the depth of her breath to make it silent, she stepped away slowly, her dark dress blending into the dark, melting into the shadows.

"She's gone," whispered Kathleen.

Judith turned her face to the doorway. Her eyes were wet. She spat the food out of her mouth onto her plate and cried silently.

Kathleen chewed more slowly than before. She swallowed and pushed her plate away. And then she stared into the formless blur in front of her eyes.

XIII

THAT DAY HAD brought death in the form of Donaldson's corpse. The next day there passed from tongue to ear, gathering the dust of warped details along the way, word of Mrs Holman's death.

She had died of two accidents, of three diseases and of domestic violence before her death became general knowledge. The people of Blood Gully easily accepted that Donaldson had been murdered. There had been so many throats slashed it was easy to accommodate knowledge of another. Now the murder was easily overshadowed by the mysterious fading away of the young, mystical Mrs Holman.

People said she was so cold she froze to death. Doctor Morrison said that was impossible. Even so, never had anyone seen a woman look so miserable before she died, and with so little reason.

"This place is under a curse," said Mrs Ross. "People die without reason."

In the Bushman's Arms Dancer Hughes was trying to answer questions about the dead woman. There were many things Dancer did not know, particularly those on the medical side. All Dancer could say was Mrs Holman might have died from a cracked heart — if it wasn't completely broke.

"If she ever lied down on the floor, Holman would have walked all over her without noticing."

That's what Dancer said. He didn't get much response to this observation, but he was unbothered.

"What do doctors know?" snarled One-eyed Albert Ross. "They said Tom Shannon had rotted lungs and one day he coughed up a wee bit of tobacco no bigger than this. And he's been good as new since."

"Well, if any woman ever froze herself to death, it would be that one, or Dirlsky's missus," said Bluey Miser. "I'm not surprised neither of them ever had any young 'uns."

One-eyed Albert Ross went a brilliant red and looked at the floor.

"I don't trust doctors neither," said Eight-toes Marler. "They cut off my two toes for no reason. They was good as gold, just suffered a bit of arthritis after that horse stamped on them. Great walloping pudding-heads. Cut them clean off! Clean as a bloody whisker."

The small mob of men all shook their heads. The toe-cutters had done Marler poorly. He should have got a better deal.

"They wouldn't even let me see them after they cut them off," Marler grieved, poking his booted feet into the open and looking from face to face.

"Wouldn't even let you look at your own toes?" said Dancer Hughes with his hand pointing like a pistol into the corner of the ceiling adjacent to the street. "That's disgusting."

"They reckoned they was too rotted to even look at. Bastards. That's them all over," said Marler, stroking his thigh. "I told them straight, I told them if I could look at their ugly faces good enough, I could look at my own toes."

"I'd rather go to gaol for a week than to hospital for one day," interjected Bluey Miser.

"You wouldn't know," said One-eyed Albert. "You never been to either one."

Miser did not answer. He didn't have time to. Marler was still going on.

"I tell you they are mongrels, those city doctors. Morrison isn't too bad. But he's bad enough. Never go to Morrison with anything that's out of your sight."

"I can vouch for that," said Dancer. "Straight out with the knife. He ought to have enough cut-offs now to open a pie shop."

"Those bastards," Marler said, looking at his battered boots. "They said the rot almost spread from the toes up into my leg and they'd have to cut off my whole leg soon."

Marler slapped his leg soundly.

"Look at that! Good as new. The horse never even touched my leg till I give it the kicking of its shitting life. Poor dumb bastard."

"They're a bloody menace, doctors," said Miser. "They're like a cross between bloody parsons and butchers."

"And priests, into the bargain," said Albert.

"I tell you what," said Marler. "I never went back to get my leg cut off, but they'd have cut it off alright. Good or bad. If any horse ever treads on my foot again, I know where I'll go. . . ."

"Where?" asked Dancer.

"To old Price, that's where. He's a wonder on the aching jaw. He's magic."

All heads nodded in agreement.

One-eyed Albert shook his.

"My missus nags me something fierce about all that lot up on the hill. I don't mind the odd one dying. Less there is, the less harm they can do. Might give my ears a rest."

"Would have been better if Holman had carked it," Bluey Miser snickered.

Dancer Hughes suddenly looked with fright toward the door.

"What about Dirlsky?" Mad Mick O'Reilly asked.

Miser grinned and looked around.

"Ah-ha!" he laughed. "Can you picture his face?"

Eyes glanced up to Suggestible Humphrey. He was attending the bar, where Sarah sat, with her legs wide apart, smiling at the men. Humphrey wiped the benchtop with an old shirt torn in half. There was no sign of Mrs Donaldson.

"I'd put up with them. I'd put up with them twice over, if we could get rid of that old dragon up on the hill," Miser continued.

"Who? Mrs Gill? She's not a bad old bitch," Dancer

Hughes muttered, glancing at the open doorway where there was the shadow of someone out of sight; then the shadow moved away.

"Not if you like a bad old bitch she's not," said Miser. "Her carriage ran over my dog, you know big old Gouger. Squashed him flat. Never even stopped. Never even slowed down. When they can run over a man's dog like that, you don't know what's next. They think they can just walk all over you."

In this fashion the town prepared for the funerals of two citizens of substance. One the wife of the Inspector of Police, the other a tavern-keeper — one respectable, the other disreputable; one beautiful and rich, the other cruel and debauched; one cold, one burning...but now both united in the eternal democracy of death.

WORD TRAVELLED FAST once it left town. The curse had struck again. The men in the hills, with tangled beards hiding their faces, looked into the sky. There was no cloud. They watched the huge solid city of branches above them shiver, then waver, then twist with a horrendous, graunching scream of tearing timber... The falling roar split the skies open to the hidden stars. And the old, old heads with the young faces swore that living in town was unhealthy, then they licked their lips with nicotine-stained tongues at the delicious thought of guzzling grog in taverns...the thought of clinging girls...and the fights and the laughter. And they swung their axes at the huge red meat, slogging their sharpened iron into the huge red monsters of the hillsides and splashing red dust with every chop.

Word travelled here. Word travelled there. When Price told Doyle and Murphy, he didn't even look up, he just kept cleaning his teeth-fixing tools, then he wrapped them up in a lump of barber's towel. He got up and put them away. Danny Doyle was bathing his eyes in a sordid solution.

Murphy kept screwing up his face. He stared at Doyle's smelly disinfectant as he heard Price's news.

"People round here are starting to die wholesale," Price said as he rose and walked away.

"Poor old bastard," said Doyle, suddenly spitting out the solution which had run down his face and gone into his mouth. "He didn't do a lot of harm."

"Not for want of trying," said Price, behind the head-high hessian partition, banging closed a shallow drawer.

Murphy sat silent, his eyes shocked, his face hanging loose from the bones of his head. Mrs Holman had been pronounced dead. She...she...she...

Murphy's mouth went dry. He sucked his tongue for moisture. He stared sadly at where Price had been sitting before. Price yelled out from behind the partition.

"We'll have a great time. They may even have two funerals on the one day."

"Hey!" Doyle yelled back. "They could put them in the same hole."

"Nah. That's adultery," shouted Price.

Doyle chuckled and dabbed at his eyes.

"I'll give you a warning, Murphy," continued Price, coming out from behind the partition as Murphy sat, still staring at where Price had been sitting. "Never miss a funeral in a small town..."

AS MRS GILL'S servant girls scurried grubbily about their toil, the funerals of Donaldson and Mrs Holman were foremost in their minds as well.

"She had a beautiful body, Rebecca said," Judith declared. "That comes from all that horse-riding, I'll bet. I would love to ride a horse one day."

"It's nothing special," said Kathleen, suddenly turning with fear at the sound of the cat's paws stepping across the carpet.

"They'll have to be buried straightaway before the bodies go off. They may even bury them on the same day," cried Judith. "Isn't it so exciting. Everybody will be there."

"Everybody except me," said Kathleen. "It isn't fair."

Kathleen's eyes flickered as she took several short, sharp breaths in rapid succession. She twisted her face and one tear ran partway down her cheek before drying out. Then she hurled a dust cloth in fury at the floor.

BARTHOLOMEW'S BOY, the blond-headed Paul, was growing famous. He had always done a man's work. Now he did two men's work. And he did not even take time off to complain, though he had every right to.

Finally the work got too much for him. Paul could do the work of two men alright, but nobody could do that much work and do it well. The hills and Main Street were littered with thrown horseshoes, and every day some apologetic customer returned with bits and pieces of ironware which had broken, bent or come apart all over the countryside.

"We'll be back in the Stone Age if he works any harder," said Rooster Gorman, who kept a horseshoe that Paul had made for him because he just did not believe it. He could bend the thing with his bare hands. He did not show it to anyone. He just kept it. He knew if he kept it long enough he would find a use for a soft horseshoe.

Several of Bartholomew's friends sent a letter, and promptly in turn, Bartholomew sent Paul a letter to say he should hire someone to help him. Paul scratched his head. He read the letter carefully. He did not like to think Bartholomew believed he couldn't carry the forge on his own. But he was an obedient lad. Next day he gave the job to the first boy who came along. He felt like a big businessman.

He washed his hands in black-looking salt water and wiped them on a hessian bag. He turned to the new boy and smiled. Then he slammed his first into the wall. The whole shed shook and dust fell from the rafters. The youngster gulped.

"That's how you toughen your hands," said Paul.

"You could knock a horse out with a punch like that," said the young boy.

"I have," said Paul. "You should see Bartholomew go to town with his fists. Come with me."

Before they could go anywhere they were interrupted by the entrance of a grey-coloured man with grey eyeballs. His last few teeth were grey too. Only his black suit and tall, yankee-style hat broke the greyness.

Dust was still falling from the rafters. The grey man looked up. Disgust was on his face.

"Is that funeral horse ready?"

"Yes sir, Mr Wimmel. Out the back," said Paul.

"Nicely shod and ready to plod?"

"Yes sir, Mr Wimmel."

Wimmel reached his grey hand up and slapped Paul's shoulder. A couple of inches of grey cuff stuck out of the undertaker's coat sleeve.

"Nice work, lad," he said. "I have a most important engagement. Everything must go well. Let them laugh. I'll show them how a burial should be done."

Wimmel chuckled as he shuffled his scrawny figure out the back. Paul licked his bleeding knuckles and winked at the new boy standing there with clean, soft hands — possibly for the last time in his life.

Wimmel turned at the back door, and paused before he slipped through the gap between them.

"I may be doing them both on one day," he said gleefully.

The boys watched him go. The new boy smiled at Paul as he in turn washed his hands in the salty water and dried them gingerly on the hessian bag. Slowly they began to bleed from the tiny, hairlike scratches.

"Don't worry about Wimmel," said Paul. "All he likes doing is burying people. I reckon if they didn't die, he'd be just as happy burying them alive. It'd save a hell of a lot of messing around if they just burned dead bodies, I reckon. There'd be less bawling. And you wouldn't have to lug them all that way up the hill to the boneyard."

The young boy shook his head. Paul continued.

"That nag of Wimmel's will go arse-up halfway up the hill one of these times, and Wimmel'll have to carry the coffin up the rest of the way himself — and then he'll have to come down and get rid of his dead horse," he chuckled as he scrubbed mildew and mould off some old strappings. "By jeez, I tell you what. That would be something to see. That really would be worth seeing. . ."

CONSTABLE TAYLOR was lighting a smoke when part of the paperwork on the table somehow burst into flame. Taylor looked at the little blaze with a scowl. The fire burned through the corners of four pages before he could beat it into submission with his thin, smooth hands.

"Christ almighty, what on earth is going on..." said Hedges, entering the office. "Be careful, Taylor, or we'll all be out of a job."

"What will I do with all this?" croaked Taylor.

"Put it in the filing cupboard and act dumb. Haven't you learned anything yet?"

Taylor looked relieved, but not for long. The fire had earned him a brief respite from the subject that Hedges kept haunting him with.

"I was just thinking," said Hedges. "About promotion. For you..."

Taylor looked at Hedges suspiciously, then gratefully, then with disbelief. He began once more to recycle his repertoire of reactions. Hedges leaned forward onto the table littered with documents, ashes and a glass bottle with a broken neck.

"All you've got to do is tell the truth. What could be more simple?" he declared with a mutinous leer.

"Well," said Taylor. I'm only new on the job. I'm not so sure, really, Maybe Jones can help you."

Hedges sneered.

"Jones?" he laughed, deprecatingly tossing his hand at the air. "Jones is a crawler. He would crawl up his own arse if Dirlsky asked him to."

"He's experienced," Taylor ventured, hesitating.

"Experienced? Experienced?"

Taylor shrugged his shoulders. What did he care? Life was too short to flog dead horses and pursue hopeless causes.

"But old man Donaldson has proved Dirlsky a fool and a liar and a perjurer," said Hedges.

Taylor couldn't help staring at Hedges.

"Dirlsky's got no shame, he hasn't," Hedges continued vehemently. "Fitting all those murders on an innocent man." He shook his finger under Taylor's nose. "Joe Marker never killed anyone — except his brother — any more than you or I done, Taylor."

"Don't blame me," Taylor snapped back. "He had a trial."

"Jesus bloody Christ had a trial," cried Hedges. "Would you call that justice?"

Taylor shifted in his chair. His backside stuck with sweat and he had to raise himself on his elbows.

"They can't hang you for five murders if you've only done one," continued the Senior Constable. "Next thing you know they'll be hanging people who never did nothing. Dirlsky would."

"Aw, forget it, Hedges, you're confusing me," complained Taylor, wishing someone would come walking through the door.

"Think about it," Hedges glared at Taylor. "Dirlsky stuck murders on Joe Marker that Marker never done. Murders he couldn't have done. Unless he crawled out of the grave and killed Donaldson."

Taylor squirmed, watching the door hopefully, as he listened to Hedges droning on.

"There's no answer to injustice, Taylor — except justice. And there is no justice except the law."

Hedges stood back, stretching to his full height. He stood without speaking, like an unarmed Spanish matador, with no cape, contemptuously facing an adversary who had no escape and no hope of mercy...

"Are you going to report him?" whispered Taylor, looking nervously through the door into an empty street.

Hedges shook his head.

"You're an imbecile, Taylor. Me report him? Holman would say I was just after Dirlsky's job."

Taylor looked back from the door, to see Hedges with a finger pointed directly at his head.

"You, Taylor! You report him. Holman may just believe you. You're the newest on the job. You're the only one with nothing to gain."

Taylor burst into motion; he uncoiled like a broken

clock spring. He leapt from the chair, feet into the air, and fled through the door.

"You gutless pool of shit, Taylor. You'll regret this, you bastard," Hedges screamed.

The door slammed behind Taylor and the bars of the empty cell rattled.

XIV

THE DAY OF the funeral dawned like any other, but the town of Blood Gully was totally unlike itself. Even on coach day there were fewer people on the street. They came from all over. Fewer people had come to see Joe Marker hanged.

The crowd came out in all shapes and sizes, and in contrasting, clashing patterns and colours. Dark greens, blacks and blues stirred among the faded moleskins, the flashy checks, lace, frills and ribbon and colourful cravats. Rope belts, leather belts and braces held up as many varieties of trousers as there were characters wearing them.

Huley Colquoon, as always, wore his eccentric one-sided brace with the other side flapping. He slipped along the edge of the crowd and was gone, carrying one boot and wearing the other. The boot he carried had no sole whatsoever. He could have pulled it halfway up his thigh if he wanted to, but he didn't want to do that any more. He had got tired of it after a couple of times.

The smart straw hat of the tailor bobbed among the felt hats, caps and bonnets. The tailor spoke to McCartney the bank manager. Then the two man laughed, pointing up the hill toward the graveyard.

They were all present — the common and the toffs, the clean, the dirty, and the filthy...the clean poor and the filthy rich, the clean rich and the filthy poor...the down-at-heel and the barefoot, the low-heeled and the high-heeled, all stirring the dust. Here a crocheted shawl, there a walking stick, a man on crutches, a pregnant woman sitting on a chair in the shade while a man fanned her, another pregnant woman carrying a small child in her arms, wiping her face on the sheet wrapped around the child. They wore bustles and breeches, waist-coats and blouses, one-piece dresses and skirts with matching or clashing bodices. They wore their best clothes — for most, their only clothes. They wore smocks and frocks and shirts, some ironed, some patched, some tied with string in place of buttons, and all marked with dark areas of sweat.

The heavy skirts swished against each other and dragged along, skimming the dust. One poor woman dragged herself along with two little children clinging to her narrow thighs through her home-made garment. Her round shoulders were bent round over her ribs and were thrust forward, and her elbows were ungainly lumps in her arms. Her hair rose from her scalp like a thin mist of wisps, clearly showing the grey skin underneath. Her eyes protruded from hollows darkened by sagging wrinkles, while her breasts rippled where they lay over her ribs. Heads turned to watch her. Perhaps she was the curtain-raiser to the real dead.

Tom Shannon, the eldest son of the trail-blazing squatter, sat on his huge horse. Proud of his three hundred acres.

Shannon leaned over, talking out of the side of his mouth to his family, all sitting in a stationary dray.

Shannon's two vicious fighting dogs slunk under the dray. They growled from time to time from behind the tall, spoked wheels.

Shannon had been so eager to get to the funeral he hadn't had time to shave.

"I wouldn't miss this for the world, Doss," Shannon said to his wife. "Two funerals in one day — they'll root something up for sure."

A dozen sulkies and wagons were lined up on the side of the street, the horses between the shafts, alone or in teams of two or even four, stirring in the cruel heat.

One-eyed Albert sat under a peppercorn bush with only his pants legs and thick-soled boots in the sunshine. Albert's deep, flat voice shook the peppercorns...

"Heh, heh. The last time I saw two funerals go together, it ended up in a race to the grave. You never saw anything like it."

Several voices joined Albert's laughter from the same

hiding place. Mad Mick O'Reilly stood in the sunshine, talking to the peppercorn bush.

"Wimmel reckons he's got everything under control. It can't go wrong, he said. That's the sealer for sure," he laughed. "I thank God I've got eyes to see this day."

High up in the corner of the graveyard a lone woman sat. Her head rocked in rhythm, sweat dripped from her face and her eyes stared excitedly at the dirt of the tiny new grave. The priest's assistant walked away from her, shaking his shining head.

Price's dilapidated cart rattled into view at one end of town.

"It's bad luck to miss a funeral in a small town," Price was saying. "Just look at this crowd."

Blind Danny Doyle behind him grunted, and Murphy said, "Blood Gully must be a real lucky place, then."

A GROUP OF cedar cutters stood at the edge of things and smoked their pipes. Over behind the Bushman's Arms, round the back of the buildings where it was quiet and deserted but for the occasional short-cut taker, Huley Colquoon lay in the grass behind an overgrown drain which had not tasted rain in six months.

Huley had his soleless boot in one hand, and with the other he scratched his flaky scalp. He had forgotten how long he had been sitting there, but when he saw Mrs Donaldson fling a basin of dirty water in a grey arc into the dead grass, he knew he hadn't missed the funerals yet. He looked at the sun and guessed there were hours to go...but you could never be sure, you can't always trust the sun, he thought. Sometimes, when no-one was looking, the sun stole inches across the sky in a few moments, it took short-cuts across the sky to shirk many hours of work. Huley knew this was especially true in the cold of winter, which Huley betted the sun hated. Hot things don't like cold things. Fires hate cold water. Huley knew that the winter days were shorter than the summer days because the sun took short-cuts in the sky. Huley got scared the sun might

117

rob him again and that through no fault of his own he would miss the funeral. He looked down and admired his good boot.

When he heard Mrs Donaldson's voice he was re-assured. Peering through the grass he could see her, wearing an apron over her Sunday dress. She was talking loudly to someone Huley could not see because there was nobody there. He strained his eyes.

"And that hypocrite old priest tried to talk me out of it, but I told him," said Mrs Donaldson. "I said, Who do they think they are? Just because he is the Inspector of Police does he think he owns the graveyard? Who is he? Does he think his wife is too good to be buried on the same day as my husband, or just in the same hour? Or is it the same dirt? I gave it to him both ears."

Mrs Donaldson pumped water noisily from the well-head and Huley could hardly tell what she was saying. The water was a long time coming through, and when it came it came slowly.

"I'm not saying my old man was any angel. But he was as good as half of them. And he's as good as any of them dead. But old Father Mitchell can't see past the end of his blue nose when it suits him."

Mrs Donaldson finished pumping water.

"He's worse than the first priest," she said. "So I says, Listen here, I send down my share of church taxes to pay your brandy bill. Don't that make me respectable?"

Mrs Donaldson disappeared through the door. Huley could still hear her voice but could not understand a word. Then she came out again, followed by someone.

"Just 'cause I sell a bit of grog and have a few girls here doesn't make my husband unrespectable. That young policeman got his throat cut and they didn't scorn him, did they? Old Holman don't object to the odd sweetener. And if he's good enough to share in the spoils, let him share the graveyard, I say."

She sloshed the water over her legs, holding up her skirts.

"But still the pie-arsed bastard wouldn't see it my way."

Looking like a princess of darkness to Huley, Marianna appeared behind the veil of the long grass stalks, her long, lush hair spilling loose and the sun shining on her long, bare arms. She laughed like a devil woman and Huley heard her. Could it be true? He looked at her hair. It was a glossy, dark blur. Was it her hair he had found in Donaldson's hand? He sank a littler deeper in the grass.

"So I told him straight," said Mrs Donaldson. "Look, I said, I'm pretty straightforward. I don't hide much, but some around here do."

Marianna stretched her dark arms and swelled her breast.

"So I told him a few things I know about him," said Mrs Donaldson. "You should have seen his eyes pop out. And then I told him a few things he didn't know. I told him about Holman's little tricks with that poor little girl up there. By the time I finished his tongue was starting to pop out. You should have seen the poor dear's face."

Marianna stretched on the washing table, her skirt pulled high to bathe her short, thick thighs in the sun. Her thighs were less dark than her arms. She murmured something and nodded in Huley's direction.

Mrs Donaldson looked up from where she was splashing between her legs and turned to the wall discreetly.

"You having a good old look over there, Huley Colquoon?" she yelled. "Haven't you got a mother to go home and look at?"

Huley blushed and sank down closer to the ground.

"In the end," said Mrs Donaldson, "I had to bribe the old bastard. If I'd known it was that easy I wouldn't have tried to reason with the old fool."

She sloshed water from the basin in Huley's direction and walked inside after drying herself. Marianna squinted and gazed into the sky like a lizard soaking up the sun. She sucked the warm air into her lungs, letting her legs laze wide. And Huley hid, watching her, smelling the sweet, dry grass, gripping the boot with no sole in his hand, thinking he had better go.

A GANG OF BOYS in bare feet ran down Main Street, chasing a terrified, yellow-looking dog with a rope trailing from its neck. The onlookers got out of the way. Saliva dripped from the dog's trailing tongue. It kept tripping on the rope and falling. Each time it frenziedly scurried to its paws and skipped free a cluster of human claws descended.

The people of Blood Gully shook their heads, some laughing at the profanity of such play on a funeral day, others scowling. Even the horses turned their heads to the yelping dog. It seemed to have no tail, so desperately was it tucked between its legs.

Then, without a bark of warning, Shannon's two surly killer dogs dashed into the street. They bore down on the boys, who scattered in all directions, pushing each other in the rush. As the larger one slammed at full speed onto the neck of its yellow victim, both tumbled in a cloud of dust, locked together, violently snarling, growling, gnashing and squealing. The yellow dog had a shallow rip in its side, smeared with blood.

The people of Blood Gully screamed and yelled and laughed, shouting encouragement to the dogs and jumping away from the fray.

"Mongrels!" Murphy snarled. He leapt down from Price's cart and ran toward the dogfight.

Shannon stopped laughing when Murphy's boot sent the smaller of his dogs sprawling. The crowd roared. But Murphy's second kick had no effect on the larger dog. It sounded as if the man was kicking a large pumpkin. The dog was solid sinew, bone and muscle. It lifted the yellow dog off the ground by the back of the neck; and its jaws slipped with deadly determination toward the throat.

Murphy kicked it again. The big dog swung with a thud into the dirt.

"What's he doing?" asked Danny Doyle, but Price didn't answer as he climbed awkwardly from the cart, cursing.

The cheering, jeering crowd poured from both sides of the street. As Price pushed his way through, Murphy was squaring off against the big, snarling dog. It was showing its foamy fangs with blood all over its muzzle.

Murphy's eyes had narrowed. His outstretched hands were begging the beast to move toward him. Then he began crouching, gently springing on the balls of his feet, taunting the huge animal with a whisper. The dog spread its front legs and tore at the air.

The crowd tittered and snickered. The animal snapped to its side, growling at the yellow dog; then it began snarling at the man again.

Senior Constable Hedges shoved his way through to the front of the crowd. He quickly glanced down at the yellow dog lying between the man, crouching like a street-wrestler, and Shannon's snarling mongrel.

"What's all this?" he asked.

The yellow dog's eyes blinked at the forest of human legs.

"Get back," Shannon growled at his dog, as the crowd stepped back to let the big squatter through. "Go on, get!"

The big dog backed away. Hedges stared at Murphy.

"You're new here. Passing through? Where you come from?"

"He kicked my dogs. He hurt one..." said Shannon.

Murphy was crouched, panting deeply. He gave Hedges and then Shannon a sleepy, bored look. His casual, taunting smile returned as he stood up slowly.

Shannon waved his hand in the direction of his retreating dogs.

"He hurt my dogs."

Hedges looked up at Shannon's bristle-covered face, then he turned to Murphy. Murphy swallowed, nothing showing on his face.

"You, now!" Hedges said to him. "Start talking."

The crowd pushed forward to hear the talking. Hedges could feel Murphy's heavy breath as the latter remained silent.

"He's staying with me," shouted Price, drawing to the front.

"Hedges!" yelled one voice in the crowd. "You going to have a go with your truncheon, or will we bring back the real dogs?"

Hedges heard the roar and sarcastic cheers from the rear of the crowd.

"Look! Get him out of here," he snapped at Price. Then he turned to Murphy himself and jerked his thumb at the yellow dog. "And you take this thing with you."

Sam Sodge looked down from the Havelock balcony, laughing at the rabble's games.

"There'll be a riot," shouted the town's leading man excitedly to his fellow gentlemen gathered inside as he abandoned his perch.

Hedges gritted his teeth and looked above the heads.

"I don't want to see you two in town again today," he said to Price and Murphy. "And tie those mongrels of yours up to your wagon, Shannon," he added. "On short ropes."

Immediately, the hateful expression that Shannon had been showing Murphy fell from his face and a pleading look took its place.

"Senior Constable!" Shannon protested, plunging after Hedges into the crowd. "They're working dogs, you can't tie them up. They need their exercise. Hedges!"

Murphy bent down over the yellow dog, his shadow looming large over the quivering, bleeding wretch. He fondled its snout. The dog licked him.

"I don't see why we've got to suffer because you want to play Jesus Christ to some stray mongrel. Now we'll miss all the fun," Price grumbled to Murphy as he flopped back up onto the cart.

"What happened?" Doyle asked.

"We've just been ordered out of town for the day."

"What??" yelled Doyle.

Murphy hopped in with his rescued dog and waved away the flies drinking at the ragged edges of its wounds.

"Let's get out of here before there's more trouble," muttered Price.

"I told you there would be some excitement around here when Murphy arrived," whispered Doyle.

Murphy stared at the wounded dog and watched the crowd from the corner of his eye as they began to move. Then he folded his arms and leaned back on the side of the cart, letting his eyes glide along the rooftops of the buildings. Already the town was falling apart. There a plank, here a sheet of iron coming loose...odd posts starting to lean this way or that. Murphy saw the men gathered on the balcony of the Havelock Hotel. One of them moved his lips silently in the distance, above the street, and his companions, red-faced in their coats and collars in the shade, began to laugh.

"There's the rascal who started it all...there he is making his getaway," chuckled Sodge.

The woman in the graveyard sat there still, mad with grief, beside the fresh, small grave. She sifted the blood-red dust through her fingers as Huley Colquoon, trudging strangely, with a boot on his right foot and none on his left, started to push the wonky wheelbarrow with his mother in it up the hill.

Sam Sodge came down the carpeted stairs of the Havelock Hotel to lead the town dignitaries as the funeral procession got itself into order.

Wimmel climbed onto his cart with a flourish of his coat-tails and gave the order sedately.

"Proceed," he said.

XV

A GIRL WITH sad eyes skipped, counting, alongside Wimmel's black-painted wagon, upon which rested Mrs Holman's shiny coffin with its polished metal decorations. The coffin was smothered with flowers, many of them wilting in the warming sun.

The wagon was pulled by Wimmel's feeble horse and Paul the blacksmith walked nearby, watching his work clomping up and down musically in the dust. He watched the horse's every stumble, and when the tired old nag paused to catch a breath, he smiled conspiratorially.

The sad-eyed girl gave up counting when the score reached twenty twelve. She was tired and the whole hill lay before her. She stopped skipping. The procession began to trudge uphill even as others were still joining the end of the line in town.

Some had not waited. One of the tree cutters, Cedar Joe, sat drunkenly in the shade halfway up, and other scattered souls dotted the hillside. Huley Colquoon was leaning against the handles of his mother's wheelbarrow. Wimmel's horse kept pulling its load, and behind its cart was an unpainted wagon pulled by another sick horse.

On this wagon lay Donaldson's plain coffin, without metal decorations, and with a single bouquet of bushflowers and lacy fern tied to the lid. Two wreaths lay in the dirt further downhill. They had fallen from Mrs Holman's wagon and been tromped to bits by the following horse. Ahead of the main crowd rode Wimmel, pointing ahead to the graveyard and chatting to Bernie the graveyard labourer about all the traps and pitfalls which lay in wait for them.

"Whatever you do, make sure you've got a good, solid

grip on it. That polished wood slips out of your hands like lightning. Bang!" Wimmel said, wincing at the thought.

Paul the blacksmith's boy walked alongside. He hoped Wimmel's horse would drop dead. He had waited so long to see it. And what difference did it make to the poor old thing if it died halfway up the hill, or tomorrow in some stock pen? It would probably be a treat for the horse to drop dead right now, he thought, that way it wouldn't have to pull the heavy wagon all that way up the hill.

Huley looked back down the hill at the parade — moving slowly in the sunlight like a little human fire, the dust raised about the wagons and people like smoke. He could see the priest's sulky racing across the ridge-line to the graveyard and overtaking the long stream of trudging mourners, followed by Mrs Gill's carriage and Major Stumic's sulky. Other carts and wagons were still leaving from the edge of town. Huley wiped the sweat across his face and leaned on the barrow handles, resting as the column of mourners breathed its cloud of dust.

"Get moving, Huley, before they catch up and pass us. You know what happened last time," cried Mrs Colquoon.

"Gawd Mum. . .have a look. . .looks like an army."

"Get moving, Huley. Quick, go."

"I can't, Ma, not yet. I'm too. . ."

"Get moving, Huley," Mrs Colquoon screamed.

Halfway up the hill, the procession had broken into an ever-slower gaggle of groups proceeding at their separate weary tacks and paces. When Mrs Donaldson passed Huley she shook her head and stared at him so admonishingly he felt ashamed. And with that shame he pushed the barrow harder than ever. But the barrow went just as slowly and his arms got tired. Then the barrow stopped all by itself.

"Hu-u-u-ley," Mrs Colquoon howled. The second hearse was already out of sight ahead of them.

At the top, Father Mitchell, dully dressed in his sheeny black smock and looking most uncomfortable among the flies which flocked to the oasis of his dribbling face, waited to move his missal cover until he was satisfied with the size of the audience. They were still streaming up the hill. Father Mitchell knew from experience that some would not reach the top of the hill at all.

Still, it was obvious he could not wait forever. Even as the procession wandered over the hill and through the graveyard gate, he opened the gleaming leather binding and flicked the purple tassel marker flamboyantly off the sacred pages. The leather cracked, the smooth white pages gleamed in the sun, and the purple tassel dangled, swinging.

"Brethren and friends!" he said, surveying the sea of suffering faces. "It is today we are gathered here under the kindness and caring of our Father..."

As he spoke, the priest glanced up at the sky, and outward toward his congregation — a multitude of inquisitive Pharisees. His eyes caught Mrs Gill's. They exchanged discreet nods. And there was the Inspector beside her... the dignitaries standing in solemn fashion around him. If Inspector Holman fainted from grief he would be prevented from falling by a solid wall of friends, behind him and to both sides. The only way he could fall was forward, into his wife's grave.

"It is not every day, thank the Lord, that we must bury two of our own...two of those who have been with us..."

The service continued. "Life is suffering, and suffering is life. Amen, like it or lump it..."

Begrudgingly, Father Mitchell waved his hand and turned his eyes to include a smaller party, standing midway between the second grave and himself. Mrs Donaldson was gazing at him, two girls standing by her, one with dark arms and one with small eyes. The priest took them in with a glance and dismissed them with a bitter thought as he turned back, thinking that if he had known she would bring those...little...harlots...with her, he would never have consented to conduct the funerals together.

His voice betrayed no sign of his thoughts.

"Doth not nature indeed teach us that the body is born, and must die? Doth not nature itself teach us that the flesh is weak...and indeed, an unfit abode for the Christian soul, once we realise the destiny which the good Lord in infinite perspicacity has provided?"

He closed his eyes and raised his hand with a benign, patriarchal gesture, and the few murmurs in the crowd died away. Mrs Ross broke a piece of tooth from the power of the moment as the muscles in her jaw clenched with a spasm. She stared at the priest's pink, quivering eyelids. She put her hands to her own belly and prayed to the Catholic God — certain he was a relation of some kind to her own, the Anglican God.

"Faith is the assurance of things hoped for..." cried the priest, opening his eyes and spreading his hand out over the grave. Inspector Holman stared down into the cool, raw hole in the ground which was to be his wife's future bed.

"...And..." the priest cried, his cheeks quivering with passionate belief, his hand turning over above the grave as if grasping the reins of the entire crowd, and his fist drawing straight to his heart, knocking the dangling gold cross out of the way, "...faith is the proving of things not seen."

Mrs Ross felt her knees begin to give way as below the crest of the hill Huley Colquoon's mother screamed at him again.

"For Christ's sake, Huley. Faster. The thing'll be started any minute..."

A deep, slurred voice called out from the shade of a dying-looking, gnarled and withered bush-tree.

"Huley! What have you got there, I wonder?"

It was stinking Cedar Joe, sitting next to a pool of vomit which had been promptly claimed by swarms of flies so big and well-fed Huley could see their greasy blue bodies from yards away.

"Help me, Joe...I can't go no farther," panted Huley.

"I can't help it if you've got no father, Huley," drawled the drunken bushman.

"Help me, Joe...help me push the barrow."

"Su-u-u-re. I'll be helping you, Huley...and your pretty mother."

Mrs Colquoon said in her most no-nonsense voice, "Tie a knot in your face, Cedar Joe, and help my boy. And none of your tricks, you bloody drunken good-for-nothing."

"Yes ma'am," said Cedar Joe, stifling his laughter.

Stinking-drunk Cedar Joe bent under the branches and staggered out from under the tree. He didn't look very useful. He stumbled toward them and banged into the barrow, and almost fell in with the crippled woman. To save himself, he clung to Huley and gradually they got themselves balanced.

"Come on, Huley," cried Mrs Colquoon, jigging about furiously.

Huley tried to prise himself loose from Cedar Joe. Together, they pushed and clung, leaning on the barrow handles. Then they tipped the one-wheeled vehicle over. Mrs Colquoon spilled out into the dirt with a girlish squeal. Huley collapsed crying, looking around for his boot with no sole. He looked at his hand, which had been the last place where he had seen it. It was gone. His mother dragged herself on her elbows toward him, hissing under her breath like a snake, while Cedar Joe sat there and laughed. And at the top of the hill the two funeral parties glanced out of the corners of their eyes as the priest delivered his oration.

Bernie the graveyard labourer stared worriedly at Mrs Holman's coffin and sized it up. It was bigger than Donaldson's coffin. How the bloody hell was that, he wondered. Bloody skinny little woman like that going in a huge bloody coffin you could fit the priest himself in. He shook his head. Look at Donaldson's bloody little coffin. You'd think they had to chop the man into bits to get him into it.

He ran his eyes round the inside of the larger hole. She's not going to fit in there, the gravedigger thought. They never told me they were going to bury her in a city coffin. He glared at Inspector Holman who stood proudly, sweating, and paying no attention to the imminent disaster.

Then Bernie squeezed his hands in terror, then simple disbelief, feeling the blisters stretch and burst, as he thought he heard a sound come from where it couldn't have come from. He looked at the coffin, already buried under the flowers.

It sounded as if Wimmel's cat had been accidentally locked into the coffin. Let it get buried this time, thought Bernie.

Then he heard another sound as the priest paused to find the quotation he wanted to recite.

It didn't sound like any cat he had ever heard before. It sounded more like knuckles or a hand in a glove knocking at a door, and someone mumbling with a mouthful of food behind the door.

He shook his head, hoping the sound would fall out of his ears and be gone. When the priest spoke again he could hear nothing. He breathed easier. He looked about and saw Constable Taylor beside the funeral wagon. Bernie took two steps toward him and leaned close to his ear. Taylor bent down with his whole body.

"Did you hear that?" whispered Bernie.

Bernie's big backside poked out as he leaned over further pursuing Taylor's ear.

"Hear what?" hissed Taylor, drawing away from Bernie's breath.

Bernie pointed to the coffin and gawked.

"In there," he said. Then he climbed up on the wheel-spokes.

Heads turned to the gravedigger as he pressed his head to the flowers cascading from the big coffin. He had risen above the crowd from nowhere.

"You'd never see Holman get up there to kiss his wife's coffin," muttered Hedges. "What's Bernie think he's doing anyway?"

Hedges began to thread his way among the mourners to drag the offender down. It was the sort of behaviour he expected from Huley Colquoon, not from respectable... well, sort of respectable people.

He drew alongside Taylor and drove his elbow into the Constable's ribs.

"Get that bastard down," he snarled without moving his lips, smiling at the faces staring at him. Father Mitchell watched him carefully as he continued speaking.

Bernie jumped down as Taylor looked helplessly toward Hedges. He pointed to the coffin and gawked.

"In there," he said, then he climbed up and put his ear to the coffin again, sprawling himself among the flowers in the wagon. The dangling back flap swung as Wimmel's horse shifted stance. The wagon wheel turned and the spoke Bernie was balancing on suddenly pointed to the ground. Bernie fell and crashed against the spokes of the wheel, dangling by his fingers from the wagon-side.

The priest raised his voice. He had just explained that he was not one to harbour prejudices against other faiths, and that in this heart he believed the Lord looked down upon all his good citizens equally, so long as they were respectable people.

"It is sometimes more grief than we feel we can bear," he shouted. "But! Bear it we must. And that is when we must turn to the comforting arms of prayer. For instance, the Apostle Luke tells us..."

Mrs Ross nodded her head in time to the priest's voice. She could hear the growing clamour behind the funeral wagon, but she could see nothing.

"Something's moving in there, I swear it," Bernie hissed as Hedges dragged him away by the collar, the poor gravedigger shuffling alongside to keep up.

The priest had stopped speaking in mid-sentence with a fatherly smile of rebuke. Before he could make another sound, the crowd saw Hedges dragging Bernie the gravedigger toward the gate. Then they heard the screaming and the running feet. And then they saw Cedar Joe as he ran through the graveyard gate.

Hedges let Bernie go and jumped aside. Bernie fell to the ground and Cedar Joe jumped over the horizontal gravedigger like a wild bush horse. Then Huley Colquoon appeared, his loose brace flapping, his one boot making a lonely sound as he rushed in pursuit. There was no sign of Huley's barrow or his mother.

"I'll kill you, you bastard," screamed Huley, galloping through the gateway behind Joe.

Joe giggled as he ran with his head half turned. He saw Bernie sit up dizzily to look at him, with his back to the gate. As soon as Bernie sat up, Huley ploughed into him head-first and rolled in the dirt.

Cedar Joe only had time to see Huley fly through the air. He himself did not see what was coming. With his head turned toward Huley he ran straight to the two open graves and the mourners and crashed into Wimmel's horse, which lashed out with a warning hoof.

The bent bits of nail hanging out tore Joe's head open like an orange. He fell, out cold, against the horse's fidgeting legs. The horse shuffled away backwards and the wagon wheel drove into the piled-up dirt and carved through it. The edge of the grave caved in and the wheel plonked down, half into the hole. The coffin slid back and over the wagon edge, screeching on the wooden wagon tray, falling toward the hole and coming to a thud, clunking at the edge of the hole in an avalanche of flowers.

"Hey," yelled Bernie as Wimmel grabbed the horse and tried to soothe her before she bolted. "Something moved inside that coffin."

"Shut up!" said Constable Taylor out of the side of his mouth.

Bernie looked at Taylor and opened his mouth wide in protest. Cedar Joe lay bleeding, and Huley stood panting like a dog, all pumping belly and open mouth. Then Cedar Joe began to pat at his blood-soaked hair, and the murmur of the crowd was punctuated with outbursts of giggling.

Inspector Holman shoved Constable Taylor out of the way and walked round the wagon, stepping over Cedar Joe's legs.

"My God," hissed Mrs Donaldson to Sarah. Sarah's small eyes twinkled. Marianna stood staring at the one the men called Rebecca the Goddess, wondering what the little pale girl had that attracted such adulation.

The priest stared at the fracas. Behind him, far in the corner of the graveyard, the lone woman sat untouched by the whole world, for the whole of time, and in all ways. She kept moving her lips as fast as her blinking eyelids as she spoke to the fresh little grave.

"Do you hear it? Do you hear it?" cried Bernie, pointing with a thick, scarred, brown finger at the coffin.

Inspector Holman pushed him out of the way and stalked to the coffin where it overhung the wagon. He thrust his head among the flowers and put his ear to the shiny, darkened cedar casket.

Cedar Joe lay propped on one elbow, watching his

blood drip into the earth. The crowd gathered around him just to watch him bleed.

"Where's Doctor Morrison?" someone finally asked.

"He never comes to the funerals of his own patients," a voice replied.

They watched Cedar Joe bleed. Huley Colquoon looked at the spots of dripping life joining together in the dust.

Suddenly Inspector Holman stepped up and away from his wife's coffin, his face still and without colour.

"Open it," he gasped dryly.

BOOK II

A SAVAGE
CALM

XVI

MILES DEEP IN the grilled hills, upon a prominent ridge facing across an inaccessible gully, sat the black figure, sprinkling dust into the almost still air, and he sang the children's song. From this perch, the dust fell out of sight toward the tangled, parched undergrowth below.

To the south the open paddocks of Shannon's station could be seen. And beyond that, the white man's town, out of sight, along the road sewn hidden into the bush, among the further hills.

DAY BY DAY the sun grew hotter; day by day the stunted, downtrodden weeds and grasses overran the native vegetation. As the stirring earth pushed up its mountains, time wore them down to hills. Time made all things, and the wide open spaces of the universe allowed them to be. Time was a loaded cannon barrel and the world was its bullet, fired a million years ago and still flying. Human life grew on the galactic projectile like a carnivorous verdigris.

Time ate like a pestilence into human souls and spread their shells among each other upon the ground in a cruel pattern of futility, wherein he that had time and looked for time lost time. He that had a wife and looked for joy thereby diminished his wife and lost her. She who allowed her carousing husband to tempt the dark night, and at the same time wished him dead, lost him. Those with full bellies who snatched food, love, land and life from others wore the shades of Hades across their shifting eyes.

To one time was money, to another it was love. To the farmer with his orchard, time and straw made mellow apples. To the woman with her nerves and hopes bundled

135

like dirty washing in the corner of her soul, time and a bitter mouth and an aching body made tomorrow. Time bled one to death and drowned another. Some drowned in the water, some drowned in sorrow, some drowned in the frustration of their own misfortune. Time turned sugar to salt, and salt to tears. Time flew, and its feathers fell like axe-blades. Time was a file that wears and tears iron and rock as easily as human hearts, but it made no noise other than the murmur of wounded voices. It made no noise but for the snoring of dreaming dogs. It made no noise but for the fire-like crackling of axes echoing over the hills, and the whine of the sawmill.

Time wore all things out, wore out this spouse, that dream, those chances, and these memories. Soon, without realising it, those who now lived and learned would be worn out and forgotten as though they had never lived. Precious few truths ever emerged from the slime of days, doubts and dealings. Time was the healer which could cure all things, most of all — life!

A MANGY BROWN DOG lifted a paw and wiped one eye, and the workers of the world began to speckle the parched earth with sweat as they beat and cajoled their dusty, unco-operative animals to work. The men of the hills, the town folk and the farming people buckled as one under the oppressive heat, under a cloudy sky that refused to utter one calming word of rain. Greased paper windows turned to dry tatters in the still air.

"By hook or by crook, this country will grind the life out of us. Those who don't just give up and die will be turned mad by the heat and kill each other, just you mark my words," said Mrs Ross.

One-eyed Albert staggered round the table in his underclothes and left his breakfast, as if he was going to vomit.

"A man can't eat in this heat," he said. "It'd bust his insides. *I'll* be in that grave she left empty up there if it keeps up."

Mrs Ross bit her thin lip. For when the heat is too

much for eating, it is also too much for working. And she knew that if they were ever to have a place of their own. . . .

Time seemed to stand still for her. It seemed a year of real time since Joe Marker was hanged.

TIME STOOD STILL, burning its mark on all that dared live within it. But the timepiece in Jansen's hand seemed oblivious to this. It still moved. And equally oblivious was the coach from the outside world. There it came, crashing along as it rolled into town, horses and coach all together.

"Dead on time," Jansen said proudly to Sergeant Dirlsky who had followed him out of the coaching office, into the crowdless street.

"It must be hot," said Dirlsky, wiping the sweat off his face. "Not a soul has come out. Even Huley Colquoon hasn't showed."

Jansen and Dirlsky closed their eyes and bowed their heads to the coach dust overpowering them. They held their breaths.

The coach driver touched his hat as he swung down from his driving perch into the airborne dust.

"Empty again," he called to the two statues of flesh standing in the street with their eyes closed, not breathing. "It's a scorcher. No-one would come here in their right mind."

His words brought the two statues to life.

"Ho, ho," laughed Jansen. "What about you? You come here."

"No I don't," laughed the driver. "I'm always moving."

The driver walked round the back of the coach, spitting out a big gob of brown mud.

"Watch his face when I tell him about Mrs Holman," Jansen chuckled to Dirlsky. "His eyes'll pop out."

PRICE mended his boots in sulking silence, glaring from time to time at the dying yellow dog outside the door under a piece of mosquito netting.

Under the chimney of slabs and tin, crouched in the fireplace with the blackened pole across it and the sooty pots hanging from wire hooks, Murphy made a billy of tea. He had a knot in his guts as big as his fist, and it was growing. Murphy told himself he had no reason to fear. They were looking for MacGuire everywhere, maybe. Why here, though? This is nowhere. No-one would come here in their right mind.

Price gave the sole of his boot one last almighty thump. The bootlast jumped on the floor.

"Not only did I have to miss the funeral, I had to miss the bloody funeral of all time," he hissed at the bootlast. "It must be just as bad as living in Jerusalem in the time of Christ and missing the crucifixion."

"How about a mug of tea?" said Murphy, as the hot, sweet, wet smell filled the room.

"No," said Price.

He jerked his boots on and stamped out of the hut. He found Danny Doyle sitting on the ground in the shade of the cart.

Price had to drag the poor old horse to her place between the cart shafts. She kept turning her huge, sad-eyed head toward him, and still he continued to harness her. Her tail flicked endlessly through a cloud of flies which included Price's face in its territory. At least on the road, he thought, the breeze will keep away the flies.

But on the road the flies were just as bad. Danny Doyle held his hand over his blind eye-sockets. The stillness in the air seemed to travel with the cart, and the flies travelled with the stillness, clamouring to sweat like bees to honey. Most of all they loved the juicy, blind eyes. Sometimes one of the pests would get caught in Price's nostril, or in his eyelashes, or in the hair in his ear, and he would squash it there before flicking it away.

The days had passed with the heat unabated, and the unstirring, repressive heat had endowed the flies' buzzing with a brain-poking tone. Price tore at his eye with his finger to get a wild one. They worried him so much as he drove that he hit his face with the whip handle. Then he saw a glint of light high on a ridge. He looked hard, over the heat haze, and saw what seemed to be a black man. Price strained his eyes. He did not trust them at a distance any more. Yes, it was a naked black man, with hair longer than any woman's. Then something glinted. It looked like a sword or a dagger. Price kept looking, but whatever it was it had gone, and didn't come back. The ridge line was deserted.

"Nah!" he said.

"Nah what?" said Doyle, sitting there still with his hands over his eyes.

"Nothing," said Price.

"You don't even like telling me that much, do you? What the hell is bothering you?"

"It's just that he doesn't own this place. And he shouldn't act as if he does."

Doyle thought awhile.

"What about me?" he asked.

"You're different."

"How am I different? We're all different."

Price shook his head without answering. He shook the flies off the reins where they sat riding along. He looked up to the ridge. There was no sign of anyone at all, only the illusion of moving shapes among the branches. Now that he was closer he could see the little birds among the branches high above him, clinging to the shade of the leaves with their little beaks open. There was nothing to be seen.

The heat kills by degrees, he thought. Starting with the brain.

THE DAYS were almost too hot for spreading gossip, but news of the extraordinary gala day of funerals travelled far and wide. Everyone had an opinion.

"Never before has such a miracle occurred," said Mrs Ross, drowning out her husband's agnostic mockery. "Not since Jesus rose from the cross..."

She raised her hand and touched the whitewashed hessian ceiling.

"Not since Jesus rose from the cross wreathed in a garland of angels..."

One-eyed Albert slapped his sweating belly.

"Don't make me laugh," he cried. "It's too hot..."

"It's no laughing matter," she scowled. "If you were more of a respectable, Christian-living man maybe you wouldn't have such bad luck in life."

She glared at the humble shack about her.

"My luck's not so bad," he struck back. "At least they haven't brung me home with my throat ripped open like old Donaldson. Touch wood."

One-eyed Albert touched himself on the head.

"Don't talk like that. You'll tempt fate," said Mrs Ross with a chilly shudder as sweat dripped off her face.

"Yeah, well, maybe it wouldn't be so bad," Albert drawled. "Anything'd be better than this stinking heat."

"I TELL YOU one thing," laughed Rooster Gorman. "I wouldn't mind being buried in that coffin. One minute she's cold as a fish. Put her in. Bang on the lid. Open it up. Hey presto!"

Everyone looked at him. He grinned and sucked smoke. They watched him slowly pull the pipe from his mouth, as though he liked the taste.

"Hey presto, she's alive," Gorman whispered.

"It's magic alright," said one of the other men. "I haven't seen nothing like it since Tobacco Williams found that gold nugget inside a piece of watermelon he was eating in the street."

THOSE WHO HAD seen it nodded their heads. Yes, it had really happened, a woman resurrected as she was lowered into the grave.

"Let the unbelievers mock us," cried the priest. "I saw it with my own eyes. And I have written to the Bishop. That should get some action. This town will be flooded with curious travellers."

"Make sure you send that letter on the next coach. I

can't wait to see what the reaction is," said Sodge. "This could be good for the town if we play our cards right."

THE WHOLE THING was a bit over Huley Colquoon's head. He wasn't sure what the fuss was all about. It seemed mostly as if the problem was they dug too many holes in the graveyard. The way Tom Shannon explained it to Huley, they had dug the first grave for Donaldson, but it was too small. Mrs Holman, he explained, rode up to the funeral in Wimmel's cart because there was no room in her own carriage. The fact that Wimmel had an extra coffin on the back of his cart just meant she rode up in the coffin for comfort.

"Simple," said the squatter, and everyone in the street within earshot roared laughing.

Huley blinked his eyes as though somebody had shoved a cabbage into his brain and he was choking on it. "But they said she was dead," he said.

"Sure, sure," said Shannon, dismissing the point and raising his voice so loud he began to cough at the end of it. "But that was before. All that's changed now. She's alive."

For Huley it wasn't so simple. It was pretty strange. He didn't like the way Shannon's dogs slunk under the wheels of the wagon, growling. And every time Huley tried to go away from them, Shannon made him stay there.

"Stay there, Huley! They like you, boy!"

"Leave him alone, Tom, he's no harm," said Doss Shannon.

"I thought you told me you like to have a bit of fun," Shannon laughed. His wife blushed and hung her head.

People laughed all round. They had Huley in the middle of a circle. Constable Taylor was in the front row. Huley swallowed, getting ready. Any minute now he was just going to put his head down and run. Things got so strange sometimes, Huley just had to run. Like the time he ran away to the next town. That was the best time he ever knew. That old black man sure was the best friend Huley ever had. Huley couldn't ever remember that old man

141

laughing at him, not even once, not even behind his back. He felt sorry he had come back to Blood Gully. He wished he had a father to look after his mother so he could go away and escape. He was so busy thinking that he didn't hear Shannon's voice till it was right against his ear. Shannon's hand touched him and the dogs growled so loud he could fell their breath on his bare trembling foot.

Without warning Shannon was talking to, and resting his hand in, mid-air. Taylor and two other men were bent over holding parts of their body where Huley's bones had struck them. Huley was racing clomp, clomp, clomp down the street, screaming with all the joy in his heart at being free of them back there, all behind him, pointing at him and roaring with laughter.

Huley loped off to the edge of town and lay down in one of his more secret patches of long, dead grass. Strange things could happen, he knew that better than anybody. Because somehow or another, Huley saw them all, or so he was thinking. Things happened that were so strange.

Huley's mother had sworn him to secrecy. And that was the only thing that stopped him blurting it out all over the street to get even with someone. Some things were so strange he never heard another soul breathe a single word about them, especially the people who did them. Like when he was stealing plums from the Holmans' orchard, and through the window he saw the Inspector wrestle Rebecca the Goddess onto a bed, and he almost fell out of that tree watching what happened next.

Huley pressed his face against the squashed grass, and he remembered how sorry he had felt for the Goddess. And how one day he hoped someone would do it to the Inspector. It was such a strange thing, Huley could hardly believe his eyes, much less tell anyone — except his mother, who told Mrs Donaldson, and she said not to tell anyone or the police would kill Huley. Huley was standing there while they talked about it. And he never forgot a word of it. The bit he remembered best was the bit that scared him worst.

"Do you mean they'd hang the boy?" said Mrs

Colquoon, with her face screwed up the ugliest he'd ever seen it.

"If he was lucky," said Mrs Donaldson.

Huley knew what it was to be lucky; it was bad. He rolled over in the grass which shaded his face from the sun and fell asleep.

MURPHY sat in the doorway talking to the yellow dog. Sometimes the dog would raise its head and try to listen. It hadn't held down any nourishment since its fight, and it was already half-starved then. Its skin clung to its shivering bones.

The man looked down to the creek and the bushy rise on the other side where a ramp had been cut into the high bank on Shannon's property, hidden behind the trees. There were some hens making their way across the yard. The yellow dog raised a swaying head to watch them, and wagged its yellow tail weakly.

Murphy thought to himself, he would like to see Shannon's mongrels coming up through the creek. He figured he would feed their guts to the yellow dog, and make it recover on the meat of its enemies.

"You know what I'd like to call you, boy?" he said. "MacGuire, I'd like to call you. How would that be? Nice name for a homeless dog."

He patted the yellow head by leaning way forward. The dog didn't move. Its dry, sticky tongue lapped at his hand. The eyes rolled toward him. The tail tip lifted a fraction...

Later, as Murphy sat there he noticed the dog had stopped shivering as it slept. He felt it. It was dead, underneath its green mosquito netting. The yard dogs took no notice as Murphy buried the yellow one.

PRICE'S CART was halted in the shelter of the trees at the top of a rise. He and Doyle were arguing.

"MacGuire buggered it up. We missed the whole show. For a dog! There'll never be nothing like it again."

143

"I don't believe none of it," said Doyle, wiping dust out of his eyes with a rag. "And the bit I believe least is about that woman. The dead don't rise up again. Only in story books..."

"Unless Holman is up to something."

"Anyway," said Price, "that's none of my business. What is my business is my place, and he walks around as if he owns it. Bloody MacGuire and his dog. And how long is he staying? Indefinitely? What's that mean? Forever? Or longer?"

The horse shifted forward and the cart moved. It was sudden and Doyle dropped his rag; it fell on his lap, onto the bench and down to his feet. He felt for it with his hand.

"You've got to stick together all the same," he said. "Just because a man might not like the stink of his own shit don't mean he's got to cut his arse off."

"I'm not saying that. It's just he don't..." said Price. "He just don't...oh, I don't know..."

"Well?" said Doyle. "Spit it out while he's not here. It might go away."

"It won't go away. Not till he does."

"Are you going to tell him?"

"Tell him? I don't even know him," said Price. "I don't know what he's capable of. I'll let him know without telling him. I'll make him want to go."

XVII

WHERE THE WIND blows no-one knows. When the air is still, all that is known is that the wind is elsewhere. And where the truth lies — no-one knows that either.

The big man in the cedar company, Sam Sodge, was thinking, however, of what he did know. He lay with his face bathed in sweat and his mind dancing with figures. His body was swollen with heat. The gold ring which was loose on his finger most of the year was now tight on swollen flesh.

He thought of thousands of superfeet of cedar, and hundreds and hundreds of pounds. He felt his wealth growing as he lay there. He felt dozens and dozens of men under his command. He felt the town growing around him and he smiled at the thought that all this made him a great man. Where others died, he lived, and where others eked out a pitiful existence unfit for cultivated men, he prospered. It was true — money did grow on trees.

He thought of the railway; and as he sweltered in the full spite of summer, he thought of the man-made dawning of the railway era...the bright sunshine of the railway which he longed to shine down on Blood Gully with all its power. He thought of all the curious travellers who would come on the railway to see the coffin which had brought a dead woman back to life. It felt as if everything just had to go right. The place had everything going for it. And it was all going well for him. Mrs Gill couldn't live forever.

Outside, the signboard of the hotel blistered in the sun; and in the street, little moved. Occasional whirlies of dust rose, whizzing in crazy spirals...and then died away. A load of chalk-dry branches in a slow-moving two-wheeled cart rocked past the shops. Beside the cart, a man and a dog dawdled, their heads hanging, the horse's nose blowing puffs in the dust.

Up on the hill, in her bower, the widow Gill felt the slightest whiff of breeze from the north, too hot to enjoy.

The servants, Judith and Kathleen, were taking it in turns to rest.

Kathleen was silent, sulking at having missed the excitement of the funerals and Mrs Holman's resurrection. Yet she wanted to ask all about it. She wanted to know.

"You were there. You saw it," she said to Judith.

"Yes. But what's happening over there now?" Judith replied as she looked up.

Walking up the graveyard hill was a woman. The long, hard walk slowed her down, but she hurried through the tinder-dry grasses, past the place where Huley Colquoon's mother had fallen out of the wheelbarrow; under the full weight of the sun, she trudged toward a tiny grave where the turned earth was already burned grey in the heat. The lone woman's face was a totem of grief so deep that nothing else remained.

ACROSS THE HILLS floated the sound of a day at a time. Price watched Murphy and where Murphy pissed Price pissed later, marking his territory. Where Murphy tidied up, Price made a mess. Where Murphy made a mess, Price cleaned up. If Murphy got out of a chair, Price moved it.

When Doyle heard it going on, he grinned and looked away with embarrassment.

"Are you trying to give me the rub?" said Murphy without warning.

Price swallowed fast.

"Eh? No? Huh? Not at all. I don't know what you're talking about," stammered Price.

"I'm not stupid," said Murphy. "You even pissed on the grave of my dog. Just let me know if my money isn't good enough, I'll take it somewhere else. I may be going soon anyway."

Price stared, perplexed. He looked as if his own dog

had died. Then, without a word, he walked out of the hut into the full heat of the sun without his hat. He rigged up the cart and drove off, through the gate and down the road.

"Where's he gone?" asked Murphy with a menacing voice.

Doyle sat with his head against the wall wafting his sweat-slicked face with a raffia fan. He laughed.

"He gets like that," said the blind man. "I thought he was crazy when I first came here. I think sometimes he goes off and digs up a bone to chew somewhere. Usually he just goes away and gets drunk."

Murphy grunted suspiciously.

"I reckon he'll be back...tonight, or tomorrow... friendly as anything," said Doyle. "He likes you to let him think you can't live without him."

"Huh!" Murphy grunted, "He needs a woman..."

"He reckons he's too old," Doyle laughed. "Too cranky more like it. It's this heat, it does strange things."

Murphy glared out into the yard. His face tightened and his eyes narrowed. His lips pressed together, going hard and thin. The whole appearance of his face changed.

"It always happens. You should have been here two years ago when they had to bury the first priest. Two people dropped dead in the heat walking up the hill to the graveyard."

Murphy mumbled something indistinct. He walked out of the dark hut and looked down the sun-washed road. Then he went off into the bush and came back with a pistol and a bottle wrapped in a cloth. Doyle smelled the shiny metal but said nothing when Murphy carried it into the house. Murphy concealed the weapon in his bedding.

"And how long do you think you'll be staying around?" Doyle asked.

Murphy shrugged, "Months, weeks, days, who knows? I could be dead by then, if Price takes it in his mind to lag me."

"He wouldn't do that," said Doyle. "You wouldn't say that if you knew him."

Murphy scanned the blind man's face. He felt cheated.

147

Nothing showed. Either Doyle was telling the truth, or...

Price was far down the road, under the high sun. He shook his head and blinked. The sun was fierce. He reached for his hat to pull it down over his eyes, but the hat was gone. Then Price realised what was happening to him. Sunstroke was creeping up on him — the curse of the open road.

Not far ahead was a gully where the road twisted down and back up through perpetual shade. He urged the horse on. She turned her head groggily to the sound of somebody rustling along, down through the old corroboree grounds. The sound drifted away. Price swayed, looking into the bush. He heard the sound again and screamed at the top of his voice.

"Come out and show yourself, if you're in there."

There was a burst of bush, a crashing of branches, and pounding and cracking twigs as the unseen kangaroos scattered free. The horse turned her head as she clopped along, dragging her burden. Price turned his frightened eyes the wrong way and stared as the cart rocked toward town.

FATHER MITCHELL sat with great worries on his shoulders, staring down from the balcony of the Havelock Hotel. Major Stumic sat there with him. They held their drinks wearily.

"Honestly, Major, I can't even meet her eyes any more without losing my composure. She came straight out with it and told me things about myself I thought nobody knew...well, almost nobody."

The Major shook his head in sympathy.

"She's a menace, Father. She gets her customers drunk off their heads over there on her cheap, poisonous rot-gut, and then she throws them out to come over here when all their money's gone and cause trouble," muttered the Major.

The priest looked into the Major's big, dull eyes.

"You don't understand, Major," he continued. "She knows things about me that I can't even tell my friends.

God knows who she might tell. Or what she might tell them."

"Well she can't touch me. So far as I know," said the Major, his confidence fading with each word.

"You should have heard what she told me about the Inspector!" whispered the priest. "I couldn't even repeat it to him. I don't believe it, of course. But what if it got around?"

The Major made Father Mitchell smile gratefully by saying, "You're quite right Father, something should be done. I'll talk to Sam about it. She's a menace, that woman. Unchecked, she could destroy this town, now that old Donaldson isn't around to keep her in check."

The priest sniffed as he smiled. Then he sneezed, spilling his drink over his lap. He stood up, trying to dry his clothes with his handkerchief.

"Damn! Now everyone will think I've damn-well wet myself."

"Don't worry," said Major Stumic, "wait here till it dries..."

SERGEANT DIRLSKY sat in the police station with his feet up on the desk, in exactly the same way as Senior Constable Hedges opposite him. They both smoked, spat and sweated freely. The floor about the waste-basket was lightly sprinkled with ashes.

"I don't know why they think MacGuire should be here," said Hedges, looking once more at the document which the coach driver had handed over to him. "We haven't had any trouble here in ages. Nothing out of the ordinary, I mean...nothing serious. No bank robberies or anything."

"Yeah, well, that's his style," Dirlsky replied, stretching his hand to take back the piece of paper. "He likes banks, and he don't mind blowing off the odd head while he's at it. He's killed three policemen so far, and seriously wounded one civilian."

Hedges puckered his lips and shook his head.

"Nothing like that around here, not in years, only the

five throats cut open like watermelons..." he said maliciously.

Sergeant Dirlsky shook his head solemnly. He shoved his hands deep into his pockets and blushed.

"I wouldn't mind a nice juicy watermelon right now..." he said.

Hedges directed a supercilious grin at his sergeant, and Dirlsky looked away.

"You had a big grin on your face when you pulled that stunt on Joe Marker," Hedges said. "You must have thought you were going to get a medal."

"You get no medals in this job," Dirlsky muttered. "All you get is jealousy. From above and from below."

"Don't worry," Hedges laughed, as Dirlsky stood up and grabbed his cap. "You can always blame MacGuire for murdering Donaldson."

Dirlsky stamped out of the office in a fury.

Jansen, standing in the dusty shade in front of the coach office, heard loud laughter from inside the police station as the sergeant emerged. As Dirlsky slammed the door, Jansen saw old Price slumped over the reins in his cart, driving slowly into town without moving. There was a condemned look about the old man. His head was bare and burnt by the sun. His old horse dragged the cart inevitably toward the shade cast by the Bushman's Arms.

"He's got twenty years older in two weeks," said Jansen as he walked across Main Street.

"It's this heat," said Dirlsky.

"Hey, Price," Dirlsky yelled across the road. "You missed the funeral!"

Price turned his bare head slowly and stared through Dirlsky, then he looked away, continuing on. The horse plodded with her head low.

"What's up with him?" Dirlsky asked Jansen.

"It's the heat. It's got to everybody."

MAD MICK O'REILLY slapped his coins on the bar in front of Mrs Donaldson. He walked back to the table, leaving spots of beer froth on the floor behind him.

He looked at Price lurching through the door.

"I've never seen anything like it...they all but had her in the ground...she could have been buried alive! I'll bet this heat is at the bottom of it..."

The other men at the table stopped in mid-laughter when they saw Price's heat-struck face looming through the darkness of the tavern. They had never seen him look so old, but they did not say anything; they just looked at each other.

"It's the bloody heat," Cedar Joe said. All the side of his head under the dirty bandage was caked with blood-tarred hair, and the raw and gaping wound was already breaking through the sealing of friar's balsam. "I told you before — people go mad."

Outside, Jansen was waving an envelope under the coach driver's nose.

"See this? You know what it is?"

"What?"

"It's a letter to the Bishop."

"So what? Do you want me to eat it?"

"It's written by Father Mitchell, telling all the facts about Mrs Holman's funeral."

"So what?"

"So! Now you must believe me," said Jansen triumphantly.

"It's true," swore Dirlsky, crossing his heart with a finger.

"If everything I heard was true," said the grizzled old driver, "the whole world would be dead twice over and we'd all be rich."

Jansen and Dirlsky smiled at each other helplessly.

PRICE could see Murphy's face where he stared at the tavern wall. He couldn't figure how a man could just move in like that, take over the place, and then just piss off when he felt like it. Bugger everyone else.

"Two can play at that game," Price muttered.

The men looked at him strangely. Price closed his eyes and poured the fiery drink down his gullet.

"Damn you, Murphy," Price muttered under his breath, barely able to hear his own voice for the noise of the fools behind him talking. Little did they realise they were the cause of all their own troubles. They had a share of the blame, but they carried on as if it was all done to them. That's what made him maddest of all.

All he could think about was Murphy. His jaw ached from grinding his teeth together. He could hear O'Reilly and Cedar Joe carrying on like a pair of old hens fighting over a nest.

"We've never had things so good," said Cedar Joe.

"How?" snarled O'Reilly. "Have a look at you!"

Price heard O'Reilly stand up, then he heard the madman's voice.

"Hey, Price. What do you reckon? Have a look at this."

Price turned. O'Reilly grinned at him.

"Just have a look at Cedar Joe. Just have a look at it."

Cedar Joe turned in his chair, the top of his head bandaged in a syrup of dried blood.

Mad Mick O'Reilly stood back admiring the bandaged man. Price just looked blankly at both of them.

"What's up with you, you bloody oaf?" Cedar Joe asked his companion, patting the top of the bandage to calm an itch.

"You know what you look like to me?" laughed O'Reilly. "What do you reckon, Price? Don't he look like a half-unwrapped steamed pudding?"

Cedar Joe looked hurt. Mrs Donaldson turned her back to them as she rinsed out a bucket of ashes and spit, and smiled at the wall. A smile crept up one side of Price's face and ran off the other.

O'Reilly winked at Price.

"I knew you had it in you," he said.

Price went to tip his hat, but it was gone. Mrs Donaldson turned to him, speaking loudly so the men at the table could hear her.

"It's nice to see a gentleman around the place who

knows enough manners to take his hat off when he is indoors."

Price turned away from the men and fiddled with a small rum glass.

"I'm not any bloody gentleman," he muttered.

"Hey!" yelled Cedar Joe, touching the top of his head as if to make sure. "I haven't got my hat on. I must be a gentleman too."

Mrs Donaldson opened her mouth wide. She turned and glared at them all just as Freddie Fairburn rushed in through the door.

"Thank goodness you're still here," he said, patting Price on the shoulder. "I just heard you were in town."

Price shook his head as Freddie talked to him, leaning onto the bar and licking his parched lips.

"You're a modern man, Price," said Freddie, his freckles fading in the dull bar-room. "I was wondering what you make of all this funeral business. I don't know what to believe...or who to believe. Everyone's got a different story."

"Piss off, Freddie," said Price coldly, without turning his head. "I've got troubles of my own."

"You've got troubles, Price? You?"

Freddie walked away, stunned. His lips were moving. He sat down by himself, without a drink.

Price pushed the last quarter inch of spirit away from him and walked out without saying goodbye. He found his horse standing where he had left her, shackled to the hot dirt at her feet.

"SHANNON was right," said Doyle, leaning over a bowl of water, washing his eyes as they heard Price's cart coming. "A man is better off dead than blind. You can't even see what you're doing."

Water ran down his arm to his elbow and dribbled onto the floor as Price's cart rolled into the yard. Murphy sat watching the door. He licked at his lips with a busy tongue.

Bang! Price stamped onto the verandah and looked down to where there used to be a yellow dog. Poor bastard, he thought, it never had a chance in the world.

"Gidday," he said as he hung at the door like a stranger in someone else's house.

"There's some tucker on the stove," said Murphy. "We let the fire go out because we didn't know if you were coming back."

Price ate up. He was so drunk he loved the whole world. He smoked his pipe with his mouth still full of food and stared at his blind cousin.

Price had to admit Doyle was a rather handsome man — a good, strong, honest face, with a nose as solid as a plug hammer. Price smiled, thinking Doyle's nose was not unlike a plug hammer in shape... The heavy brow was permanently marked by the band of a sweat-stained hat. Even overnight, with the hat off Doyle's head, the hat's mark remained, ready for when he put the hat on the next morning.

Without his hat Doyle's naked head seemed shaped like a woman's. Doyle's beard was in the same wild, overgrown style of his eyebrows and entirely covered his lower face. Price thought Doyle was a blind, bearded saint. Doyle could easily be the model for the Chinese carver who made the little ivory Buddha gods. Price had a little Buddha himself, so he knew.

He sucked his pipe and reached for his tobacco pouch. Strange how a grown man could take a fancy to carrying around a little Chinese doll, he thought. Well, it wasn't really a doll so much as a lucky charm. Inside the pouch he felt the smooth, white marble god, stained black with tobacco juice. The tiny sculpted figure was only as big as the top of a man's thumb, but the beauty of it was that the little thing had a little face carved into it.

Price smiled as he rubbed his thumb over its nose. He remembered the light-brown Chinese trader who used to travel in and out of town years ago selling cheap hardware and leaving behind a plague of leaking buckets.

Murphy walked outside and looked around, then came

back in. He saw Price pluck the little black Buddha out of his tobacco pouch. Price sat fingering and admiring the thing and putting it away in the pouch, then pulling it out again. He had the only one in town. No-one else had bought one, even thought the Chinese trader had had a boxful. The little god did no harm, which was more than he could say for many people.

Murphy walked over to his cot. Doyle stopped breathing. His hair tingled. His head turned, following Murphy's footsteps.

"What are you up to?" Doyle called across the room.

There was no answer.

"Murphy," he snapped. "Answer me. I know you've got a gun over there."

"So what?" Murphy said, pulling the bundle out from its hiding place. "Do you want a university degree?"

At Doyle's words and the simultaneous sight of Murphy's bundle, the smile fell from Price's face. He stared at the three hats behind the door, and wondered if he would ever wear his again.

Murphy unrolled the bundle on the wet table.

Price's eyes were fixed on the pistol.

"What are you doing?" Doyle said.

Murphy picked up the bottle and grabbed Doyle's hand, and shoved the two together.

"Ask no questions, hear no lies," he said, as Doyle's face rose in a smile.

"What have you got there?" said Price, still looking at the pistol.

"What's up with you, Price, haven't you got eyes?" said Doyle, pushing the basin sloppily out of the way and spilling more water onto the table.

The warmth of the wine ran down the gullies of their minds. The three men talked till they were halfway through the bottle.

"Don't worry. If you behave yourself, there might be nothing to worry about," Murphy said, smacking his lips to the liquid's sweetness.

Price then poked his nose toward the pistol.

"I don't like that," he said.

Murphy picked up the offending object and shook it in his hand to savour the weight. Price could tell it was loaded.

"I don't like it either," Murphy replied. "It's very inaccurate over ten yards or more. They never hit anything you want, but they make a noise and blow holes in people, that's the main thing."

"Very funny," said Price.

"You want me to go?" asked Murphy, holding the pistol at arm's length to exercise his arm.

"I don't know," said Price, licking his drink-sweetened lips. "Let me think about it."

"Fine," Murphy said. "That's all I need, is to know what's going on. I can take care of the rest."

He rolled up the pistol and topped up the tin mugs from the bottle. He put the bundle back, hidden in his bedding.

The subject of conversation changed with every mouthful of drink.

"Look at me," said Doyle, opening his hands to show them. "I earned my living going blind over a block of stone..."

He leaned on the table, turning their way and prodding his finger in a scattering of spilt sugar.

"...over a block of stone, a chisel in one hand..." Doyle raised a hand as if holding a cold chisel, then he raised the other. "And a hammer in this one...and the glare of the sun burning, burning off the rock into my eyes."

"It's cruel," said Price, breathing smoke out with the words. "But it's done, isn't it?"

Murphy looked into the depths of his mug, half listening.

Doyle wiped his mouth and nose with the back of his hand, then he began to pick up bits of sugar on the tips of his fingers and lick them off.

"They fried the eyes out of my head," said Doyle.

Murphy looked at the blind man's face, with his fried-out eyes.

"My back was saved by my eyes," said Doyle bitterly. "A fearsome cost to pay. If we'd had the eight-hour day in my time I might be a whole man today."

"Bugger what Shannon says," said Price. "You're useful around here."

Price glanced uneasily at Murphy. Doyle talked on regardless.

"Those employers have hearts of stone," he said. "It was like working granite to chisel the eight hours out of their hides. They didn't like it at all. Took years. Bloody years..."

His voice trailed away. Murphy lit up a smoke.

"At least they're reliable," Murphy winced away from the smoke stinging his eyes.

Doyle flopped back and sighed. He flicked his hand hopelessly and slapped it down, onto the edge of a plate on the table. The wooden-handled knife on the plate catapulted into the air, and a crust of bread hit Murphy between the eyes.

Murphy and Price laughed as Doyle swore and the knife landed on the table.

"Shot him between the eyes," laughed Price with glee.

Murphy wiped his face. He looked at Price. His eyes were cold. Price became silent in mid-laughter. He returned his eyes to the floor.

Murphy's knuckles whitened as he gripped the bottle neck. He topped up Price's mug, then charged Doyle's.

"You're drunk," Murphy said to Price.

With a peculiar smile frozen on his face Murphy stood and raised his glass. His eyes stared ahead as he spoke.

"Let those who do no harm, not be harmed," he said.

"I'll drink to that," said Doyle, "whatever good it may do."

Price rose to his feet, shaking drink from his mug with a splash. He swayed where he stood and raised his drink above his head.

"To the bloody poor black and white, yellow and brown bastards of this world who get kicked from pillar to post from one end of the bloody world to the other."

He sat down with a whack, almost missing the armless chair. He blushed and then drained his mug with one guzzle.

Murphy grinned at him. "I think even MacGuire would agree to that," he said.

XVIII

"MY FATHER WAS a gold-toothed man..." said Rebecca.

"Where is he now?" asked Judith and Kathleen simultaneously.

"That's all I know," said Rebecca shaking her head and sniffling.

The three girls were sitting along a bend in Blood Creek downstream from Price's and Shannon's farms, on unowned land. It was nearly time to go back. They had to prepare evening meals. They did not want to go back... not ever.

Kathleen got up and strolled away. Rebecca lay her head upon Judith's shoulder and stared up into the trees. She told Judith how she mortally feared her master, how she dreaded to be alone in the house with him.

"He uses me," she said. "But I don't want to talk about it. It would spoil the day."

Judith held her breath, waiting, but Rebecca didn't cry. She cradled Rebecca's head in her lap.

"You're so beautiful," she said.

"No I am not," said Rebecca. "I'm as ugly as a person can be. You don't know what I've done."

"Don't be silly. You're beautiful. Everyone says so. All the men look at you when you walk along. I've seen them."

"Of course. They're all like dogs. And you know it."

Judith's eyes darkened, and her voice lost its former brightness.

"I know what men are like," she said matter of factly. "Some *can* be nice."

"Yeah," said Rebecca.

She thought about it. The old gardener, Mr Hughes,

was a nice old man. But she had even caught him peeping through the crack in the wall when she had a bath.

"The weather can be cold and rainy too," she said, finally. "But it isn't, is it?"

The water in the creek sang softly over rocks, and the leaves in the trees tinkled against each other. A flock of parrots burst into the air and swung low overhead, screeching away.

Judith watched ants crawling up her leg among the long, fine, fair hairs. She flicked off the ones that bit her.

"Look at them," she said. "They look like cedar cutters crawling up a hill."

"Where's Kathleen gone?" said Rebecca, looking away.

Kathleen sat among damp shadows in a curl of the creek, watching a dragonfly hovering between a draping fern and its reflection on the water. She put her hand down and pressed an imprint into the cool, soft, damp earth. The creek had wasted away to a trickle in the heat.

She thought of Mrs Gill and the mysterious power of her wealth; the cedar company that made her rich; her dark clothes that scraped along the carpet, with the sleeves buttoned tight at the wrists, and the neck buttoned at the throat; her broad velvet sash; and the way she moved, swishing about like a crinoline ghost; her waist padded out with corsets; her hands clasped upon the perfectly laced table cloth, among the silver and gleaming china; her des- iccated features pursed sanctimoniously... Even with her eyes closed, Kathleen could see the old woman glaring at her.

And Kathleen's thick, dark brows frowned together in anger as she pictured the landscape of toil, of labour and drudgery that was her world, as she dragged herself up the never-ending mountain of time, a mountain of carrots, onions, turnips and potatoes, scrubbed, peeled, cut, diced and stewed... She thought of the fowls flapping pathetically in the dust in their vain quest for relief from the heat. They loved whoever fed them their scraps and garbage, till the one they loved came and cut off their heads and let their dribbling blood coagulate in clotted strands from their severed tubes... She held her breath at the smell of their scalded feathers...then her mind smelled the roasted meat when she placed it in front of the old woman... It made her feel sick.

"Kathleen!"

She heard Judith's voice and stared at the dragonfly hovering near her. Its wings flashed like fire, its body was red and it darted toward her like a warning.

AND, from a distance, the three girls were watched by the cool eyes of the wild, black man whose hair was as long as theirs. The man's heart was beating to the music of the water as it ran over the rocks, as if forever.

THERE WAS NOWHERE to run, and nowhere to hide, and no obvious reason to do either. By lunchtime the air was too hot to breathe. In a partitioned bedroom lined with old chaff bags, Doss Shannon sat sewing and sweating. The hessian chaff-bag walls were papered with newsprint. The walls had been like that the very first time she had entered the room. That was the time Tom's father had dragged her in there and had opened her legs up against the door.

She had never said a word, to save causing trouble. Old man Shannon never did it again. One day, after she had had her first child, the old man had said he had done it only to test her.

"To test me for what?" she had asked, wondering what use a test like that could be — standing up against a door with both hands held behind your back, a mouth full of bad tongue and having to cop it sweet whether you liked it or not. Men were all the same!

"You're pretty smart, Doss," the old man had replied. "You can work that out."

She still hadn't worked it out, and years had passed, years and years. She couldn't count them. Her lips trembled when she thought of the years since her children had ceased to need her, and subsequently had ceased to

care what she thought of them, and told her so in no
uncertain terms.

The door banged open. Tom Shannon barged in
limping. He stood in front of her, standing there in one
boot, till she looked up. She smiled.

"Hello."

"Where's my boot?" he said, "And what are you
grinning at?"

She gave a girlish giggle.

"I started off thinking about last night!" she said. "It
was just like old times."

He flicked the bedspread up to look under the bed,
and left it all disturbed.

"Maybe for you it was," he mumbled, picking up a
pile of his discarded workclothes and tossing them into the
middle of the floor. "Where's that bastard boot?"

"Look in that pile of clothes," Doss pointed. "Usually
good pickings in there."

Shannon located the boot and shoved his foot down its
throat.

Serenely, Doss Shannon sat in the cane chair beside
the bed. When her husband had slammed the door behind
him she squinted in the half-light and made one last stitch
and tied off the ends after biting the cotton. She fiddled
with the buttons under her chin and opened the top of her
dress and looked for the little teeth bruises on her breasts.
The smile on her lips rippled with tingles as she ran her
finger over the smooth flesh, feeling the sweet tenderness
of the bruising and the slight firmness that lingered... The
moment had been so short-lived, but she could not
complain. She put the sewing away in a basket. She did not
try to close the lid. It had been thirty years since she had
been able to close her sewing basket.

She did up her dress buttons and looked at the walls.
Sometimes a piece of newspaper would take years to fall.
Usually, though, she would have to tear off the loose pieces
each week. Each week there were always more. Sometimes
they fell off in clumps and her husband would stick on
more.

She sat there peacefully, in the dull gloom of the coolest room in the house. Outside, she knew by now, it was too hot to breathe.

BEFORE NOON they had said the temperature was over a hundred; by lunchtime they stopped talking at all, and just sat with their mouths open.

"It's like a wooden oven in there," said One-eyed Albert Ross, coming out of his hut into the hot, still, open air.

Nobody answered him. He kicked a dog away and stole its place. The dog stood forlornly in the sun looking at its spot, now filled by Albert's bullying backside.

THE HEAT drew dreams out from the back of their minds. Dancer Hughes remembered things that didn't fit together, like the first priest...and like Shannon's wedding, when Doss had been the fairest of the fair. He remembered the dancing till sunrise to the accordion and fiddle...the dust rising and choking the dancers who danced on regardless upon the bullock-dung floor. Those too drunk to stand had danced on all fours, or else they had fallen in heaps like moths outside the stable doors.

All the young women with an eye for a good bit of land and a hard-working man were jealous of the lucky girl who had hooked Tom Shannon. Doss took it all serenely, as if she would have married Shannon anyway, even if he was a pauper. The really disappointed girls went around for years talking about Shannon, saying, "He was no fool when he married her — he had no use for a woman with any brains."

ON THE MAP, the Shannon farm was as straight-sided as if it had been carved up with a knife — except where Shannon's abutted the odd-shaped sliver that was Price's farm. Price's land was so small they couldn't even write his name in it. They had to write his name outside it. This was an endless delight to Tom Shannon, who had bought out his own brothers when old man Shannon had died.

This had almost sent him broke. He sold off nearly everything that wasn't tied down or stuck in the ground. Then he had to sell two small blocks, one of which was miles away and didn't hurt. The other was a little sliver of land on the farm. It was separated from the house by the creek.

Shannon put a big price on the second parcel — top quid he wanted. He worked out what the land was worth in pounds, added a bit and called them guineas. Everyone laughed.

"Let them laugh," he said. "I can wait."

They were still laughing when he couldn't wait any longer. He began talking to a black-market dentist...that's what the man had called himself, saying he'd learned to pull teeth out in the navy. Years later, when he'd got to know the man as Price, Shannon heard him say he'd learned to pull teeth from watching veterinarians. Whichever way you looked at it Price turned out a funny fellow. He turned up at Shannon's place with a smile on his face and opened up his big fists. Inside them were two big wads of paper money. Shannon remembered licking his lips when he saw them. He used to lick his lips years later when he thought of them.

Price's money smelled like dirt. But Shannon didn't care where it had been. He needed it. Price closed his hands around the money and they began to talk.

"Let's go and look at it first," Shannon suggested.

"I've looked at it," said Price.

First, Price called the guineas pounds, then he told Shannon what the land was worth. And, to make matters worse, when Shannon told Price how much he needed to pay the bank, Price laughed and said he had been talking to the people in the bank. Then he told Shannon how much he really owed the bank; and he made Shannon an offer — to the penny, it was exactly the amount he needed.

"So long as you don't tell anyone how much you paid," Shannon said. "Tell them you paid my price."

It was a deal.

164

Years later, when the bank's old cleaning lady died, Price came up to Shannon at the funeral and whispered in his ear.

"Remember when I told you about people in the bank telling me how much you really owed them?"

Shannon didn't like being reminded of Price's bargaining him down so far. But after he learned the truth, if it was the truth, it didn't make the memory more pleasant.

"That was her," Price said, nodding to the woman's grave.

He asked Price how much he had paid the old crone, and Price replied evasively, "She asked me not to tell anyone. I shouldn't have told you this much."

Then Shannon abused Mr Jones the bank manager for letting his business secrets waltz all over town.

"I appreciate your raising this matter with me in confidence, Mr Shannon," said Mr Jones. "And I do hope the matters we discuss here remain absolutely confidential. But the fact is, what your anonymous friend has told you is impossible. We take precautions..."

Shannon lost his temper and stood up.

"I don't give a damn if you take to your missus with a horse-whip! How did the mongrel find out?"

"Do sit down," said Mr Jones. "Please, Tom. Sit down."

The bank manager wiped sweat off his brow. It was winter time. It was the coldest winter since the British had colonised the land. That's what everyone said. Some said it was the coldest winter in human history. The old crone had been found frozen to death in front of her burned-out fire, her shivering dog still curled round her feet trying to keep her warm.

"Tom," said Mr Jones, "I don't know what your friend has told you, but it is not true."

The bank manager opened a thick ledger. He turned the long blue pages so fast that Shannon couldn't find his own name. It was all just a blur of careful ink-writing. Neat columns of names and figures. Shannon could see that much. Only the name of Sam Sodge caught his eye, and that only because of the huge figure in red written alongside Sodge's column. Many smaller figures were in red, but Sodge's was like a fortune.

"As you can see," said Mr Jones, "we have many people who trust us. Small accounts, large accounts, and those such as your own, which fall in between. Now if we could not assure our clients of confidentiality, then where would we be?"

"All over at the other bank," Shannon laughed; then, remembering where he was, he apologised.

Jones did not laugh.

"As you say. It would be unfortunate..."

"Well, alright," said Shannon looking respectfully at the big book. "You satisfied me. But I thought red meant you owed the bank money."

"It does," smiled Jones, closing the book gently, like a priest closing a church Bible, and brushing dust off the gilt embossing with his hand.

"Well, someone's made a bad mistake," said Shannon, shaking his head, feeling sorry for the bank. "They've got Sam Sodge down for a fortune in the red, and he's the richest man in town...oh, except for the widow Gill, but she doesn't bank here."

"Mrs Gill does have an account here, actually," said Jones, opening the ledger to prove it. "But, just as a point of information, sometimes large debts, or borrowings as they are sometimes called, or, for that matter, credit..."

"I missed that bit after the debts. Can you say that again, slower?" asked Shannon.

Jones tried to make it clearer.

"Sometimes a large debt is a sign of prosperity."

Shannon shook his head like a churn.

"Sam Sodge owes the bank money?" he asked, dumbfounded. "I thought he owned the bank."

Knowledge certainly could be a burden, especially confidential knowledge. Shannon felt like running down the street like Huley Colquoon, screaming out, "Sam Sodge owes the bank a fortune, Sam Sodge hasn't got a bloody brass razoo to his name."

When he caught himself thinking such a thing, and worse, feeling good at the thought, he felt ashamed. He realised there had to be a code of honour in business. Confidences must be kept or the whole shebang would crumble and the blackfellas would take over the land again.

No, he thought, whichever way you look at it, that Price was a funny fellow. Having him for a neighbour was like having a circus clown down the bottom of your paddock. He was the fastest-ageing man in the district, was old Price. The older he got, the crankier he got. And the crankier he got, the funnier he got.

Tom Shannon was a happy man. He had a full belly, plenty of land, plenty of stock, a few kids to disown and a wife with big soft breasts who never gave him cheek. It was paradise on earth.

The sun shone down on him. Being happy was only part of it. Knowing he was happy was even better.

Even the town was an amusement, with all its fights and funerals and hangings...heh-heh, he thought, and its resurrection. Hah-hah. He'd seen it with his own eyes, which made him one up on Price. Heh-heh, Shannon chuckled at the thought of plaguing Price with it.

XIX

THE HOLMANS' KITCHEN was in a mess when Rebecca opened the door. The mess — no, not the mess, the work involved in cleaning it up — made her gasp. Mrs Holman was sitting at the table in a winter robe. The flesh on her face and hands seemed gone from under the skin. She had no colour. She was shivering and shaking and her walking stick lay on the floor.

A huge, buzzing blowfly flew in through the door as Rebecca looked in horror at her mistress shivering there. The buzzing insect flew straight to the cup of cold soup in Mrs Holman's hands. Rebecca laid her hand to the flyswatter immediately and waved the fly away.

Mrs Holman's voice croaked.

"Don't blame me for all this mess." she said. "You can thank the knight in shining armour for that."

"Yes, ma'am," said Rebecca, glancing timidly from the corner of her eye as she slipped into her apron.

The woman sipped the cold soup. Her eyes were lively and clear. That's the way they were when she was pulled from the coffin. Clear but unmoving. They did not even move when Doctor Morrison was brought up from town and he lit a match right in front of her eyeballs. Later, as the woman's body gathered strength, the frozen eyes began to move.

Mrs Holman's eyes haunted Rebecca. The servant girl lay awake at night, determined to scream if her mistress came to the room. But she wondered what would happen if she screamed when the Inspector came to her room.

"I've got to build up my strength," said Mrs Holman, sniffling into her soup and sneezing as she put the cup down; then she began to cough, almost falling from the chair. She held the table with both hands to steady herself. "When I'm strong enough, I'm getting out of here. If you've got any sense you'll do the same."

"Yes, ma'am."

"Rebecca," said Mrs Holman. "Come here. Sit down."

Rebecca did as commanded.

"There is no need to call me ma'am. I'm not the Queen of Sheba. When we're alone you can call me Agnes."

"Yes, ma'am," said Rebecca. "Do you think you should lie down?"

Mrs Holman grabbed Rebecca's arm.

"Don't breathe a word of what I've said to anybody, will you?"

"No, ma'am."

"You see," continued Mrs Holman, "I'm just like you. Only they don't know it yet. I don't belong here, yet I've got nowhere to go."

"Yes ma'am," Rebecca said with a trembling voice.

Mrs Holman put her face in one hand, with her elbow on the table. She rested her other hand on her hip.

"Could you get me my stick, please, Rebecca? I'll fall down if I lean over."

As the girl got up with a clatter, Mrs Holman watched her.

"You poor dear," said Mrs Holman, taking her stick from Rebecca. "You're...I made you cry..."

"No, ma'am. I can't talk about things," she cried, trembling all over. "Please don't ask me. I only do what I'm told. That's my place in life. I don't ask any more..."

The girl bawled. Mrs Holman tried to stand and crumpled at the knees. She pushed on the stick for balance and it propelled her sideways, into Rebecca's arms.

"I'll help you," Rebecca said to her mistress, swallowing her tears.

The girl and the woman walked and huddled together, clutching each other and crying, not belonging but with nowhere to go, both powerless, for the length of the hall.

FLIES of all kinds — little clean bush flies, bigger, dirtier house flies, giant greasy blowflies and vicious march flies — gave the air a steady hum as they conducted their commerce between the manure of all species and the kitchen table.

Devil-whirlies ran up and down the streets and through little yards of dust and wilting gardens.

Father Mitchell checked his calendar as he walked into his bathroom to shave. He hummed a bawdy theatre song. As he scanned the dates scrawled with notes, he saw that the travelling Anglican parson would return to town soon to conduct his monthly service. Let them build a church here, he thought, let them come. There is plenty for everybody. Sam Sodge was right. Blood Gully was on the brink of a huge expansion. When the railway arrived it would be a commercial fiesta, and where there is wealth the church is strong. He could feel the future breathing down his neck like a fire. In the emotional haze of optimism he saw a cathedral looming before him. As he began to hum again he nicked his neck with the razor.

"Bastard!" he hissed, watching the blood start to run in the mirror.

TOM SHANNON picked the dust from his nose as he rode to town the long way. He whistled when he came to a shingle rooftop showing through the bush. The door, marked *Pox*, was just visible through the trees. A voice came from behind him. He turned to see one of the Cooper twins standing with a rifle cradled in his arms.

Shannon halted his horse by twisting its head with the reins and heeling it in the guts.

"Mr Shannon," said the hermit.

"Hey, when are you boys going to bring around that jug you promised me?" said Shannon, almost dragging the horse's head off to stop it bolting.

"Hey, Shannon!" said the hermit's voice, this time behind him.

Shannon turned to see the other twin on the other side

of the road. The second twin held a blunderbuss with one
hand, the muzzle aimed harmlessly at the sky.

"Why don't you boys stand together once in a while?
A man would screw his head off if he talked to you for
more than five minutes," said Shannon, growling at the
horse as it started to veer to the side.

The horse twirled round twice before Shannon brought
it under control.

"You oughtn't to treat a horse like that, Shannon,"
said one of the Coopers.

"It might get it over you one time," said the other.
"They're not as stupid as people treat 'em."

"Look," said Shannon. "I can come back this way. I'll
pick up the jug on my way."

The twin he was looking at shook his head.

"Uh-uh. That's not right. If we let everyone come
along here they'd start nosing around. And we'd have
nowhere to go."

"There's spies everywhere," said the twin with the
blunderbuss. "We caught one of them snooping around
here."

"He didn't find nothing, though," said the one with
the rifle.

"That's enough of that, now," said the other one, as
Shannon turned his head from one side of the track to the
other. "We found out he's staying at Price's place."

"We followed him," said the one with the rifle.

"That's enough of that, I told you, Geoffrey," said the
grizzled hermit with the blunderbuss. "Anyway, I never
thought Price was like that. You better watch him,
Shannon. Price is your neighbour."

"Hold on a minute there, you two," said Shannon.
"I'm not. . . ."

"Yes, you are. You sold him the land."

"Anyway, that one at Price's, his name is Murphy, we
found out."

"He's the police spy," said the twin with the rifle.

"That's enough of that now, Geoffrey," said the one
with the blunderbuss, after waiting for his twin brother to

finish speaking. "There's getting to be a plague of lawmen. There'll be nothing left by the time they're finished."

He spat onto the road and disappeared. By the time Shannon turned his head in the other direction there was no one there either.

Shannon rode along, disturbed by the Cooper twins' attitude. If they did move on, then he would have to buy his illicit grog off Mrs Gorman.

So when he reached the Gormans' place he stopped to have a look. Gorman's two-roomed hut was walled with a mixture of wattle and daub and first-cuts from the mill. Round the place, sections of built-in verandah served as a dormitory for the Gormans' children.

Rooster Gorman was a charmed man, Shannon thought. His herd must have numbered an easy fifty, and his family was the largest in the district. But Shannon shuddered when he thought of Mrs Gorman's face. She never went to town any more, not since she had had the accident, when the last baby, had kicked over the spirit lamp and burned the whole of her face.

Old Rooster's heart was almost broken. He cried about it until his wife's face had healed and she could see again out of both eyes. One eye took six months to heal.

Doss Shannon had made her husband accompany her to visit the poor woman. That was the last time he ever went.

"Wouldn't be so bad if she was a bloke," Shannon told Doss. "But she used to be so pretty. Now, I can't look at her."

Shannon shuddered every time he thought of the woman. And old Rooster was always talking about her, making it worse. He would describe the accident in detail — how the woman had bent over face first into the flames and pushed the baby clear off the edge of the table in courageous sacrifice...and how her hair had flared like a torch and she stood there almost peacefully, except for the agony on her face behind the curtain of billowing flames...

"God knows, I moved as fast as I could," Rooster blubbered like a baby at the bar, and everyone else just stood not knowing what to do. "I never moved so fast in my life. And it...it was...it was as if I was crawling... crawling, and I couldn't go any faster...and she's just standing there like this..."

Gorman had stood up there in the eerie, yellow lamp-light, his face shining with grief, his clawed hands begging for help.

"She was burning in front of my eyes," he screamed at the crowd. "And I couldn't get there..."

Shannon's blood had gone cold in his veins. He would never forget Gorman's face in the yellow light, the mad, red skin and the agony in the eyes. And then Price walked out and Shannon thought, if Price is game to make a run for it, so am I. He followed Price out and Price staggered into the middle of the street and started to cry like a baby.

The women went around for years saying that if a man had done what Mrs Gorman had done he would have got a medal. Shannon got tired of hearing it. And once when Doss had dragged him to something or other he got drunk and gave the whingeing old biddies an earful.

"It'd want to be a mask they was giving her, not a medal," he told them.

Their mouths fell open.

"I know it might have been a cruel thing to say," he told Doss afterwards. "But you've got to admit it's true. What good is a medal when you look like that? Who's going to look at the medal?"

Doss refused to speak to him for a couple of weeks. When he got tired of the peace and quiet he just told her straight.

"Cut all this cold-shoulder business, or tomorrow you can get the hell out of here."

When Doss went into the bedroom later she found all her things in cases, packed ready by the door. Next morning the first sound Shannon heard was Doss asking him what he wanted for breakfast.

As he sat there on his horse, serving his sweat to the flies and jealously appraising Gorman's herd, Shannon saw the eldest Gorman girl walking toward him with her head up. Her arms and the front of her dress gleamed in the sun and her breasts were almost bursting out. She looked just like her mother had done — once.

Shannon shuddered as he recalled how pretty Mrs Gorman had looked when she had a face. He touched the brim of his sweat-darkened hat.

"Hello, Anna. What are you doing?"

"Nothing, Mr Shannon. Just keeping my eyes open. Are you going to town, Mr Shannon?"

"It must be a bit hot for getting around in the heat of day without a hat on," he told the bare-headed girl.

"Hats make you go bald," she said.

Shannon blushed. He felt the rush of blood tingle the bald patch under his hat. He smiled at her.

"You're just coming into flower," he said. "I suppose it won't be long before they're marrying you off."

"Time will tell," Anna Gorman replied, scratching a flea bite on her hip as she looked at Shannon suspiciously. With each scratch her skirt rode up a fraction. Her feet and legs were filthy, scratched and dusty.

Shannon stretched his neck and swallowed. His Adam's apple bobbed like a duck in a pond.

"Watch out for snakes," he said. "They're everywhere in this weather."

Anna Gorman watched Tom Shannon riding till he was gone; then she went and sat in the shade of a twisted, scarred tree, with the charred signs of ancient fires burned into the trunk. She picked up a pipe and sucked at it. She relit it, puffing out clouds of smoke.

"Bloody snakes?" she laughed, rubbing her bare feet against each other. That was a funny one. She had seen plenty of people bitten by snakes but not one had died; fancy a big lump of a fellow like Shannon being scared of snakes, she thought.

THE SUN went down behind the hills. The hills changed colour, from blue to black. But the sun left its heat behind.

"Do you think Rebecca is beautiful?" Judith asked, as

she and Kathleen lay sweating on their timber bunks in the cramped corner of the verandah next to the kitchen. The wire screens had been repaired by cotton where they had rusted through.

The bunk-out had two entrances — one from the kitchen, and one from the other side. Sometimes a draught would come through there, but not now, even though both doors were half open.

"Do you have to ask me that a thousand times?" answered Kathleen, pulling her nightdress over her head and exposing her naked belly and her sweat-soaked drawers.

"I think she's the most beautiful girl in the world," said Judith, emptying her lungs of breath. "She is so ge-e-entle and so pretty."

"O-o-o-h!" moaned Kathleen. "I feel like Joan of Arc. I'm burning."

Judith sank back into her mattress and melted into the dark, beginning to dream even before her eyes closed. Her body tensed and sweat ran off her into the sheet... She was carried to a corner of herself, a corner she shied from, where all was god-like and devil-like power, all was candle-lit.

Her bones cracked without pain as the dream devoured her like a dragon.

The dragon's lowered face... mouth full of spit... close to her. Stinking breath. Dirty eyes. Burning breath, putrid and foul. Deafening laughter. Laughing, leering. Sharp, hard hair. Spasms from outside her, filling her. Her eyes pouring tears. Sickening body fumes. The dream so cruel with mystery unfolding, and enfolding her. Unspeakable fumbling. She felt an urgency overwhelming... fear, horror, and hideous terror.

Time dangled suspended, as the dream lasted forever in all directions.

Judith felt the penetrating shock. She bent against her own body. Demons walked through her, slashed at her and spat in her. The breathing fire scorched and blistered her. She no longer smelled of herself, and the wind turned

175

hotter and hotter and the ground became too hot to stand on, and leaves burst into flame around her. She felt the hand go up her dress. She felt the hand go over her mouth, with her arms pinned against her sides. The smoke scorched her eyes. She screamed but no sound came out. She ran, she crawled; when her whole body was crushed she crawled with her fingers digging into the dirt...her own flesh...

She moaned and thrashed about in the sweaty tangle of her sheets. In her dream she struggled and slashed at the choking hand with her teeth. She almost drowned on the foul, hot blood which turned to flame as it poured over her bosom, and she screamed. The blood was her own voice. She screamed, and she screamed and screamed...

"Shh. Wake up, Judith, it's Kathleen. You were dreaming. Shhh."

Judith broke into a sob and flung her arms around Kathleen, squeezing hard. She sank her face as deep in Kathleen's wavy hair as she could. She breathed its rich smell and felt her nose cold against Kathleen's neck, and she cried with helplessness.

Bang! The door slapped against the wall. They were blinded as the lamplight splashed across their squinting faces.

"What is going on here?" growled Mrs Gill.

"Judith had a bad dream. She screamed," said Kathleen.

"I could hear that inside! What are you doing in her bed?"

"I'm not in her bed, ma'am," protested Kathleen. "I'm *on* it."

"Don't be so clever, girl," said Mrs Gill. "Get in your own bed."

"Yes, ma'am."

"If this is the thanks I get when I let you have a morning off your work, I'll have to be less generous next time. If you have energy to be up screaming and cuddling till all hours, then you must need some more work to burn up your excess. That can easily be arranged. Good night."

176

"Good night, Mrs Gill," the girls said, with tight lips and lowered eyes.

Then she was gone, leaving the door open behind her. Kathleen watched the old woman limp along in the aura of the yellow lamplight. She could just hear the old woman's voice.

"Curse this damned heat," Mrs Gill hissed softly to herself, swinging the lantern as she clutched her side.

XX

EACH DAY WAS hotter than the one before it, as summer soared to its zenith.

"Well," said Kathleen, taking a tray of iced and fruited cakes to the garden bower and turning to Judith as she left the kitchen. "If you ask me, I'd reckon you were dreaming about Rebecca last night. I'll bet that was why you screamed."

"That's not true. Leave me alone," said Judith, plucking a cake from the tray.

"Don't you dare. Put it back," said Kathleen, as Judith popped the cupcake whole into her mouth.

It was morning tea time. Mrs Gill was entertaining the town's gentlemen. Father Mitchell had a cut on his neck which was encrusted with dark gold friar's balsam.

"Yes, you've done wonders in this garden, Mrs Gill," said Young Mr Callow, peering through the gnarled wisteria vines and the whitewashed latticework.

Young Mr Callow preened his moustache.

"I have a brother in London," he said. "He writes of his garden there and it could be this one here he is describing."

Mr Stewart rolled his eyes patronisingly at his junior colleague in the government service. He turned to Mrs Gill as the priest next to him tapped his fingers and licked his lips with hunger.

"Ah, London," sighed Mrs Gill. "Where is that wretched girl with those cakes? They had me up all last night with their screaming and carrying on. Sometimes..."

"They're only young," said Young Mr Callow shyly.

"This garden is an oasis of civilisation in a wilderness," said Sam Sodge. "In this place time stands still."

Mrs Gill smiled regally.

"That's very eloquent," she said.

Sodge beamed a smile back at her.

"And true."

"It doesn't come without a price, of course." She looked around toward the house as she spoke. "We need to cart a dreadful amount of water from the creek. I shouldn't be at all surprised if the farmers were to complain."

"I dare say they will, madam," exclaimed Father Mitchell. "But I have always been enchanted by this garden. A delightful repose."

The priest wiped the sweat from his brow and it dripped from his hand. He waited, his eyes on Mrs Gill's face. She smiled. The maid brought cakes, then went.

"So restrained," he continued. "It has a manner of quality that defies real appreciation. It has..."

He shook his hand open as if to catch something. His eyes searched the air for a word.

"Atmosphere?" suggested Sodge, a smile all but hidden by his walrus moustache.

"Yes. That's it," said Father Mitchell, reaching for his cup of tea. "Atmosphere. Very well put, Sam. Perfect."

"I say, Mr Sodge," said Young Mr Callow, as his hand reached for the tray of cakes before he resumed speaking.

"How fares the cedar trade these days? It's been ages since we have had a discussion, and, as you know, I must do a report."

Stewart sat scowling at him with a mouth full of cake.

"Perfectly stable," replied Sodge, as he chose a cake dripping with fluffed cream. His fingers sank into the freshly baked, warm softness.

"Our only concern is the heat. The men won't work, the beasts can't work by themselves and, God knows how, the machinery breaks down. Our overseers swear there is no sabotage, but you never know."

He placed the cake whole in his mouth.

"That doesn't sound very stable to me," grinned Young Mr Callow, his ears reddening. "But then, I don't know a great deal about the cedar business."

"Mr Callow," Mrs Gill said. "This is a social occasion. Let us not spoil it."

Stewart smiled broadly.

"Yes," agreed Father Mitchell, letting his belly swell comfortably. "Let us refrain from talk of hangings, heat, religion and business. Let us be purely social."

"Might I just say," interjected Sodge, speaking with cake still in his mouth, "the only concern that worries me..."

He bowed slightly toward Mrs Gill and turned again to Young Mr Callow.

"The only thing that worries the *company* is something which should worry all of us...everybody in the district..."

They all watched Sodge with expectation, but Sodge put his lips to the teacup he held. His fingers fondled the smooth china as he sucked the steamy liquid. Then he wiped his moustache on a napkin.

"Fire," he said. Then he gulped his cup dry, gasping as the tea scorched at his throat.

He coughed and gagged, and sat up with his face a fiery red and sweat in beads all over his brow.

"My goodness," he panted, his chest pumping wildly. "That was hotter than I realised."

He turned his face toward the young government man.

"As I was saying, fire is the only thing that worries me," he repeated.

"And me," laughed Young Mr Callow, looking round. "If there is a major fire, I have to do a report. It's one of my duties."

Nobody joined him in his laughter.

"These hills are a tinderbox. If they go up..." said Sodge without completing the sentence, shaking his head gravely amidst the unsettled murmurs.

"Quite so, quite so," the priest thrust into the uneasy lull.

The hot, sticky reality of the scorching summer had invaded the cool composure of the bower. Stewart shifted his bulk and leaned forward on an elbow.

"Father," he said, "I'm loath to broach the subject with you, but what really does lie behind the extraordinary events of Mrs Holman's funeral?"

"It was terrible!" Father Mitchell coughed up tea from his lungs. "I'm...I don't know what to say. It's... unexplainable.'

"Nothing is unexplainable," said Young Mr Callow confidently. "Some things *we* are unable to explain."

"Most remarkable," Mrs Gill said, ignoring him.

Stewart nodded. He glared at his assistant.

"It was a miracle," he said emphatically.

"I didn't think you Protestants believed in miracles, Mr Stewart," said Father Mitchell. "But of course, Doctor Morrison assures me there must be a perfectly logical medical explanation.'

"Medical explanation or no medical explanation — resurrection is a miracle in any language," said Mrs Gill enthusiastically.

She poured out more tea. Steam came up from the spout as she held the heavily padded pot.

"Perhaps it is all for the best," Father Mitchell said. "Perhaps it will remind the Inspector of the joys of marriage. You never miss your water till your well runs dry," he added, crossing his fingers over his belly and smiling with cream all over his lips.

The young government man leaned over and tugged the priest's sleeve.

"From what I hear around the place, the Inspector might have more than one well," he said.

The priest looked at the young man with horror. He turned helplessly toward Sodge, and Sodge peered at Young Mr Callow with loathing eyes. Stewart sat still with his mouth open, his eyes motionless with disbelief. He closed his mouth and opened it again, as Callow looked apologetically at Mrs Gill, his face beginning to blush. Beads of perspiration began to show along his hairline. Stewart spoke, a smile flickering on his face like a candle-wick drowning in its own wax. With each forced raising of the corners of his mouth, his eyes twitched nervily.

"Well," said Stewart, not taking his eyes from his assistant. "Quite honestly, it pains me to have to listen to an inexperienced man. A man who has not known a

181

wife...a man who has never known the pressures and demands of married life, sitting in judgement upon another man's conduct of his own most private affairs. I'm afraid I have to say it...it..."

Stewart shook his face and sweat flicked off it.

"I can't say it. I can't bring myself to say it, so strongly do I feel. A man who has never known a day of married life!"

Sodge blushed. Callow turned as red as the cherry sitting on top of the last cupcake in the silver tray of crumbs and blobs of cream.

"FATHER MITCHELL will be here this evening," Inspector Holman told his resurrected wife, as she lay grey-faced and deep-eyed in bed, staring at him.

Six pillows were bunched up behind her. Her bottom sank deep into the mattress, and a quilted eiderdown covered her from the foot of the bed to her waist.

"Stop staring at me," Holman said with a friendly voice. "Is that all you can do?"

His wife looked away from him. She seemed not to breathe any more. Her shoulders did not rise and fall, her chest remained sunken. Sometimes Holman regretted giving the order to open the coffin. They might as well have buried her alive.

"So! You can hear me, after all," he said triumphantly.

Mrs Holman tensed; she just sat staring.

"For God's sake, woman, can't you speak?"

She narrowed her eyes, without moving her face, just as if she was really dead. Only the eyes remained alive.

"You don't realise how lucky you are. If I hadn't told them to open the coffin, you'd be buried in the ground. You would have suffocated."

The woman's eyes sparkled with hate.

"You were just lying there. If I hadn't slapped your face, who knows?" Holman continued, pointing at her with a trembling finger. "You damned well looked dead."

Only one nostril moved on his wife's face, but he saw it and shook his head.

"Don't think you'll beat me," he said, smiling hard and biting his tongue between his back teeth. "You moaned something last night. Don't tell me you can't talk. For God's sake, Agnes, stop staring."

"What did you call me?" Mrs Holman asked suddenly.

He heard her voice; he couldn't believe it. He hadn't even seen her lips move. He became frightened with the thought that they hadn't moved — that some live thing in her dead body may have spoken with her deserted voice. A weird foreboding made him shiver all over. When she saw him shaking, Mrs Holman's eyes widened. Her back straightened and her shoulders rose. Instinctively, Holman stepped backward and shook the dresser.

"You talked?" he asked, unsurely.

"What did you call me?"

He saw her lips move. He heard the almost forgotten sound of her voice again.

"Call you..." he repeated after her.

"Yes."

"I don't know..." he said.

"So you do know my name after all," she replied.

"Don't be ridiculous," Holman sneered, relieved. "Do you have to stare at me like that? You make a man feel like a fool."

"And so you are."

He smiled.

"I'm glad you can talk. Don't worry, you'll be up and about in a few days. Father Mitchell will be here this evening...Rebecca!" he yelled.

Holman listened to the Goddess rushing down the length of the hall. He kept smiling at the open doorway till Rebecca showed.

"A cup of tea for Mrs Holman."

"Yes, sir."

"And you drink it," Holman said to his wife. "You'll need all your energy if you don't want to end up where you very nearly did."

Rebecca's skirt swept round the doorway as she went out. Holman stepped over to the bed and stood looking down on his wife.

"Do try to be human by the time I return," he told her.

"Human!" she snarled. "You wouldn't know the meaning of the word."

Holman's voice was tinged with a vague tone of menace when he spoke.

"Be careful," he said. "Don't say anything you might regret at a later date. You have a whole life ahead of you — don't spoil it for yourself."

"Spoil this!" She waved her hand at all of it, as if it was a bad smell. "You're making fun of me."

Rebecca stood near the doorway holding the hand-sized silver tray. She was afraid to go in, too afraid to knock on the door jamb, even more afraid to be heard walking away. She watched Holman's shadow dance through the open door, across the hall and up the wall. She was watching it grow huge when he walked straight out of the door and almost crashed into her.

"There you are, Rebecca," he smiled when he saw her.

"You're tired, you're yawning," he said with concern. "Here, give me that."

He took the little tray from her.

"Go and sit down for five minutes and rest your legs," he told her.

Rebecca compressed her lips and lowered her eyes.

"Yes, sir," she mumbled uneasily.

"Here is your tea, dear," Inspector Holman said turning to his wife and avoiding her eyes. "Don't let it go cold."

XXI

FLOWERS-OF-TAN, the mould growing on dead wood, began to die in plague proportions, dried out and destroyed by the air they breathed. The stockpiles of sawdust around the mill were taller than the little huts and shacks of the town. Their roofs were held down against a wind that did not blow by huge woody pumpkins, and lumps of log, rocks and boulders.

One-eyed Albert Ross had a half-busted cart wheel on his roof. The weight of it had buckled the rusted scraps of iron. One-eyed Albert had tried to sell the wheel to Price.

"It's a hickory wheel," he had announced.

"Hickory wheel? If it was a hickory wheel it wouldn't have broke," replied Price.

"That's the trouble with Price," One-eyed Albert had complained to Danny Doyle. "You can't sell him nothing, unless he wants to buy it."

"How much do you want for it?" Doyle had asked.

Albert had told him, secretly, putting his face along-side Doyle's. Their blind eyes had almost touched.

"I got it for nothing," Albert whispered. "You can have it for half a crown."

Doyle laughed.

"Alright, a shilling," chuckled One-eyed Albert.

"I'll give you sixpence for it. Take it or leave it."

"Sold," said One-eyed Albert. "Give me the money now. And come and get the wheel down when you want it."

"Don't be ridiculous," said Doyle. "You'll have to get it down."

"I can't get it down," grunted One-eyed Albert. "If I got up there with my fat guts, the whole thing would come crashing down."

So the wheel stayed where it was.

Now One-eyed Albert sat in the shade of a drooping peppercorn bush in Main Street. At home his wife wondered where he was, while the broken wooden wheel on the roof dried out in the blazing sun.

One-eyed Albert was half asleep with the heat, mumbling away to Paul, Bartholomew's young apprentice.

"It's so hot," One-eyed Albert said, "I'd sniff a dog's backside to get the breeze off its tail if it was wagging. That's why they do it. Of course. Keeps the flies off their faces. Amazing what you can come up with if you think long enough."

He started to groan. Paul nodded his blond head.

"What do you think of this?" the boy said.

He handed One-eyed Albert a horseshoe. He had scratched two words, "Good Luck", into its rusty coat with a nail.

"That's fine, mighty fine," said One-eyed Albert, regarding the item scrupulously, taking almost twice as long as a man with two eyes would need to look at it. "What's them words say?"

"Good Luck."

"Hmmm," said One-eyed Albert, getting an idea. "I wouldn't mind one of them for my missus. What are you going to do with it?"

"It's for someone," said the lad, taking the horseshoe back.

He held the beaten iron softly in his hardened hand and wiped One-eyed Albert's dusty fingermarks off it with his apron.

"Someone who?" asked One-eyed Albert.

But Paul wouldn't tell him.

BEHIND THEM, over the tops of the shacks and behind a few trees, lay the mill, now silent.

From the balcony of the Havelock Hotel, staring into the future, Sam Sodge looked at the mill, its unpainted roof scorched raw in the sun's glare. Though the mill had now stopped, he could still hear the big saw roaring, tearing into the timber, forcing the sap out of the wood in a steamy lather.

The whole town still bathed in the squeal, a sound that embodied the raw energy of industry, the roaring spirit of commerce.

Dancer Hughes too would hear the sound — a distant, high-pitched, constant howl which rang in his ears even though the mill had been still and silent all day.

Dancer thought of Tobacco Williams and the girl who had cried at his hanging before she married the hardware merchant's son and went away. Then he remembered the Marker boys. He remembered the way Inspector Holman had smiled as Joe Marker, hanging at the end of the rope, began to spin.

Dancer recalled Joe Marker's mangled face. Jack Marker — the poor bastard — should have known better. Served him right, what happened. You never fart in anybody's face. That's asking for trouble.

Dancer shook the sight of Joe Marker's body out of his mind, along with the gunned-down, ruined body of Jack Marker as he was dragged dead from the tavern in a barrow covered by canvas. In his mind's eye Dancer could see right through the canvas. Blood kept dripping down from the barrow as the police pushed it down Main Street.

With these horrible thoughts gone, he recalled the massacre of the blacks, even though he hadn't been there — and he did not regret missing it. Then he wiped the sweat out of his eyes, thinking of poor Mrs Colquoon the day Tom Shannon had called her for everything in the street, in front of everybody.

"Go on, you bloody old cripple," Shannon had told her as he turned his back on her and rode away, with the whole town listening. "If you were a horse they'd have shot you years ago."

Dancer's time-wandering mind saw Mrs Colquoon's knobbly fist shaking in fury at Shannon.

"Come down here and say that, Tom Shannon, you

gutless big spoiled bastard. Come down here where I can get you. You're such a mean mongrel, even your own brothers wouldn't work for you," Mrs Colquoon had yelled back.

Huley's face was pop-eyed. Dancer stared at it all again inside his head. Probably Huley would have shat himself if Shannon had got down off the horse. It wouldn't have been the first time Huley had done it. The worst time was when Huley had been found tied to a tree outside town with his back torn to deep shreds like a convict flogged and left to perish on the triangle. Huley couldn't — or wouldn't — say who had done it to him. When they cut him loose he fell into the hands of his rescuers, who recoiled from the sticky, greasy shreds of his back and the foul stink of his messed trousers that were by then soaked with blood.

"They just kept laughing and calling me names," Huley cried as he lay healing on his belly for days. "They said it was just like flogging a blackfellow."

Months later, when people asked Huley all about it, wanting to hear the gory details, Huley could hardly remember a thing. Sometimes the scars on his back would hurt, but then, sometimes his teeth ached, and to Huley it was all much of a muchness.

How long ago was that? Dancer wondered. It was before they hanged Nancy Ogilvy. That's how long ago it was. Huley must have been no more than a boy. The kid's going to be a handful when he grows up, Dancer figured. What would he be now — about twenty?

Dancer thought about his own age — well over a hundred; and probably, at the rate he was going, he would make two hundred. And times were getting better. He could remember Mrs Colquoon, almost shaking herself out of the barrow, whipping a stick against the side, screaming, "Faster, Huley! Catch the no-good bastard."

"You're a thief, Shannon. You robbed me just like you stole that land off your own brothers! Try and deny it!" she had screamed as Shannon lowered his head, hiding his face in the shade of his hat brim; only his blushing ears could be seen.

THE HEAT brought a thirst no drink could allay. It was a giant mangle crushing all that time fed into its huge tumbling rollers.

The silence of the shut-down mill enveloped the town and all its surroundings like a shroud. The huge form dominated a landscape which had been slathered smooth; now, faded to the edge of death, naked and unprotected, it was sucked dry by the thirsty sun. The giant, dark bulk of the mill was as dour as the widow Gill's face...

Price had been drinking for days on end. Each morning he staggered into the dusty heat and spewed till nothing came, and then he tied his gizzard with cramp, dry-retching. He slept wherever unconsciousness found him. He stank. When Mrs Donaldson told him he needed a good tubbing, he looked at her as if she was a stranger.

"Dirtiness is a relative thing," he slurred drunkenly.

His eyes shone from his dirty face like two embers in an ashtray. The whites were red with blood, the skin of his face had become a splotchy mess of ashen flesh darkened and faded at once.

Price didn't care one way or another. On more than one morning he lay in the dust, clutching his throbbing liver through his ribs. "Come on, you bastard. If you want it, here it is. Come and take it," he cried. And no-one wanted it. There it lay, heaving, and swallowing bile, breathing with short, uneven, painful breaths...his body. No-one came to take it. He dug his fingers into the dust as if to get a grip on the world. As his fists closed and his face contorted, the dust flowed through his fingers. He might as well have tried to seize hold of a running stream of water with his bare hands.

For the umpteenth time, holding a drink in his hand Price lurched around the Bushman's Arms. Like a man learning to walk. He felt a stabbing pain between the eyes. Fire ran down his face, or so it seemed, as tremors ran through his features, giving off a glow of madness under his sheen of sweat. He staggered to a chair where he slumped, regaining his strength. He could not remember the last time he had slept. It wasn't like sleep any more.

"I've seen so many of them go like this," said Mrs Donaldson. "If ever there really is a devil, I'll wager he comes in either a keg or a bottle."

"Or a police uniform," said Mad Mick O'Reilly, slapping money on the bar.

None of them could see, Price thought. None of them knew. None of them could say one encouraging word. They were no consolation at all. Well, he thought, if they're too stupid, if they can't see the light of day. His eyes rolled, and with a firm effort he steadied them, slumped where he sat. I'll show them, the lot of them, he thought. MacGuire, Shannon, the thieving bastard who sneaked onto his farm one day and stole half his hand tools...

"He walks around as if he owns the place," he snarled, wiping the dribble that came out with the words. "Bloody MacGuire, the bastard...he..."

Price stood stunned at the words he heard coming from his own mouth. His mouth dropped open. He saw himself as a grub, boring the soul out of his own life, betraying a man who trusted him.

"Get him out of here," Mrs Donaldson whispered to Suggestible Humphrey as she looked fearfully to the door.

A great, visible melancholy overcame Price. The whole of life was only an accumulation of errors and aggravations. He shrank in height as his stomach muscles started to flinch. The spasm made its purpose clear when a wild, chundering spurt spewed from his mouth and ended drooling from his whiskers.

Mad Mick O'Reilly laughed.

"Come back and see me when you've stopped eating," he yelled, slapping Price on the shoulder.

"Get him out of here," Mrs Donaldson screamed, as Humphrey put his hand on Price's shoulder.

"Before he comes out with something less recent," giggled Sarah, who was standing at the bar.

The girl pulled an ugly face when Mrs Donaldson told her to clean up. But she did not have time to protest. Mick O'Reilly, leaning beside her on the bar, reached down and rubbed the side of her far breast with his arm around her back.

"After you clean that up," he winked. "And wash your hands first."

"Oh," the young girl said, folding her thin arms speckled with scurvy sores. "We are getting toffy."

At that moment Price turned and Humphrey's hand slipped from his shoulder.

The drunken man lowered his head like a bull in a Spanish bullfight and lunged across the room. He didn't care if they tore him limb from limb. Better if they did. Maybe if pain could get through to him, other things would in its wake. Maybe if he thrashed about in the depths of his gloom he could fight his way to the surface and things would become real, if they ever had been at all...

As Sarah unfolded her arms and rose from the bar stool, Price slammed into O'Reilly's back, his shoulder thumping into the big man. Sarah and O'Reilly screamed as one. A bloodthirsty roar rose to the ceiling in the misty bar as Price bounced off Mad Mick's muscular body and fell to the floor like a heap of dirty clothes. O'Reilly just stood there, arched backward, his hands reaching behind him, the scream still visible on his face; slowly bending, he lowered himself to one knee and pushed away Sarah's helping hand.

"No fighting!" yelled Suggestible Humphrey. "Remember the Markers."

"Out! Out!" shouted Mrs Donaldson, flinging her finger repeatedly at the door.

Hands grabbed Price from all directions, raised him from the floor and bore him to the door. They dragged him into the dusty roadway and let him fall.

Price crumpled without resistance. He lay crying into the dust which was under him and all over him. It was in his mouth and nose and eyes. It was in his belly and his lungs. He felt like a blowfly drunk on sheep's blood, rolling upside down, unable to lift its filled belly.

He rubbed his nose and looked at the blood that was left smeared on the back of his hand. It was the colour of mud. He looked up and down the empty street. He could hear the cheering from the Bushman's Arms as Mad Mick rose painfully from his knee.

Sarah walked behind O'Reilly with a dustpan, a bucket of cold water and a moulting mop. O'Reilly rubbed his back and shook his pale face, wincing again and again as he rubbed the hurt.

"I thought my number was up that time," he grinned sadly.

An uproar of laughter erupted around the bar.

XXII

HIGH IN THE inaccessible gully sat the black man, deep in the conquered territory surrounding Blood Gully. A mass of hair dangled from his scalp in matted, knotted locks that surrounded his young, mystical face. Once again he sang the children's song, and then he beckoned the wind toward him from the north.

DAYS HAD COME and gone, but it made no difference. Dust hung motionless in the air. The only breeze that ever came was too gentle, and worse, it was from the west, fired up by its long journey over the outback.

The road-making, town-forming serpent burrowed inland from the coast, devouring all, tearing down the flesh of ancient forest to the flesh of the earth.

And in the heart of the serpent, in the peaceful little town, two dusty boys in rags and bare feet stepped out from sweltering shade into the blaring sun as the young Stewart boy came along.

Young Stewart was eating an orange, and threw the peel away when he saw them. One of the two barefoot boys picked up the dusty orange scrap and wiped it on the leg of his pants, then he began to suck it.

"Where you going?" he said, standing up close to the well-dressed youngster.

The two dusty boys would have been the same height as young Stewart, except for the difference made by young Stewart's heels.

"I said, where are you going?" the boy snarled again, scabs all over his freckled face, his shaved head colourless in the blazing sun, his little hands like claws knotted into fists.

"To the store," said young Stewart.

The bald-headed boy handed the orange peel to his barefoot accomplice, pressing his scabby face close to young Stewart's oiled and carefully combed hair. The barefoot boy with tangled hair sucked and gnawed the orange peel, never taking his eyes from young Stewart.

"Don't lie to us, fancy pants," he said, not taking the peel from his mouth. "You're not going to the store."

"Honest," said young Stewart, the front of his starched shirt caving in as he breathed.

"Show us your money."

"Look," said young Stewart.

The moment he opened his hand the coins were gone. Gone with a flash of flesh. The barefoot boys were running as fast as their starved, sore-speckled legs could carry them.

IN THE BUSHMAN'S ARMS the men culled their memories, to reassure themselves that time did move. They recalled the year that the mysterious curse had struck at calving time.

"It almost ruined me," said Ten-cow Miller, and Shannon smiled.

There had been so few calves. Many were born dead. The strong ones had hobbled their first steps and then died. The men wondered why they refused to drink and starved themselves to death. Only the weak had survived.

"It was like a disease," said ten-cow Miller. "A plague or something."

"Whichever way, it was a curse," said Price.

"It's the cedar," said old Rooster Gorman. "They don't leave any. They've cut it all out and took the life out of the ground. It'll never be no good no more. Not where they've been through. Up the back of my place you can watch the hillsides just wash away."

All heads shook.

"That was when it used to rain," Gorman continued, still shaking his head. "Last week two of my pigs died. Two in one week! The heat dried their tongues out and they swelled up till they choked."

194

Danny Doyle turned his face toward each voice in turn as they spoke of the extraordinary storms that had struck when it used to rain, with beautiful sheets of lightning falling across the wide black sky. The lightning would explode on the hillsides and send up sheets of flame in return. Then the rains would put out the fires.

Sweat rained down their burning faces as they spoke.

"No," Price said. "You've got no worries with the land. You look after her and she'll look after you. It's the same the world over. You don't abuse what you use. Shannon wouldn't know about that but it's true."

Shannon snickered as faces turned his way. Doyle turned toward the snicker.

"From what I hear, Price, you was abusing all and sundry last week," Shannon said.

Price scowled and looked down at the floor where he had emptied his stomach. Murphy sat, arms folded, eyes open, without moving, ignored and forgotten by all by the open door. Airborne dust barely moved in the shaft of sun-lit haze.

"Last week is gone," said Gorman.

"I can live with what I did last week or any other week," said Price, looking up.

There was brooding silence. Footsteps moved about them behind the bar but they were so quiet the men only felt the vibration in the floorboards. Doyle shifted uneasily and reached for his pipe.

"Don't it sound peculiar without that screaming mill howling in the background?" he said.

Ten-cow Miller looked amazed.

"Hey, you're right, you know," he exclaimed. "I knew there was something different."

"What's happened to that mill?" Shannon called out.

"Haven't you heard?" Price replied.

"What do you mean?" said Shannon. "I want to know why the mill has stopped. That could affect us, you know."

He glared at Price, then at Gorman and Miller. Then he turned to Mrs Donaldson, who sat on a stool behind the bar. She shrugged and began scratching at herself under the counter. Doyle slapped his hands around on the table like a man fumbling in the dark, till he touched his tin of matches. He picked it up and began to puff at his pipe, holding a lighted match to its bowl and sucking the flame out of sight, down and in, drawing the heat and smoke down deep inside himself. Mrs Donaldson looked at their faces.

"The heat burned out the bearings on the big saw," she said. "Sodge put off all the men. They all took off. Into the bush."

She wiped her chin on the back of her hand and kept talking.

"They've gone hunting for food. Some of them took their families. The others just sit at home, I think. I don't know how they are going to manage. They haven't got the price of a drink."

"Sodge is a bastard," said Doyle, with his pipe gritted between his teeth.

"They'll be better off out in the bush," said Price, fingering the carved marble Buddha charm in his trouser pocket.

Shannon laughed as Mrs Donaldson moved around behind the bar, leaning heavily on her knee with one hand and clutching at her side.

"For heaven's sake, Price," Shannon chuckled. "Sometimes they way you talk about the land and the bush, you'd think they was gods."

Price looked at him with glazed eyes.

"You can't deny it," he said. "When you've got that title in your hand, no man can touch you. No man can tell you what to. do. There's always a crop of apples or potatoes you can sell to get spending cash, and the land gives you everything you need if you let it."

Shannon scoffed and Miller joined him, both snickering at Price, who grinned in reply.

"I don't know how you survive, Price, I honestly don't," said Miller. "And maybe it's none of my business. But I reckon you make more out of harvesting teeth than anything off your land."

"You take a bit of work here, a bit there..." Price started to explain.

"Go hungry here, go hungry there..." echoed Doyle.

"Sure," Price cut the blind man short. "And be a bloody free man while you're about it. No-one can touch you on your own land."

"You won't buy many horses with a cartload of apples and spuds," scoffed Miller. "Eh, Rooster, how many horses do you reckon Price can get for a cartload of spuds?"

"Or apples?" laughed Shannon.

Gorman didn't answer. "Remember that time there was a flood of butterflies?" he asked.

"They came in oceans," nodded Miller. "And the birds ate the lot of them."

It had been a good year, they said, as Mrs Donaldson sat with her mouth opened toward the ceiling, gasping with relief that the pain had stopped. Bent, old, muscly Rooster Gorman got up and walked stiffly to the front door. The year of the butterflies was so recent, that good year, but it seemed so long ago. Gorman leaned in the doorway, feeling the open heat drying his face as he stared into it, watching the large devil-winds whirl by in Main Street like a wave of immigrants moving into town and taking it over. Dust flew high into the air and fell down in a slow-moving haze.

"That was a good summer. Lots of butterflies that year," said Gorman, turning his back to the heat coming through the door and rejoining the table. "Hardly seen a butterfly this year at all."

"Mr Gorman," groaned Mrs Donaldson from the bar. "Can you do us a favour? Close the doors."

THE DAY'S HEAT rose off the ground in a haze as the sun blazed down, trapping life. Huley Colquoon leaned in the shade of the camphor laurel tree, picking filth from under his toenails and sniffing it. The shade lay around him like a blanket.

Murphy got up and left the Bushman's Arms. He stood awhile, out of view from the open back door, by the wash-table, staring out into a field of long-dead grass. He heard the tavern door close behind him, and he began to walk.

He grinned as he saw Huley in the shade of the camphor laurel. Huley had his eyes closed behind his dangling fringe of hair. He did not look up. He picked more filth from under his long toenails and sniffed it.

"Does that smell good?" Murphy asked.

Huley looked up and grinned.

"I wasn't eating it," he said. "Anyway, what's your name?"

"Murphy."

Huley held out his hand timidly. Murphy looked at it. It looked as if it had never been dipped in water in its life. Murphy stretched his own hand toward Huley's. As their fingertips touched, Huley pulled his hand away.

"You thought you had me then, didn't you?" Huley said, with a friendly smile.

THE DIN OF male voices continued to rise and fall in the Bushman's Arms. The chink and clunk of bottles continued to break the tedious monotony of mumbles. The heat continued to draw ancient smells of stale alcohol and sweat from the woodwork.

Price looked round at the faces of his companions.

"Where the hell has Murphy sneaked off to?" he shouted above the rumble of conversation.

Before any reply could be made Mrs Donaldson shouted from the bar.

"What about a few sandwiches?"

The men looked at her in surprise. She saw their faces ageing before her, hungry and haggard, like old weeds withering in the darkness of a cave.

"Too hot to eat," said Shannon.

"Do you want a man to burst his insides?" Miller asked.

"What about the rest of you?"

Nobody wanted anything to eat.

Mrs Donaldson shrugged. Shannon picked up the thread of the conversation.

"My old man was there. We had the skulls on the mantelpiece and all," he said. "They slaughtered the lot of them. Down at the bend near my place. Good job too. We don't have none of the trouble like they had at Chinaman Flat that time."

"You can still taste the blood in the water if you've got imagination," said Price.

"You cannot!" Shannon scoffed.

"You've got no imagination, Shannon. How would you know?"

"Me either," said Miller. "Only bloody women and policemen have got imaginations. And that's where all the trouble starts. What about you, Doyle? I suppose you're going to tell us you've got imagination next."

Miller and Shannon roared laughing. Gorman sniggered.

"I've got no imagination any more than I've got eyes," Doyle said as his face turned to Miller. Miller stopped laughing as soon as he heard the blind man's voice and saw the slits of white between the quivering eyelids.

"But I know what Price means," said Doyle. "Only I don't call it imagination. I call it something else."

Miller and Shannon both looked at Rooster Gorman. They had nearly forty head of cattle between them — not to mention pigs and sheep and horses — but Gorman had more than Miller and Shannon put together. But then Gorman had more mouths to feed than the other two combined. Mrs Gorman could not feed them out of thin air, Shannon told his own missus. Even if Mrs Gorman was brave and deserved a medal.

Shannon had noticed the Gormans were eating their sheep faster than the flock could breed. Next they would be starting on the cattle, and then they would be finished. Even though his wife didn't think it was funny, Shannon did.

As he sat in the Bushman's Arms, Shannon was imagining the Gormans eating themselves out of house and home. It made him laugh as Gorman spoke to Doyle.

"What do you call it if it's not imagination?"

"What I call it is intelligence," said Doyle. "Simple, commonsense intelligence with a touch of human decency."

Gorman rolled his eyes and grinned. Miller guffawed and shook his head. Shannon spluttered.

"Of course it is," growled Price.

Price's raised voice drowned Shannon's laughter and overpowered Miller's guffaws.

"Sometimes a blind man can see clearer. You just don't want to admit it. You two are what's wrong with this country and every other country that ever existed. You think nothing happens outside the fences of your own property."

"You talk such a load of shit sometimes, Price..." chuckled Shannon. "You should write it all out one time and send it off to one of those places where they make newspapers. They print all that sort of rubbish. They'd probably pay you for making a fool of yourself."

Price shook his head as Shannon continued.

"Heh-heh, don't insult me, Price, you're too funny for that. You don't bother me in the slightest."

"Well I *should* bother you," Price replied. "You're bothered by the wrong things. You ought to broaden your mind. You should be like Danny. He's been in the city. He's been surrounded by news and knowledge from all corners of the country...and the world. He'd still be there — except he went blind over a block of stone."

"It's true!" exclaimed Doyle. "And when you're no good to them they just throw you away. You're nothing. You're just rubbish, that's all. I'd be in the gutter now if it wasn't for Price."

"That stoneworking is no Sunday picnic," said Gorman. "I started off in it, but I threw it in. They wouldn't catch me again. Breathing those grits tears your guts apart, it does. Your hands end up feeling like they're part of the hammer and chisel."

Shannon raised his eyes to the ceiling.

"Until they end up feeling like they're part of the stone," said Doyle.

"It's a sin," said Price. "The land isn't that cruel, only man is that cruel."

"Here he goes again," Shannon laughed. "I could listen to you all day, Price. You go for the bait every time."

Mrs Donaldson watched them sitting there, getting slowly drunker and more short-tempered, like six hairy old spiders... Then she rose and turned and went out the back door.

HOOFBEATS POUNDED across one slope after another as Mrs Holman's horse galloped, foaming at the mouth, with suds of sweat all over its body. The woman's mouth was dry, her lips colourless and split with dryness. With every pounding hoofbeat, the woman grew stronger as the breeze of galloping speed tugged at her hair.

The beast grew nastier. The Inspector's wife broke it into a canter and took it through the scrub. Twice it tried to scrape her off its back on the sides of leaning trees. The second time it tried, the Inspector's wife dragged on the reins suddenly and veered it into the open fields where, with one fierce stroke of the whip, she sent it charging up the slope.

Murphy walked to the edge of the town and up a rise. He sat out of the sun there, sweating, and he watched the rider galloping closer as he sat in the shade-dappled, dead grass. He licked his parched lips and drew the pair of sweat-saturated cloth socks from his feet. His feet glowed pink and soft. They were embossed with the texture of the cloth.

He strained his eyes and held a hand across his brow like a shelf for shade. He crouched in bare feet, alongside his sticky socks and boots, and he squinted. He swallowed and licked his lips like a lizard. Suddenly the veins in his neck and temples stood out.

The rider was a woman. No! It couldn't be. But yes, it

was. She galloped across the dangerous ground as if charging headlong to a death she had been cheated of. . . .

It had to be her. And she had to be trying to kill herself. He could see her now, riding like a man, or a bush woman, with legs either side of the saddle, moving along the fenceline, with a spume of dust trailing. The dust clouds glowed pink and orange with sun-fired edges. Suddenly the horse swerved and propped. The rider slewed in the saddle and seemed to fall, slowly, hanging onto the reins and the horse's neck. She remained suspended above the ground for a moment, and then horse and all went crashing down.

Murphy sprang to his bare feet and ran down the slope. The sharp grass and stones stung his softened white soles.

The horse shambled to its feet and shook itself all over before it skipped, limping away. Murphy's legs flew over the final rise out of the gully, to reach Mrs Holman standing up and brushing herself down near the fence. Her face was turned away as she refastened her skirt.

"Are you alright?" Murphy yelled.

The young woman swivelled from the waist and turned to him with a frown. For the first time he saw that death had not entirely left her. She had a prison pallor and lips that were as grey as the whites of her eyes.

"I hope you're alright," he said, gasping for air.

"Why should you?" Mrs Holman asked aggressively, grimacing as she pressed on her hip and arched her aching body.

Murphy was taken aback.

"I find you interesting," was all he could say.

"Interesting? Why should you find me interesting? You've never met me before."

"Yes I have," Murphy replied, moving close to the fence where she stood on the other side. "I rode with you in the coach from Chinaman Flat. You didn't say much."

One side of her mouth began to smile.

"Oh," was all she said. And she started to walk away from him, along the fence-line.

"I want to see you sometime," he said urgently. "I have something important to tell you."

Mrs Holman turned her sharp little face over her thin shoulder and screwed her dark, sparkling grey eyes at him. She looked at his red face and his mouth open like a fish's, still panting for air, and she scowled.

"What sort of important thing?"

"Here, tomorrow?" Murphy answered, rubbing his dusty mouth. His hand came away to reveal a smile.

The woman looked away from him. She wiped her face on the sleeve of her blue riding jacket and unbuttoned the front of it, making a lacy show of her bosom. Then she stopped walking and turned to face him.

"My husband is the Inspector of Police, you realise?"

"I know. That's one thing I want to speak to you about."

A curtain seemed to fall in front of her face. She looked through it as if she could not see him. Her eyes became too dark even to show the grey that had been there before, her cheeks became sunken with illness, her face pallid.

"You are an admirable woman," he said.

"My husband doesn't think so."

She began to walk again along the fence-line. He followed her, staring sideways at the wrinkle at the corner of her eye. She seemed so close to him, yet the fence held them apart. But not only the fence. He felt doomed to never even touch her lips or ear with his fingers...and yet, he felt as if he knew her, as if he had even held her before. There was something about her mouth that he knew. He felt safe with her. As if he could feel the smile on her lips that did not show, and the kiss that lay so close behind it.

The horse trotted playfully along behind them, pretending in turn to run off and then to charge them.

"Tomorrow?" asked Murphy again, stopping as the track beside the fence veered away.

Mrs Holman giggled and then raised her head to the sky. She walked like a drunk, her body shaking with laughter.

"Tomorrow?" Murphy pleaded as she drew away.

She kept walking.

A confused grin faded from Murphy's mouth as he

watched her slowly disappearing over the crest of curved ground. At the top she turned and threw her head back in laughter. Her horse strolled along the fence and passed him by, flicking its long tail in front of his face as it swished away the nagging flies.

Murphy felt cheated. He felt confused as he stumbled down into the gully and up the other side of the hill. His cut feet burned as he pulled on his cool socks and damp boots. What did her laughter mean? Would he ever find out? And tomorrow, would she come? Or would she be elsewhere, still laughing at him? He didn't care if she hated him. He kicked up dust as he walked along back into town. He didn't care if she hated him, as long as he spoke to her, so long as he could test his own instincts and share with her...if only for a moment...somehow, some time, somewhere...

XXIII

HIDDEN IN THE hills, the black man shone in the shady after-noon light. Blue light flashed along the edges of his body, woven into the fine hairs that gave him a golden aura.

His voice subsided into a murmured groan. All things were true. His hands wove a greeting in the still air, inviting the wind from the north to blow.

Far above flew the last eagle, swooping and soaring in grand heavenly arcs, circling, circling, higher and higher, toward the sun, looking down upon the wrinkled landscape and the town that was like a scab in the centre of a spreading, festering wound.

MAJOR STUMIC smiled at the small gathering in the Havelock Hotel parlour. He raised a midday gin in salute.

"Mr Stewart won't be long now," he said.

The men were waiting for Stewart to bring all the details. They planned to set up a town council, and needed authoritative advice.

"We've established ourselves by now, surely. All we have to do is make it official," said Jansen, looking at his watch.

All agreed.

Inspector Holman sat in a chair that dominated the room. As Sam Sodge entered the parlour from the balcony, Holman rose and stood aside.

"Why do you call the hotel the Havelock?" Young Mr Callow said to the major. "If you don't mind my asking."

Stumic spread his thick lips into a smile. He did not mind being asked. He said so. He told the young man how he had run away from his birth-country and become a soldier of fortune. Young Mr Callow bowed his ear toward the major, listening carefully as the noisy bodies sent waves of heat through the room.

"You were a mercenary?" he asked.

"Precisely," said Stumic, tapping Young Mr Callow's arm.

Stumic's greatest honour had been to serve in the British imperial army. Especially in India. It was the invincible army of a great empire, the most feared army in history.

"It was Sam's idea, to tell you the truth," Major Stumic finally explained. "We are both great admirers of Major General Sir Henry Havelock. General Havelock led the troops to crush the Indian soldiers who mutinied at Cawnpore and Lucknow. Traitors! We taught them. Strong leadership — that's the secret of a stable society."

Stumic smiled in Sodge's direction as Young Mr Callow nodded and sipped his wine. He could almost smell the blood as he spoke...the heated roar and sweat of battle, the smash of bone and slashing of flesh. He smiled and sweat poured from him as if he were there again, young and slim, hard-bellied, wild and vicious.

"I was there," he said. "In both charges. In the first wave. But I never talk about it. We were always there... we mercenaries."

Stumic shrugged with his final word and stared into the mid-distance at some point close to the floor, among the shined footwear.

"Gentlemen!" Sodge called out. "Mr Stewart!"

Stewart stood in the double doorway. He had a fistful of documents. He raised the papers and a muffled cheer went up. Sodge pushed his way toward Stewart. The two men shook hands vigorously while the gathering clapped.

AS THE CONVERSATION continued in the darkness of the Bushman's Arms Rooster Gorman pounded the palm of one hand with a finger of his other hand. He missed his hand once, and prodded twice as hard next time. Like all

those listening, he sweated profusely, the stain darkening
his shirt. His eyelids were sagging, and his eyes were laced
with threads of blood.

"It doesn't matter how you look at it," he said. "I'm
not saying you're wrong. It's an irony, that's all."

"An iron-y! What's that?" Shannon sneered. "Fancy
city talk for a blacksmith or something?"

Gorman sat back, ignoring Shannon's remark.

"Anyway, I reckon it's an irony," he continued.
"Everyone's been fighting for the eight-hour day, and what
good has it done them in the long run? They just end up
working harder and harder for a little less time..."

Everyone stared at Gorman's finger, poised in the air,
ready to pound again into his hand to make a point.

"Rubbish," said Doyle. "How can they make you
work harder than flat out?"

No-one answered, so Doyle answered himself.

"I'll tell you how. By working you into the grave,
that's how."

"Like convicts, eh?" smiled Shannon.

"The working man is only one cut above a convict,"
snarled Doyle.

"That'll change," said Price. "That'll change."

"Oh yeah," Shannon said. "And who's going to
change it? Get them to change the weather while they're at
it."

Doyle's head clunked back against the wall.

"A man might just as well be in chains as blind," he
said. "That's what they done to me."

"Hurrah!" came the muffled shout from the Havelock.

"What on earth is that?" asked Miller.

"It's those bastards over the road," said Shannon.
"They're having a meeting. They invited bloody Dransfield
the squatter, but they never invited me."

"Just go anyway, if you want to go. Stumic won't
throw you out if you're buying drinks," Price said.

"Nah," said Shannon. "It'd be nearly over by now."

"You wouldn't have liked it anyway," said Price.
"They'd have looked at you as if you were dog-shit if you

207

opened your mouth. At least here we let you get a word in edgeways."

Shannon smiled at Price as if he was going to be sick.

"You're right, you know. They couldn't have stopped me from going in."

"Sure," grinned Price. "It's just like in America. Equal opportunity..."

"That's right," said Doyle. "And let the Devil take the hindmost."

"Well, at least this heat doesn't play favourites, even if God and the Devil do," chuckled Gorman.

IN THE HAVELOCK PARLOUR, standing beside the elephant-legged teak table, Major Stumic declared that he was most honoured to be recognised as a leading citizen...yes, he was unashamed to repeat it. Indeed he had already done so a number of times, and on each occasion he had proposed a toast — to the prosperity of Blood Gully.

When Inspector Holman proposed a toast to Queen Victoria, Major Stumic swelled up to his full height and thrust his chest forward nearly as far as his belly. It was a proud moment. The Queen's name filled the room with magic. Stumic shuffled his feet and swayed with the poignancy of the moment. The Queen's name rolled from the men's tongues.

"We are not just talking about incorporation, gentlemen," said Sodge, one foot on the leather of a chair and a drink in his hand. "We are talking about the future. Not just of ourselves, but of all those whom we represent. We are talking about prosperity, civilisation and wealth."

There was a murmur of approval.

"We need men of vision. Men who can see the future. Men who can turn wilderness into prosperity. And there is only one way that can be done — and that is the way it will be done, I assure you," continued Sodge. "The way of the future, gentlemen, and the way we must go, is the railway."

"Hurrah!" everybody cried.

"Friends, are you with me?" Sodge cried.

"Yes!" the crowd answered, with a single, booming voice.

Inspector Holman led the applause. Stewart stood proudly, with one hand on Sodge's shoulder, and swung his sheaf of papers in the air. He smiled round the assembled faces.

"Sam Sodge for Mayor," shouted Stumic, amid the clamour.

Young Mr Callow looked sideways at Stumic, who was grinning like a snake, his eyes blinking. Soon the circle of faces became breathless and quiet, blazing with the warmth of ambition. Stumic seized Callow by the shoulder and blurted out into the young government man's ear:

"Do you think the railway will really come?"

"I know less about the railway than I do about cedar," said Young Mr Callow.

"I hope you don't think I was presumptuous," said Major Stumic, rising from the chair and swaying. "But I felt it beholding upon me to offer myself, as a man of rank...indeed...a man of rank, as you may be sure the Inspector would appreciate, well commoded as he is, to the exercise of authority, that I, as a man of commissioned rank, not as a hotelier, not as a publican...no, not as a man of alien origins and a mere mercenary..."

Stumic had turned away from Callow as he spoke and had raised his voice. Now he addressed the room's occupants at large. Callow still sat behind the Major, listening and watching the smiles fading slowly from the faces of those who were witnessing Stumic's soliloquy.

"Yes, my friends...my friends and...I have, and shall...to...not as a...as a...but...as a soldier and a gentleman...as a commissioned officer in her majesty's forces, do swear to do my duty."

With his last word, and with his arms outstretched, Stumic collapsed backward on top of Callow.

"It's the heat!" shouted Stewart. "Open the window."

"Get him out on the balcony."

"Into the fresh air."

Young Mr Callow bundled Stumic out of the parlour and into a cane chair on the balcony. As Stewart joined him the young man asked, "Why on earth did they call it Blood Gully anyway?"

Stewart stopped in his tracks and swallowed. He looked deep into Callow's eyes.

"Come over here," he said, leading Young Mr Callow to the railing. "Look over there."

Stewart pointed far out across the hills.

"Out there is the creek where they had the final battle with the natives. The men had tried to run them off before, poisoning a few, flogging a few, shooting a few...just to teach them a lesson. You know, just as a warning. But nothing worked."

Stewart shook his head sadly.

"It was a terrible battle. I heard it from the last police inspector down at Chinaman Flat. Terrible. Fourteen men against a hundred savages. Six men lost their lives, I was told — only farm hands, fortunately — but the savages were slaughtered to a man."

Stewart slapped his hand on the railing and held his palm out to catch the rays of the sun.

"They called the battle ground Blood Creek. And that is how the town was named."

Behind him Major Stumic burped.

"I foresee the day when the Union Jack will fly over every nation on earth," said Stumic, opening his eyes.

"Even over your own homeland, Major?" asked Stewart.

"Even over Austria," replied Stumic. "Even over the United States of America once again."

Then he closed his eyes, burped again and grinned like an orchestra-lover at a big concert.

MURPHY walked back through the streets, still seeing the sick woman's bloodless face. As he came toward the Bushman's Arms, he could hear Price's voice. He walked out of the sunlight, through the gloom, toward the voice. The soles of his feet felt on fire in his stiffened, dried-out boots.

"And I found skulls and bones over there too," Price was saying.

"Where is this?" Murphy asked, his eyes adjusting to the dark.

"You know where. I told you," Price said.

"Where have you been, anyway, Murphy?" screeched Doyle, as Murphy nodded to Mrs Donaldson's raised eyebrows.

She began to draw him a frothy beer.

"There's skulls everywhere around there," said Gorman. "Everywhere! The place is cursed, just like One-eye's woman says."

Gorman waved his arm, slashing through the tobacco smoke hanging in a thick cloud.

"Are you buggers still carrying on about that massacre?" grunted Murphy. "Anyone would think nothing else ever happened around here."

"It wasn't a massacre," said Shannon. "It was a battle."

"A battle?" laughed Price. "They slaughtered them all. It was like a kangaroo hunt."

"That's true," nodded Gorman. "I've seen the little skulls."

"Anyway," said Miller, dribbling from the corner of his mouth, "you can't undo the past and you can't bring back the dead. So no sense having regrets."

Murphy sat down in a trance, an almost tranquil look on his face. Shannon stared at Doyle as if the broken-down stonemason's blindness was a personal affront. And the boring heat bore down on them all. Miller poured sweat like a corned roll in a boiler.

Mrs Donaldson stood there, with Murphy's money in her hand, wiping her wet hands on a towel.

"And who is this MacGuire you were raving about last week?" she asked Price. "What has he done to get you so stirred up?"

Price burst into a convulsion of coughing.

Shannon stared snakily. Doyle turned his ear to the room, his face serious, suddenly looking coolly sober.

A smile froze on Murphy's sweaty face; instinctively, his eyes darted to each door, as Price recovered from his coughing.

"Mrs Donaldson wants to know about this MacGuire fellow you were telling her about," he said. "We're all ears."

Price half-turned toward Murphy, but did not meet his eyes.

Murphy searched Mrs Donaldson's face, as she searched Price's, and Doyle searched the silent darkness for signals he could comprehend.

Price stood up. "I don't know nothing about no MacGuire...", he muttered, slipping his tobacco pouch and matches in his pocket. "It's no good asking me what I was talking about a week ago. I probably didn't know at the time."

"That wouldn't be unusual. That wouldn't be unusual at all," chuckled Shannon.

"You two coming?" Price said as he turned, looking only at the blind man.

Doyle slid out from behind the table and slid his feet warily along the uneven, board floor. Murphy smiled to Mrs Donaldson with a shrug, and followed Doyle.

Shannon watched the three cousins going, then he looked at Mrs Donaldson as she stared, not at him and not at them, but thinking. Then Shannon's eyes turned to the empty door and the hot, empty dirt outside.

XXIV

PRICE'S CART CREAKED and shook from side to side. Murphy was leaning over Price's shoulder, staring him in the side of the face and shouting in his ear as if he was going to kill him.

"You bastard, Price! Thanks for letting me know!" Murphy bellowed. "I could be tied over the back of a horse by now, and I wouldn't have known what hit me."

Doyle sat stonily, still and silent. Murphy sat back down in the back, slumping with disgust.

"Nothing happened, anyway, that's the main thing," Doyle said.

"You'll have to get me a horse tonight," Murphy said. "A good one, too. One that will carry a good load all day and all night."

"You don't have to worry about Mrs Donaldson," said Doyle. "She's alright."

"So is Price," said Murphy. "Just get that horse. I don't care if it costs twenty pound. I'll give you the money when we get back."

"No need to be like that," mumbled Price.

"Where will you go?" asked Doyle, over his shoulder.

Murphy sat thinking awhile, as the cart trundled down a slope with the horse's clip-clop always ahead. He rested back, his arm along the side, stretching his neck in the breeze as the cart built up speed. The dark bush on either side of the track hung heavy, still and hot.

Murphy thought of tomorrow, supposing that he would see it, but wondering, would he see her?

"I'm sorry, I really mean it," said Price. "I don't know what came over me..."

"The story is," said Murphy, ignoring him, "Cousin Murphy could not stand the heat. So he has temporarily departed for the south. He will write when he gets there."

"Where will you go?" Doyle asked again.

Murphy just laughed. He let his head go back and he laughed.

The hot sky fell dark fast. Murphy heard his own laughter, and it made him think about the police inspector's wife, and her laughter.

"A man must be a bloody fool," was all he muttered.

AS THE SKY GREW DARK, the black man raised his hands to the star-like eyes of ancestors peering down. Now he would dance for them, and their sorrows would bathe in burning vengeance.

Dead flowers of cedar rotting upon the dirt turned to dust under the pale soles of the black man's bare feet. The deep brown worlds of his eyes turned slowly in all directions, listening to the voices of the leaves whispering warnings of the coming wind. He spoke to the stars by name and they answered, their silent whispers tingling in his skin.

In his veins flowed the ancient river of blood. Nearby lay a large military dagger, with the hilt-end of the wooden handle stained black with human blood. A white man's weapon, the blood that of white men.

MRS GORMAN'S FACE was a swirl of healed agony. The ridges and ripples of scar tissue had set like smooth, soft leather. The colour of the shiny, poreless skin was grey. Bone-white specks and threads of skin stretched between one part and another. The lid of one eye drooped open like a torn pocket, and the eye wept an eternal tear. Her nose was a spur of cartilage with a tent of skin drawn across it. Her hair was drawn back tight in a plait, wound up into a bun at the back of her head. Not a hair was out of place.

Mrs Gorman's lashless eyes blinked. Only one closed. She straightened her springy body. Her breasts showed hard through the thin cloth wrapped about her. The long, loose sleeves revealed scars which ran from her hands up her arms. As she looked at the back of her husband's head her hairless eyebrows frowned.

Old Rooster Gorman, back from the Bushman's Arms, sat at the head of the table as the evening plunged into darkness outside. His brood of eight stared adoringly at him. Mrs Gorman sat down next to him at the table and looked at him. He smiled at her and then turned to Anna, the little girl who looked so like her mother had once.

Mrs Gorman watched her husband. He was drunk, but still respectable. He had swooped on his dumplings and mashed potatoes, leaning forward over his plate with the hunger of a toiler, though he had hardly moved a muscle all day. The constant sweat of the heatwave dripped from his nose onto his food.

Mrs Gorman watched the drips fall. The yellow light made her face look like carved and decorated gold.

"Feels good eating dumplings," Gorman slurred drunkenly. He chewed his food with relish, beaming smiles at his children. As he continued speaking he cast a conspiratorial glance toward his wife.

"It makes me feel that tonight I'm going to have a beautiful dream."

One of the toddlers squirmed with delight.

"So," said Gorman. "Don't any of you kids worry if you hear me laughing and carrying on in my sleep — I'll just be having fun in my dream."

Gorman looked at his wife, who stared back blankly, her eyes sunken in the sea of scars.

"You watch me now," he continued, turning back to the children. "Learn to sop up your gravy like this and don't let any go to waste."

Gorman wiped a chunk of torn bread expertly through the thick, hot sauce.

IN THE MIDST of the roaring silence the black shape crouched in the darkness. The man's arms moved, drawing in an invisible net, drawing it deftly from the sea of darkness as he fished for the wind to come.

JUDITH sneaked away from her chores to meet Rebecca in the corner of the garden; and together they watched all the brilliant red, orange, crimson and scarlet spreading like a huge fire across the sky. The two girls sweated in the fierce heat radiating from the baked earth. Rebecca's golden-brown hair fell like a cascade round her shoulders as she turned her head to admire the whole horizon. The glow flashed upon the surfaces of her face, as though her cheeks had ignited.

As the darkness rapidly closed around them, Rebecca showed Judith where she had burned her arm on the stove when Inspector Holman had walked into the kitchen suddenly and frightened her. In the dying glow of the sunset, the blisters seemed to seethe with pain. Judith kissed the arm above the wound with religious devotion.

Rebecca told Judith how, when the priest had called on Mrs Holman for the third time, the resurrected woman had refused to speak. And then when the priest had left, Mrs Holman and the Inspector had had a terrible row.

"What did she say?" gasped Judith.

"She told him that he had let her whole life go to waste," said Rebecca. "And that he never shed a tear of regret about it."

"Phew! She said that?"

"Yes."

"And then what?"

"Well, I missed some."

Rebecca stared regally into the blackness.

"I was listening through the door and I couldn't hear well. But he told her that there was nothing to regret. Then Mrs Holman got mad and told him that she had her whole life with him to regret. And she said she wasn't going to waste her new life dancing to his tune."

"What else did you hear?"

"No more. He just told her she had lost her senses. He said she lost them in the coffin. And she said she had found her senses, that she found them in the coffin."

"What?" Judith screwed up her nose and the rest of her face.

"She said she found her senses in the coffin. She said that was the first time she had ever got out of his control."

"And then what?"

"Nothing," said Rebecca, her face fading into the darkness. "I thought I heard him coming, and I ran."

Judith walked alone toward the big Gill house and went to her verandah bunk.

"Rebecca says Mrs Holman goes riding every day," she said as the candle flame died between her licked fingers.

"Thank heavens today is over," sighed Kathleen, lying on the bunk opposite. "Will this heat never end? I feel as if I'm living in an oven."

"Did you hear me?"

"Yes, I heard you."

"Well?"

"Well, what?"

"Don't you think it's scary?"

"No."

"You must not have a soul, Kathleen! How would you like to be buried alive?"

"As long as it's in the shade," moaned Kathleen.

"You're dull.'

"Good."

"What are you going to dream about?"

"I'm going to dream of you losing your voice and my hands getting chopped off so I don't have to do any work. Things like that," said Kathleen as she lay in the dark, pulling her nightgown back and forth over her head like a sail-fan.

"You're not nice."

"Well, who could be as nice as Rebecca?"

"Are you jealous?" Judith asked as she peered playfully toward the dark form under the flapping nightdress.

"Jealous of Rebecca? Don't be such a fool. I pity her," sneered Kathleen. "When I think of what she has to go through with that mongrel Inspector over there, it makes me sick. I'm not jealous of her. I'd love to take her away."

"If Mrs Gill dies," said Judith, "we might be able to stay here in this house, and Rebecca could be our maid."

Kathleen said nothing. She just lay there in the dark, fanning herself with her nightgown. She heard Judith chattering, and then all was quiet and still. The only movement came from her own breathing and the deep, sleeping sighs of Judith in the other bunk...and then the mournful wail of a dog in the town below.

AND AS THE TOWN SLEPT the dark, owl-like eyes vigilantly scanned the darkness and the hand-like black feet felt their way stealthily over the bush floor and gathered the kindling that lay there. The night kissed the ears of the lone gatherer with the sounds of the living bush.

The man built pyres of twigs, bark and leaves at the bases of the trees, all the while singing under his hot breath an urgent song. He sang it in time to the beat of his blood, which ran in time to the clear water running over the stones in the creek, which ran in time to the twinkling of the stars. The dry kindling rustled as he built up the piles around the tree trunks on the gully leading to Gorman's farm.

JUDITH sat bolt upright in her bunk in the dark, stiff with fear. She was still half-dreaming. She felt cold sweat all over her. And it had all been only a dream. She could still almost see the faces staring down at her, but it was only a dream. She could feel the start of day approaching. It was not too early to get up.

She stood outside the house, looking down to the garden and up to the sky from where the new day's heat would pour down. The dull light of false dawn stretched over the trees, and the shadows that filled the world thinned out as they stretched.

The rising sun began to show with a flaming spear into the sky. Judith could hear a bullock team moaning up a hill somewhere, getting in hours of work before the tortures of daylight. She could hear the loaded jinker graunching in the distance.

THE DAY'S EARLY HEAT rose and fell like waves beating upon a coastline. Price had not yet returned with a horse. Murphy's blanket roll was stowed in the shade against the wall. He had to move it out of the sun for the second time.

"I'll miss you, Danny," he told Doyle. "But when the time comes to go, you can't stay."

"Something like that," said Doyle. "But I'll miss the excitement you've caused around here. Price needs a bit of a stir-up, he gets himself a bit stuck to the bottom of the saucepan sometimes."

Murphy laughed, wondering if he would have a chance to see again the face that haunted him. Would she even go to meet him? He could knock at her door and ask to see her. And if the Inspector heard about it too late, there would be no-one to suffer any consequences.

"How's that sky look?" Doyle asked.

"Nothing," said Murphy dispiritedly. "Not a cloud in sight. It's going to be a hot day's ride."

Would that cunning old bastard Price finally turn him in now that he had a fistful of his money and no prospects of getting much more? Murphy walked several paces and picked up the pistol and checked it quickly. Having satisfied himself that he could not be taken alive, he strolled into the sun again and looked down the empty road.

He watched Doyle's face. The blind man looked nervous.

"Any smoke?" Doyle asked.

Murphy reached into his pocket and handed his makings across.

"No," said Doyle, shoving it away. "In the sky. No smoke in the sky?"

"No. Not that I can see." Murphy looked all the way around. "Why? Should there be?"

Doyle shook his head, twiddling his thumbs nervily, with his hands crossed on his plump belly.

"I shouldn't have stayed."

"Well, it wasn't my choice," said Murphy. "*I* trust Price, but *MacGuire* can't afford to — he's already let him down once. And to keep Price on his toes, MacGuire needed a hostage. You can understand that."

"You know," said Doyle. "Sometimes I get to feel it isn't natural to be a white man in this country. It's not right for a man to always be stretching for something out of his reach, praying for rain, waiting for the water to go down, or for a funeral or a hanging to liven things up. It's not natural here. This place isn't used to it. I sometimes feel this heat has been sent to burn us out like a fever killing off a disease."

Murphy squinted at Doyle. The blind man's face was blubbery and his voice tremored. He looked ready to cry.

"At least in the city you know what's going to happen next. At least *something* happens."

"Are you alright, Danny?" said Murphy, stepping toward him.

" 'Course I'm alright," Doyle said weakly. "I just wish Price would get here in a hurry with that cart, that's all. Just in case something happens."

"Like what?"

Murphy's voice snapped like a gunshot. His eyes levelled suspiciously at the blind man.

"Oh, say a bit of a fire, or something. It happens," said Doyle. "You know, I wouldn't like my chances running through the bush with no eyes to guide me."

Doyle laughed as he spoke. It was cold self-mockery.

"Probably wouldn't notice the smoke till the flames were licking my backside."

"Don't get carried away," said Murphy. "The sky is as clear as a bell."

"That's good. But I don't like the feel in the air. There's something different about it. It's not normal. You know how it is with Price when he's going to explode — even though he doesn't say anything, and there's no warning? You can just feel it."

"Jesus Christ, are you trying to put the wind up me or something?" Murphy said, then spat into the dirt and looked down the empty road. "You've done a bloody good job."

"Just keep your eye on that sky," said the blind man, turning his head about to sniff the still air.

IN BLOOD GULLY the full heat of day had not yet risen. Women wiped their faces on their aprons. Men hitched their trousers tighter. Children vomited up milk and eggs before the food reached their stomachs. Babies moved their mouths, sucking for air and crying silently, their voices too weak to leave their dried throats. Sheep lay down to breathe easier and died. Pigs tore their backs to bloody shreds scratching mad itches on fences, and then they lay in the steaming prison slime of their pens, driven mad by vermin bites.

XXV

THE STONES IN *the open sunlight cracked on the glazed earth where they lay shining. The cloudless air sizzled. Trees bent double with fatigue. Shadows were slashed by sunlight as it reflected off the rock.*

The black man sat hidden on a shaded overhanging outcrop above a gully, so inaccessible that felled trees could not be retrieved. Below, wallaby and kangaroo lay as always, on a small crumb-speck of their former terrain. They too panted with exhaustion before the sun was high.

The black man sang and beckoned to the north, and as if by miracle, a dry gust of gully wind answered him. The red meat of his tongue moved between his gleaming teeth as he smiled sweetly.

He rose and crept along the animal tracks. Beside a mound of long, dead grass, in a line of similar mounds, he proceeded to rub a stick between his hands so that it spun faster and faster. The stick drilled into another piece of wood, and soon the friction dust gave off a trace, and then a wisp, and then a puff of smoke. And as it did so, from the north there began to blow the suggestion of a hot, dry wind. With nimble toes, the black man pushed the fine, unravelled grass and bark fibres toward the point of the wooden drill.

Softly now he hummed, shaking his hair and beckoning to the north, drawing his hand toward his heart, again and again...

He held the tuft of smouldering grass and touched it along the mounds, and he blew gently till the flames ran like water down through the stiff, dry stalks; then, having lit these mounds, he shook the fistful of grass like a torch, spraying sparks in the breeze toward Blood Gully, as the burning mounds flared and blazed.

222

He closed his eyes as smoke drifted past his face. He danced beckoning the north toward the south, raising each knee higher in turn. Then he tossed his torch of tufted, smouldering grass toward the town...and its sparks broke and ran across the carpet of kindling.

The mounds of grass flared in a line, crackling as each dry blade and stalk burst alight. The sparks flew fast on the updraft, as bright as burning dust from the sun itself. Louder and louder the crackling fire-fuel sounded, and louder and louder the black man sang, calling out the names of the slaughtered ones.

He called out the names of his loved ones, so long remembered, and he pounded his feet in dance, harder and harder on the ground. And the birds began to leave the trees with fear and the scorching wind from the north blew a little stronger, and the mounds of grass grew smaller, burning out as their flames grew upwards and outwards.

Twigs caught fire as the black dancer pounded the ground. Crisp-dried leaves flashed alight as the flames took to the tree bark and the lower branches which swayed in the breeze and lowered their leaves as if offering themselves. Smoke swirled about the naked dancer like a force milling before battle around its leader, and the flames leapt to the height of an adult, and the man ran his fingers among them.

A bare trace of white smoke rose into the sky. The man ran his fingers through the flames and flicked them higher...He chanted to the fire and stamped his feet, then he flung his outstretched arm, one vengeful finger speared in the direction of Blood Gully.

Again and again, he jabbed his finger passionately toward the town. And as the flames leapt he began to see his long-lost memory-folk. The long-dead danced without moving their faces, they danced without moving their arms, only their feet danced...It was the dance of the trapped dead with no legends to carry them on and no babies left behind them.

The man watched them dancing in the flames. Their eyes were the brightest specks in the fire. He chanted. He shook his body all over till sweat flew from it. His breast muscles shook loosely. His chanting grew softer and the breeze blew harder, driving the roar of the open-air furnace to the treetops. It was the moment he had hungered and thirsted for. The dead leaves flew from the swaying trees, clashing their branches and foliage together in the blistering updraught.

The black man stopped dancing. He raised himself straight and cast his chin defiantly toward the white man's stronghold. He took one breath and exhaled, and he stepped forward to join his slaughtered family.

He stepped among the dead dancing in the flames. They gathered around him. They rushed toward him. He stepped into the flames, and then through them, and began to walk toward the unsuspecting town. The wind blew harder, hotter and drier behind him; and, leaning with the wind, the flames began to follow him.

BOOK III

THE BRUTAL STORM

XXVI

CONSTABLE TAYLOR LOOKED up at Dirlsky as the sergeant spoke, twiddling his moustache nervously.

"I tell you, I don't like it," said Dirlsky. "Whenever it feels like this, something happens."

He was staring across the road at Gorman and Shannon. The two farmers were standing arguing among the bush workers who lolled in groups in patches of shade, each in their own vague little territory, muttering. Some of the men sneered and spat from time to time in the direction of the police.

Taylor chuckled and whispered in Dirlsky's ear, "Why don't we just lock up a couple to give them a taste of what to expect if there's any trouble?"

Dirlsky smiled at Taylor. Then he rolled his eyes upward. Then he looked at Taylor again and shook his head.

"Point one," said Dirlsky, "we might end up needing more room in the cells than we've got. Point two, have you ever tried to arrest one of these bush-rats when they haven't been drinking, and their mates are sober? It's like grabbing a handful of ants."

Taylor looked up and down the street. Suddenly it looked crowded with men, yet he could only count nine in all. And that included Gorman and Shannon, who were both standing on one leg, kicking the dust with their other foot.

"Point three," said Dirlsky, so only Taylor could hear, as he checked up and down the street, "I just said I don't want any trouble today! It's madman weather."

"I TELL YOU Rooster," Shannon said to Gorman, giving him a poke in the ribs for good measure. "This weather is a

227

godsend. You and me, we're sitting on permanent water. We'll hold out, no matter how long."

Gorman pursed his lips and shook his head soundly.

"Don't you understand?" asked Shannon. "You'll be able to pick up land for two pound an acre, maybe less, after this. You'll get a good horse for the same. Don't you see? A few months of hard times cleans off the little suckers like a burn-off clears the rubbish out of a paddock."

"Hard times are bad at any time," said Gorman.

"No, no, no," Shannon said. "Haven't I just been telling you? They're a blessing in disguise..."

A breeze was building up in the air. It was hottish. It lifted the dust and carried it along.

"Well," said Gorman. "I still don't like to see people suffer..."

"People!" scoffed Shannon. "The weather isn't concerned about people. You look and see. People aren't concerned about each other. What matters is individuals, Rooster. Individuals and families. Can't you see that? This is progress. Look at the mill down there."

The mill sat down the road just outside town, a dark shape glowing in the shimmering heat, huge, harmless and silent.

"It's a mistake if you ask me," said Gorman.

Shannon leaned back and squashed up his chin. He looked at bent old Gorman and the dust lying dry on his sweatless face.

"Progress doesn't make mistakes," Shannon said. "You should listen to Sodge if you get a chance. The British Empire is supreme. It's taking over the world and we're part of it."

"Well, I'm not taking over the world at my age. You can."

Gorman held his hat to stop it blowing off in the breeze.

"I might just do that," smiled Shannon. "I just wish everyone would stop bitching about this heat. We've just got to make the best of it."

228

AS MURPHY WAITED for Price to return with a horse to escape on, he stood in the middle of the dusty yard watching the open gate and the empty road. A devil-wind gyrated down the pebble-strewn dip in the road and raced off into the bush, ripping leaves into the air.

The stiff hot breeze flicked at Murphy's shirt. Tear-like moisture filled his eyes as he stared down the road. The trees looked especially beautiful. They were proud and gaunt and green in their own grey way, and especially alive to him. The hot breeze tasted dry and clean as he breathed through his mouth. He thrust his hands deep into his pockets, impatient with Price for taking so long, and sad to go. He tried to stop himself suspecting that Price had betrayed him.

"Life is magic, Danny," he yelled across the yard to the blind man twiddling his thumbs. Doyle had no shirt on.

They heard a cart coming. The dull roar was a long way away, then nearer and nearer. Murphy sprinted to the open gate; Doyle came gingerly down the step. The blind man, his blazing pink torso bared and glowing in the open air, stumbled, but he did not fall. The sound of the cart sounded louder and louder, but it seemed to take forever to appear.

The cart was racing at full gallop, with another horse tied to the back of it. Price was screaming. At first they could not understand him. When they did their blood went cold.

"Look! Look! Look!" screamed Price, driving madly, pointing wildly over their heads. The terrified horse behind strained its neck back against the tether attaching its bridle to the cart.

Murphy turned. Stretched high above the tree-line, like a grey, jagged crack in the sky, but moving, an innocent-looking stream of smoke was bending vaguely toward him. The hot northerly breeze blew in his face.

"What is it?" said Doyle.

"Smoke."

"Oh no..."

Price swerved the cart into the yard. The second horse, whipping along behind, stumbled and almost fell. Price leapt from the cart like a young man.

"Let everything loo-argh-gh-gh..." he yelled in the air, screaming as he hit the ground.

He hit the dirt with his legs crossed after clipping the edge of the cart with his boot. His legs gave way under him with a clear snap. He screamed, clutching his shin. Murphy looked at the smoke again, now in several streams, as he knelt down to Price.

"There's a fire!" he shouted to Doyle, raising Price in his arms: Price howled and shook all over. "And Price has broke his leg."

"This place'll go up like gunpowder," screamed Doyle. "Quick, get Price in the cart."

"Let 'em go...let 'em go..." whimpered Price, between his howls.

He screamed again as Murphy lifted him like a giant baby into the cart, his leg dangling. He lay there, his tears streaming through dusty sweat and speckling the dry wood, crying out.

"It feels like it's ripped in half."

Murphy grinned grimly as he ran to let the animals go. He chased the hens out of the roost. He untied the goat and opened the pig gate. He ran down to the cow paddock and dropped the sliprails as the cow pushed her head through. He ran back for his blanket roll as several kangaroos, sounding like a cavalry charge, bounded out of the bush fifty yards away, sending leaves and dust flying as they shot off, scooting across the road diagonally, back into the bushes on the other side.

Gunshots were going off around the hills. Murphy looked at the streams of smoke. They were thicker than before...and they were closer...and there were many more of them...

"That's the warning," said Doyle. "Let the cow loose and give her a chance."

"I did."

"Well, fire the rifle off and let's go!"

THROUGHOUT THE HILLS the cedar cutters, like fleas in a dog's fur, fled among the trees. In the town a heavy drift of hot dust swept down Main Street. The post office camphor laurel swayed one way, and the hanging tree up on the main corner swayed the other way. There were dull explosions in the distance far away.

"Look," snapped Gorman ominously, as clear gunshots broke the silence of the hills and grey smoke broke the broad monotonous haze.

Shannon turned.

"Shit," he said, glaring at the far hills, as if the sound of the word was the taste of the substance itself in his mouth.

In the distance rose a monstrous, grey plume of smoke, unfolding from within itself and rearing above the hills like a huge, antediluvian serpent. Gorman spat toward it, but the wind hurled his spit back at him.

"This wind is going to shove us right down its throat," he said as the church bell began to ring. "I've got to get out there to my missus and kids."

The two men ran in different directions.

Up on the balcony of the Havelock Hotel, as the first gunshots went off, Sam Sodge turned away from the men gathered before him. His hands gripped the railing, his jaw tensed, his eyes narrowed.

"Look!" he growled from deep in his belly.

One boy turned and ran down the street, screaming, "Fire!" The hotel guard unfolded his arms and stood ready.

"Get three wagon loads of men out there and see what they can do. Make sure they get whatever water tanks they need. Fast!" Sodge yelled to him.

Major Stumic rushed onto the balcony with his hair a mess, his cuffs and collar undone and his coat in his hand.

"What's your strategy, Sam?" he cried.

"My what? For God's sake, man, send messengers. We must have everyone here. Make sure there are guards on the bank, and double the men on duty downstairs. I want Holman here. Get Stewart..."

"Mrs Gill?"

"Yes, send messages and get them all. And have my things loaded into a carriage."

THE SMOKE MOVED like strands of brushed hair blowing in the wind, the folds and streams intertwining. Mrs Ross watched it pouring from the hills and filling the sky.

She just stood there for an instant, staring. Then with a bitter face she looked down the street to where women were running out of the buildings screaming the names of their children.

Like ants, some of the people of Blood Gully were already leaving along the coach road as the church bell tolled. The number coming into town was swollen by bush men who trudged up the long, grey-red road past the silent sawmill. Cedar cutters, fossickers, ringbarkers, hermits and farming families raced together, some on foot, some on horseback, and some riding in vehicles. Those furthest behind appeared out of a luminous haze. Most carried nothing but what they stood up in.

All the dogs in creation had materialised. They ran along the road, barking at the tide of refugees fleeing the inferno behind them. Sometimes they would wheel off into the scrub to chase the disturbed wildlife. The sky was busy with fleeing birds.

Streams of smoke in the distance began to marry together and raise families of small smoke columns, whose tangled strands thickened and united, becoming a heavier and heavier grey. Without respite, the hot north wind blew.

Old Rooster Gorman galloped along the verge parallel to the road, against the human tide, toward the smoke-screened horizon where the flames licked out just above the tops of the trees.

Sam Sodge watched the road and the tide of human souls flooding into town; and he saw the lone horseman flying in the opposite direction.

"Now there's a man with courage," he muttered as he gripped the railing of the balcony.

Sodge felt the hot blast of wind spitting in his face. A challenge of nature against man, that's what it was... It was the stuff that made great men and broke down the weak.

He looked down on the rabble below, moving like a shed full of hens disturbed by a snake. They cackled and squawked and flapped their wings. The guard grunted behind Sodge and handed him a note. He opened it. The note carried only one word, written in Stumic's scrawl: "Ready!"

Sodge stared at his future among the heavy smoke clouds. He swallowed. The smoke cast a huge shadow across the mill and toward the town. He turned, and with a deep breath he strode into the parlour, between the double, curtained doors.

Sodge stared steadily ahead, his face deadpan. He saw the dozen motionless, miserable faces, crowded in the parlour, all tense, all familiar — Stewart, Mrs Gill, Holman, Stumic, the priest... Sodge looked at them. He could see them curdling with fear.

He sat in the armchair and scowled at Young Mr Callow as the junior government man slid into the parlour from the stairway. Inspector Holman stood and straightened his shoulders as Stumic mumbled.

"Good, Sam. Most of those here came of their own accord before I could even send one messenger."

Sodge scanned the faces. He made a steeple with his fingers and pressed the peak against his lips, then his nose. He mumbled into his clasped hands and stared at a point in the middle distance.

"We have already done all that we can. I have dispatched three wagon loads of men with water tanks to fight the blaze. Have they gone?" Sodge raised his eyes over the nearest heads and addressed himself to the mill manager, lurking uncomfortably in the background.

Swallowing hard, the mill manager spoke up with a quivering voice, his face blushing. Sodge could not help but notice a glimmer of a smile on the lips of Young Mr Callow, who was standing beside the manager.

"Word has just reached me, sir," said the mill manager, "that only two sizeable portable water tanks were obtainable. And the men refused to go anyway. They say it would be suicide..."

Sodge's face became transformed with disbelief. He began to lose his composure.

"The fools! Damned fools!" he hissed, and then looked helplessly around the room. No-one responded.

"Get every available man down to the mill, with both those wagons. The mill must be saved at all costs," Sodge told the mill manager. "You hear me?"

The manager shrugged helplessly.

"We've tried to make them go, but they won't. They say they won't leave town in any direction but to safety."

Sodge slapped his forehead.

"They said so, did they? Who said so? Them down there in the street? They said they won't go...so help me, God!" he cried. "Have you seen them? Go on, look for yourself..."

"It isn't here yet, Sam. It hasn't got us beat. It may not even get here." Major Stumic's voice faltered and faded as he looked at the sweating faces around the room; they stared stonily away from him. Then he stopped when he saw Young Mr Callow's smile.

"What about you, Mr Callow?" said Inspector Holman. "You seem to find something amusing."

"I'm sorry, Inspector," said Young Mr Callow. "I always smile when I'm nervous. If it disturbs anybody I will be happy to leave."

Stewart banged the table with his fist, which left a flower-shaped mark on the varnished tabletop.

"Well, I'd be happy to leave too," he said, defiantly. "This could develop quite nastily. We could have a disaster on our hands..."

"But what can we do?" Father Mitchell protested, turning from Stewart to Sodge for an answer.

"As I tried to explain before," said Sodge, as he sat looking at no-one, "we have done all we can. Now all we can do is pray."

"They've preyed on my patience too long already," whispered the mill manger in front of Young Mr Callow. He walked straight from the parlour without another word.

"We've already had a prayer from Father Mitchell," Stewart screeched. "I suggest to you all that you follow my example and clear out."

With that, he stood and bowed to Mrs Gill, who was rising from her chair.

"May I offer you a place in my carriage, madam?" he asked her. "It may be crowded, but we depart directly."

"Thank you," Mrs Gill replied without smiling, as they both walked toward the door, eyes following them. "My carriage is waiting. Father Mitchell is coming with me."

The priest rushed to escort Mrs Gill on her way.

"As you wish." Stewart bowed again.

As if he was seeing some of their faces now for the last time, Stewart turned to the others in the room before going through the doorway.

"I have a family to consider. May God protect you all."

The room behind him boiled with hushed, anxious conversations. Sodge waved his hand dismissively in Stewart's wake.

"What's the use?" he mumbled.

XXVII

FLAMES, LEAPING WITH life and drunk on their own smoke, rushed down the slopes and straight through Gorman's farm. The air stirred with the screeches and flapping of parrots fleeing in flocks as the screaming horseman rode into the smoke which poured through the bush in waves. The smoke hid everything ahead. The horse shied and resisted its rider's will. When the first flames were seen it threw the man and fled, flinging its head from side to side and whipping its own forelegs with the loose reins.

The thrown rider rose bent from the ground, coughing and choking. Dribbling from the mouth, blocking his nose and shutting his eyes, he rushed limping into the milling inferno, screaming out the names of his wife and children.

It was Rooster Gorman. His eyes were like a mad man's as he entered the furnace of his own front yard.

KATHLEEN AND JUDITH watched the approaching cloud of smoke from their own hilltop perch at Mrs Gill's attic window.

They watched the billowing smoke taking on different shapes: one minute a horse's head nodding, then a serpent, the next moment an eagle springing into flight, then a woman dancing... Then they watched old Dancer Hughes the Holmans' gardener, dawdling downhill as if it was any other day, as if he was drunk already, with his little blue dog skipping right behind him. He was carrying a chair.

As each wave of pedestrians and riders passed the arms of the rugged ridge-lines, a fresh roar of mumbling and murmuring arose. Terrible, awful, sad, dreadful, unearthly, miserable and horrid, they said it was; and much, much more.

"It's incredible...incurable...like a doomed place...like a volcano...like hell-fire...we'll all be killed...roasted alive...

"We'll all be rooned...we'll never get out if we don't go now...how will it end...where's my children...what will happen...where's the Inspector...oh God, will somebody do something..."

The fire made a terrible, devouring sound, rumbling through the skies from the distance. The blazing blizzard was a huge explosion of evil, a burning bubonic plague, a terrifying, horrifying pestilence looming insidiously. One moment the black clouds were all striped with the fire's glow, like a giant tumbling tiger. Then the flames themselves leapt, the smoke coiled and writhed, snaking like a huge live maze above them...soon to descend, crushing all beneath it without pity, trapping them all for all time. It was a dream gone bad, a nightmare come true...it was a white-hot knife plunged through the heart of every dream, gutting every hope, every passion.

A newborn child, huddled in a stranger's arms, began to cry for its mother.

Suddenly the madly thronged street erupted with the scream of Rooster Gorman's panic-stricken horse, ploughing into the desperate procession. All one side of the animal's rump dripped from deep, burst blisters. Wild eyes afire, the poor, crazed animal had to be dragged, limping and crying out, out of sight down behind the post office.

"She's done for," a man said.

The horse was gone. People escaping along the coach road turned and looked back at the glow cast by the fires of hell upon the billowing walls of smoke.

Moments later there was a deafening gunshot from behind the post office. The roar of the approaching fire was louder in Main Street than the sawmill had ever been.

And still the firestorm approached, showing only a little — just the sharp, jagged fringe of itself carving like a giant saw blade through all that stood in its path. Inky clouds blotted out the sun's natural brightness, and the terrifying glimpse of flames over the treetops, under the mountain of smoky lava, struck the watchers with fear.

They could see the brightness of the distant blaze flickering upon their own sweat-drenched faces.

Stewart the government man steered his buggy and his wife hugged their children, and they forced their way into the stream of slow traffic. A woman on foot leading four children and carrying one on her back, followed by her husband pushing a barrow overflowing with possessions, stopped to let Stewart drive his horse forward.

In the turmoiled hills, in the path of the marauding flames, around the deserted cedar cutters' camps, twigs of every thickness, tangled with the litter of ages, lay burning, ignited by the sparks flung far ahead of the wild fire. Faded-red piles of powdered dry timber lay begging to be lit. The flames slurped up the dead twigs and leaves and the bark, logs, nuts and flowers. The wind blew hot and hard and drove the fire racing up and down gully sides like liquid, splashing sparks in all directions. The fire crawled up trees and burst the the tree-top cities into mighty elevated torches. The fiery tree crowns dripped flaming litter, and squealing reptiles curled up in their ovenlike hollow branches and died.

The rest of the wildlife fled through the scrub — small things and large, creeping and crawling for their lives, scurrying and bounding, slithering, flying, loping and lumbering, the feathered, the furred, the spiny and the scaled. Some were smouldering, some stumbled in the flames. Some squealed, some grunted, some screamed, some cried. The goannas raised their heads and licked the smoky air. They flicked their tails to and fro before reaching their last moments of agony; then they twisted and seared among the sparks and the blizzard of burning air.

The cries of humans were drowned by the crashing of branches and roofs. The fences fell away like matchsticks. First one shack caved in with a roar, then another.

Men emerged, blackened and half-naked. And women, too, with blood running down their legs, too frantic to care or to notice, their faces golden from the overwhelming glow and black-smeared with the airborne soot. And then the children, their huge eyes absorbing the terror, their smudged faces dancing with fire-sparkled sweat.

"We're done for," said the man who had pitied the wounded horse, and no-one answered. The sky was dark and the inferno rose on one of the closer ridge-lines. Like torches the tall trees burst alight, first in the distance, then closer. A crazed wallaby bounded among the crowd in Main Street. The wallaby stood crouched and panting a moment before darting up the laneway toward the graveyard.

The street was flooded in disarray. As Inspector Holman's sulky moved slowly along in the stream of fleeing traffic, Rebecca the servant girl searched the crowd. Mrs Holman stared fixedly ahead as Price's cart, driven by Murphy and drawn by a limping horse with a good horse tied behind, made its way past.

Mrs Holman's eyes met Murphy's. Her mouth seemed to tense but she made no gesture. The Inspector was nowhere in sight. Murphy did not greet her. He spoke only with his eyes and one twitch of the corner of his mouth, like a quick twitch of pain. Mrs Holman stared him straight in the eye. Their faces danced together with the giddy-making glimmer of the reflected brilliant haze. Murphy flicked the reins as Doyle snarled at him to hurry it up, and in the back — his voice-box bleeding from his own endless cries — Price clutched his leg weakly and moaned. The cart and the sulky passed each other and the meeting of glances was over.

Rebecca slipped soundlessly from the back as the sulky's pace briskened. She ran to Mrs Gill's carriage from out of the retreating crowd and flung open the door without a knock. Mrs Gill's eyes were slow and glazed as they stared with chilly distaste at the beautiful young intruder. Rebecca looked about the carriage. It was empty but for Father Mitchell and Mrs Gill clutching her velvet purse and a large iron key.

"Mrs Gill," said Rebecca. "Judith and Kathleen! Where are they?"

"At the house. They'll be safe there, I've locked them

in. Mr Sodge will take care of them. Now be off."

Mrs Gill slammed the door in Rebecca's face.

Rebecca threaded her way through the crowd, over-hearing terrible rumours. Someone had seen Dancer Hughes walking around with a chair and talking to it. His brain had finally snapped, they said. The Gormans' had gone up — no sign of them anywhere. Gorman's was the first place that had stood in the path of the fire, someone said. It was now buried under oceans of smoke. Rooster had been seen galloping down the road the wrong way. He never had a chance, they muttered.

Then Rebecca was swallowed by the crowd.

As Mrs Gill's carriage jerked away from Rebecca, Father Mitchell began to cry. Mrs Gill ignored him in the carriage's merciful darkness. She did not even have to look away. She sat back and sighed. Then the carriage stopped to a crawl, forcing a way through the crowd.

"It's like Dante's *Inferno*," the priest cried.

MURPHY asked three men before he discovered that Doctor Morrison had set up a makeshift hospital in the open. As a wagonload of injured was pulling away, another wagon was being backed up to the site.

Doctor Morrison wiped the sweat off his face and replaced it with a smear of blood from the back of his hand as Murphy pulled the limping horse to a halt by the camphor laurel. Doctor Morrison washed his hands in black water.

"Price has busted his leg. He's out cold," yelled Murphy.

Doyle sat slumped as a woman walked up to him.

"Who owns the cart?" she asked.

"Him in the back," Doyle mumbled.

The woman looked at Price and nodded.

"Alright!" she yelled confidently as she pointed to the cart, though nobody answered her. "Two more in here."

The doctor was bent over a silent young man with a bandaged head and a leather burn around his wrist. His arm was snapped out of its normal shape. Doctor Morrison felt the man's blue-streaked throat with the back of his hand and removed a blanket from the man's chest.

"If he starts shivering again, cover him," said the doctor, and then he walked over to the dusty cart, followed by Mrs Ross.

Doctor Morrison was handed his satchel. He ran his fingers lightly over Price's leg, as deft as a pickpocket. Then he cut away the trousers, touching the distorted flesh. He shook his head as he did so and Price quivered.

"Get me another one of those fence pickets," he said.

A luminous haze hung above as the hellish bushfire turned brighter than a thousand sunsets at once, reddening the diabolical clouds of darkness.

JANSEN AND Young Mr Callow looked across the road from the coach office, across the raging flood of faces and souls in the street and down to Morrison's hospital.

"I'll go down and see how it's going," said the young government man.

The fire screamed all round Blood Gully like the wind of the wildest storm at sea, swarming with screaming sirens starving for the taste of terrified human souls. Inspector Holman came out of the Havelock Hotel as Young Mr Callow walked into the tide of stricken faces and the downpour of soot ash. Holman surveyed the street quickly; then Sergeant Dirlsky ran up, his face a lather of sweat, his hands jerking as he spoke, his eyes beseeching Holman's attention.

"Sir, I must speak to you," said Dirlsky. "It's time to abandon town. The blaze is almost upon us. We have thirty minutes — an hour at most."

A group of children, in the back of an overloaded wagon pulled by grunting, odd-sized horses, sang a hymn. They passed slowly among those who were travelling on foot muttering blasphemies.

"Very well," said Holman. "Make preparations."

Sergeant Dirlsky swallowed. His brow creased

downwards. He moved his mouth without saying anything. Finally, a word came out...

"Preparations?"

"You have your orders, Sergeant."

Inspector Holman spun on his heel and marched back into the hotel as Young Mr Callow started once again to worm his way across the road.

XXVIII

A BOILING CAULDRON spewed steam where it sat upon a smouldering fire, in the midst of a town boiling in an inferno. Morrison's sweat dripped into a man's burn wound just before Mrs Ross wiped his face again. Callow saw Huley Colquoon sitting nearby, dripping wet from where searchers had found him in a water barrel. Huley's only defence was that his mother had told him to get in it, after she had made him put her in the barrel next to his. They found her there, drowned. They took Huley to Doctor Morrison and sat him so he could not see his mother's waterlogged body.

"Sit there and don't move," they told him.

Callow stood there, looking, and soaking up the sadness that surrounded him in all directions. He could hear the crying. He stood like a lily on a dirt-box, his white face and white hands shiny in a sea of grimy hands and faces. Morrison looked like a grubby old tradesman. The doctor's shirt-tail dangled out of his trousers. Callow felt useless. He watched a lifeless man being loaded into a cart. A girl pushed him aside. It was Sarah, the saucy maid of the Bushman's Arms. She began to scrape filth from the burnt hands of a man who sat grunting and shivering all over, breathing in an unending, tremulous groan. The girl bit her already-bleeding lips as she worked like a watchmaker on the mangled, jellified hands of the man. He had been dragged from a blazing doorway, after a burning beam had melted into his hands as he tried to force his way inside the fire's belly, to join his family in their doom. Callow looked down at the man with his blistery hands splitting open. He felt his own fingers stretching from the pain.

Callow looked down at Sarah, her skirt drawn in and

tucked under her legs, her sharp knees bared as she squatted like a child, sweat trickling down the side of her neck from under her hair drawn into a bunch and tied in a bulky knot. She glanced at Callow — not at his face or his eyes, or his fine clothes, but only at what met her eyes — at his white, smooth, empty hands. She bit her wooden scraper between her teeth and made the burned man writhe and grunt and squirm. Callow saw the nearby faces, the closed eyes of sorrow, the open eyes of horror, the frowns of pain and scowls of bitter loss...and the blankness, as deep as souls. He looked down on the man's hideously blistered and weeping and bleeding hands. The ragged, useless pads of stripped meat suddenly sparkled in the sunlight.

"Good," Sarah said as she got up. Callow felt weak at the knees.

AS PRICE'S CART was loaded with more injured, Doyle sat like stone in front. Murphy shook Doyle's hand and then looked at Price's face.

"You'll be right soon," Murphy said, squeezing Price's shoulder.

Price opened his mouth and closed his eyes, and his teeth chattered. A man in a blanket and a pair of pants too small for him got into the cart and picked up the reins.

"Right! Get them out of here," yelled Doctor Morrison.

As the cart pulled away into the slow-flowing crowd, Sodge's voice was heard bellowing out above the street. His voice soared above the din of the crowd from the hotel balcony.

"The mill!" Sodge roared.

But rather than burning, the mill seemed to disappear in a burst of shattering light. The sawdust-and-timber-charged factory became a fountain of light. Balls of fire swelled and burst above the silhouetted shape of the structure.

Rebecca fled up the hotel stairs and through the parlour. She rushed onto the balcony and tugged at Sodge's sleeve. He recoiled as though from a leper.

"Mr Sodge," she said. "Mrs Gill said you are taking care of Judith and Kathleen. Where are they?"

Sodge stared blankly at the girl.

"What?"

"Judith and Kathleen..."

"Go away," he said, turning his glassy eyes back to the sight of his life's dream being razed.

"But Judith and Kathleen..."

"Take her away," he said.

As the guard's hands seized Rebecca she began to struggle, but they steered her to the parlour door. She saw Stumic as she was dragged by. The Major sat speechless, staring through the window at the conflagration and fanning himself with a large raffia fan.

"All I need now is a violin," Sodge muttered without hope, "and everything would be perfect."

REBECCA ran to the base of Gill's hill. There, as she broke out of the crowd, she saw Dancer Hughes, drunk as usual, sitting on a chair in the clearing.

"Rebecca the Goddess," he saluted her like a seated soldier. "The bravest of the brave. I told them there's nothing to worry about. I've got the answer."

Dancer was puffing on a big pipe that streamed powerful-smelling pale smoke. Rebecca ignored him and rushed away from the retreating column of refugees, now thinning to a trickle.

Freckle-faced Freddie Fairburn pushed the wheelbarrow loaded with his children up the road. The barrow wheel wobbled from side to side as it ploughed through the dust. A small dog ran in front with his tongue out. Dancer Hughes's blue dog wagged her tail and watched Freddie's dog run by.

"Don't go too far, Freddie," Dancer called out. "You'll be back tomorrow."

Price's cart went by, driven by a man in a blanket. The blind man Doyle was sitting beside him; and the groaning passengers, half-hidden in the back, sounded like doomed victims.

"Where's Price, Danny?" yelled Dancer Hughes as the dead-looking horse limped along.

Doyle turned his head hauntedly in Dancer's direction and said nothing.

Constables Jones and Taylor rode by on fidgeting horses, keeping the frightened column reassured and in order.

Rebecca struggled up the dark, pitted hillside, through the dead, spiky thistles and the clods of broken clay. The smoke drifted downward, almost choking her as it stung her eyes. She turned and looked backwards at the fire.

It had rimmed half of the town, swallowing the outlying huts and creeping across the trodden-stubble fields where small groups of dark, bent figures were beating out the flames with hessian bags.

The hot wind beat upon her frantic face. Then a cool devil-wind suddenly sprang out of the earth like a pair of mad, invisible snakes wrestling in a frenzy, tossing dust at her eyes and spurting dead grass in the air. She rushed upwards again.

Dancer Hughes moved his chair right into the middle of the road where he could talk to the people of Blood Gully as they fled. He was tired of yelling at them like a madman. His little blue dog followed him and sat flapping her tail in the dust.

Dancer saw Mrs Holman walking back down the road towards him. He thought, surely she has not returned to be with her husband. "Nothing to worry about, madam," Dancer said. "Everything will be back to normal directly."

Dancer Hughes raved at the people going by, then he raised his eyes and his voice and began to talk to the approaching inferno itself.

On the outskirts of the town, one tin hut was blazing like a flaming parcel wrapped in buckled sheets of tin. The post office, the Bushman's Arms and the little shops and stalls were all huddled under a coating of grey ash, speckled with black soot and piled thick like snow. On the Havelock side, toward the shanty town of makeshift dwellings and the road to the blazing sawmill, the huts and outbuildings smouldered, the shacks and cottages glowed, their dark little shapes torn apart by the flames.

Dancer Hughes did his best to placate the blazing monster. As the old gardener challenged it his face was contorted with sincerity.

"There now, you giant brute. You don't want to burn these people..." he yelled to the glowing, smoke-filled sky. "This poor old town is hardly worth any regard. There isn't anybody here you could be after.

"All them bad ones, they've gone already," Dancer yelled at the monster in the sky. "Why don't you just go off and have a rest now. That's the way. Leave these poor people in peace."

The marchers going past, even in their bitter damnation, laughed at that old fool Dancer, looking straight into the blotted-out distance, pretending he was staring the monster in the eye.

"Go on," he said, screaming out so loud spit flew from his mouth with every second word. "You big old bully. Just look at those suffering children and mothers."

Dancer jumped up and pointed at the children. He kept yelling as he sat down, glaring at some unfathomable point in the heavens. He sat down and stood up again, still yelling, and sat down.

"They wouldn't hurt you, you big bully. They wouldn't hurt no-one. They're going to die anyway. Not like you or me. You should be shamed...shamed for burning down a little place like this. You should go and..."

"Mr Hughes!" Mrs Holman snapped Dancer out of his blurred, mesmeric spell.

"Yes, sir, Mrs Holman," Dancer said, rising. "I thought you went..."

"I did," she replied. "But Rebecca was missing. I couldn't just leave her. She has no-one."

"I seen her," said Dancer. "She's alright."

He wiggled the chair to set it right. Then he brushed the seat of it with his hand.

"Have a seat, ma'am," he said with the grandness of a potentate, leaning on the back of the chair with his feet rooted to the dirt, swaying, and holding his stinking pipe in one horny hand. "Have a seat, and I'll fetch her for you."

"No thank you," Mrs Holman said. "Where did she go?"

MURPHY helped load a broken body onto another wagon. The splintery wooden planks were spattered with blood. From the top of the wagon, as he straightened his aching back, he could have sworn he caught a glimpse of what he most wanted in the world. Up at the main corner stood a woman who could have been her. As soon as he could, Murphy told Morrison that he would need to slip away for half an hour. The doctor nodded, and Murphy was soon running down the street, weaving among the slow-moving people.

Down the other end of town, Mad Mick O'Reilly and Tom Shannon ran among the burning dwellings with Constable Fraser. They looked about frantically, searching the area with their ears and eyes as the fires roared.

"Let's clear out. There's no-one," said Shannon, squinting from the burning heat.

"Dirlsky said to make sure," said Fraser. "I tell you what, though, I bet the loot feeding these fires would be worth getting your hands on."

Shannon nodded.

"As long as it doesn't get us," said O'Reilly, as the roof of a shack collapsed with an ear-shattering crash. "I think Shannon's right."

"We've done all this side," repeated Shannon. "No-one's here. It's the same everywhere. They're either safe now, or they're finished."

Their sweaty, frantic faces gleamed with the light of the burning dwellings.

"You're probably right," said Fraser. "But if Dirlsky asks, we looked everywhere. Alright?"

The two others agreed. They saw two men rush between the flames with four buckets dangling from a long sapling pole.

"Feel that," said O'Reilly as they turned back toward town, surrounded by smoke and flaming shapes.

"What are you talking about, O'Reilly?" said Shannon.

"The breeze in our faces," said O'Reilly. "It's cool."

"Hey! I think you're right," said Fraser.

Shannon scanned the burning hillsides as Fraser and O'Reilly followed his example. The flames that before had seemed to claw their way closer and closer, spurting along the ground and whooshing along the tops of the trees, now stood straight, marking time; in some places, the flames even leaned back toward the north where they had come from.

"She's holding," whispered Shannon.

Fraser and O'Reilly smiled like brothers, their blackened faces shining in the hellish glow, as the fireworks about them danced.

"Quick," said Fraser. "I've got to report this to Dirlsky."

Fraser ran.

XXIX

MURPHY REACHED THE edge of town and stood staring at Dancer Hughes. Dancer smiled knowingly at the fool dog lover, then he scowled suspiciously at Murphy and looked about the dismal parade. The crowd suddenly pointed up the hill, crested with the dark, foreboding shape of Mrs Gill's house, an overwhelming vision of gloom and authority. A sizzling, flaring spear of burning bark, in a strip longer than a burning man, was streaming like a comet showering sparks down, down, to the peak of Gill's hill. It disappeared in a shower of sparks behind the big house.

"Did you see that?" Dancer screamed as the crowd gasped.

Standing still, partway up the hill, Paul the blacksmith's boy raised his blond head to see the flaring strip of bark plunging down. Murphy left Dancer Hughes gaping, as he ran toward the hill behind the blond boy, up the steep, rugged slope.

REBECCA reached Mrs Gill's house just as the burning spear fell from the sky, plummeting down through a rain of its own sparks into the cypress hedge. Like a kerosene bush, the hedge ignited.

Oblivious to the danger at their back door, Judith and Kathleen watched the tragedy below. They stared from the attic window while the blaze tore into the rear of the building. Through the gigantic walls of smoke, they could see the violated landscape and the stream of marchers bleeding out of the town's punctured belly. They watched the town dying. They were alone. The two gardeners had flown like birds uncaged.

"Isn't it exciting?" cried Judith, clapping her hands.

250

"It's as if the world was ending. . .and we get to watch it."

Kathleen watched from the window. She stood transfixed, saying nothing, clutching a horseshoe to her bosom.

Rebecca rushed to the back door. She tripped on the step and fell in through the doorway, into the kitchen, as the cypress hedge became a ball of fire behind her. A frilled lantern on a stand crashed to the floor as she stumbled through the dark, bumping furniture.

"Kathleen! Judith!" she cried; then the hallstand smashed down on her head.

Smoke flowed through the second doorway into the hall around the girl as the kitchen began to roar with flames. First the curtains flashed alight, then the fire started to race along the walls and across the ceiling in a whirl of hot air.

"What was that?" hissed Kathleen. "It sounded like . . ."

"Rebecca!" Judith cried out.

She screamed the Goddess's name and from the distance came a muffled echo . . .

"Rebecca! Rebecca!" screamed Mrs Holman as she saw the cypress hedge blazing and the fire tearing through the verandah and the bunk-out, the kitchen, and all up the outside wall . . . the whole house engulfed in a flaming whirlpool.

The cool breeze from the south was driving the flames. Mrs Holman staggered among them as they lashed out at her, trying to drag her into their mad dance. Half-blind with the heat, she rushed to the doorway and flung herself between the flaming doorposts; she tore straight through the kitchen as the verandah crashed down, blocking the doorway behind her.

The flames behind her lit her way ahead. The Inspector's wife threw herself into the flowing stream of acrid smoke pouring into the hall like liquid darkness.

"Rebecca!" she cried, as she crashed over the girl sprawled on the floor.

"Rebecca! Rebecca!" cried the two other girls, their

voices coming down the attic stairs. They heard the roar of the burning house about them, and then they smelled and saw the smoke filling the hallway. The flames were gushing in with the draught driven into the house, licking up and along the hall ceiling. The tapestry hangings at first fenced them back, but soon they caught alight themselves and burned like fuses.

The three women screamed and screamed in the blazing house.

Through the blazing, roaring sky their voices carried no louder than the screeching of the frightened parrots in a far-off tree.

Paul the blacksmith's boy and Murphy the dog lover raced each other up the hillside, followed by two other men from the crowd below. They fled by the freshly torn shreds of dress and petticoat which dangled from a half-buried broken gate. Their hands tore at the steep slope as they half crawled and half ran, rushing over the crest and vaulting the fence into Mrs Gill's garden.

The blazing building towered before them. They raced among the ghoulishly illuminated trees round to the blazing rear.

Three other men galloped along the road winding up the far side of the hill, still with far to go. The whole rear of the building was engulfed, with the hedge, the kitchen and the lean-to laundry. Paul and Murphy swerved among the burning fruit trees and dodged the burning bower, all its white latticework alight. Then the upper roof collapsed into the attic in an avalanche of burning shingles.

The screaming stopped.

Up the marble front steps the two men ran, stomping their boots loudly, their faces dark, sooty and sweaty, leading the other two from out of the crowd. Murphy tried a window and Paul tried the door. The boy punched the doorframe with the power of a horse's kick.

"It's locked!" he screamed.

Murphy and the others rushed three times with their shoulders and all the maddened forced they could muster before they snapped the lock's grip. Still, even open a crack, the door would not budge. Someone was holding it from behind. The smoke belched from the open crack. It might have been day, it might have been night. Nobody knew anymore. Hell was permanent brightness. The curtains burned in one front window.

"Can you hear us?" Murphy shouted, only to be answered by the crackling of the flames.

They pushed the door until it moved, shoving aside what was behind it; and they found the women, lying there.

The men dragged the women from the house. The fourth they could grab only by the ankles. They could get no closer to her because of the pulsing blast of heat and the choking smoke. Then they backed helplessly away as fast as they could stumble, shielding their faces with their arms.

Peeping from under his elbow as he staggered backwards dragging the light body, and screaming from the heat, Paul saw the fingernails embedded in the door, its mirror-like varnish flickering in the reflections of the furnace.

The last woman had been caught in the fire. The others' dresses too were smouldering. The men beat out and stamped out the smoulders and the flames in the hair of the last one. They beat out the flames dancing on her face with their hands as the blazing ruins of the house collapsed with a huge, angry explosion. Embers and sparks spewed out and scattered into the smoky mist, raining down in a scorching shower with a rumbling growl, belching out a ball of white heat and another shower of red sparks.

The men frantically brushed the embers away. They had felt the unresisting bodies in their hands. They had felt the ribs, so yielding and small. They had felt the warm, soft faces...

The long-haired, pretty heads hung so low and so sadly, with their teeth showing in their open mouths. Each man looked down and searched the stricken faces for signs of life — all the faces but one. At that one they looked only with stunned horror.

"She's had it," said one of the men from the crowd with tears pouring down his smudgy cheeks as he pointed to the woman who had been disfigured by the fire. Part of her hair was still smouldering about her scarred face where the man had beaten out the flames. She lay hideous, her face naked of skin, her blistered eyes peeled to the sky.

The men's faces and the women's faces were golden carvings in the flame-light...the burnt one's face glistened like the pattern of an embossed sculpture.

Riders rode into the bright, blazing aura of the burning residence, their horses panting and fidgeting with fright.

One, they said, was Judith the dreamer. She had not a fingernail left on either hand. The one with the staring eyes and bleeding nose was Kathleen, the new girl who had come from out of town to work for Mrs Gill. She clutched a horseshoe.

Constable Fraser rode up behind the horsemen. He looked at the row of bodies.

"My God!" he cried. "It's Mrs Holman."

Fraser wheeled the horse and galloped away.

Murphy knelt by the Inspector's wife and raised her closed eyelid. He stared into her eye. He saw his own face, shrunken and reflected there.

"She's stiff," he whimpered, hearing his own voice coming from deep inside him like a stranger's. His lips trembled.

The new arrivals stood, staring. The blacksmith's boy ran his fingers through Kathleen's dead hair. He bent and brushed her top lip with the dryness of his own, feeling the blood there, still running from her nose.

There were gasps from those who watched.

"Hey, boy, come here," said one of the faces flickering in the crowd, leaping to the boy's side and grabbing him, dragging him to his feet. "Come on, son. Come away."

Murphy, still kneeling by the inspector's wife, watched the blacksmith's boy as he wrestled with the man. Paul punched the man hard in the shoulder bone, knocking him off his feet to the bright dust and easily shaking himself free. He turned back slowly to Kathleen and knelt down again. He looked behind like a dog feeding, then he bent his thick-skulled head and softly kissed her hand. It tasted cold and stank of smoke. No-one moved behind him. He read the words on the horseshoe clutched in her hand near his face. Good Luck! The words stabbed him in the guts and his breath squeezed out of his lungs with a hysterical, coughing gasp. With his eyes squeezing shut, he grasped her cold hand and pulled the horseshoe free of her callused fingers. He jumped to his feet, his face bursting with blood; he shook all over and raised his hand, growling through his teeth; he shuddered and hurled the metal boomerang into the black smoke dancing above the golden, flaming ruins.

"Christ," he screamed. "You old bitch."

Murphy knelt there forever, among the dead. No-one tried to move him. The marchers filed by and took their last solemn, precious look, shuddering.

"Where's the boy gone?"

"I don't know. He just stormed off."

"Just look at that, will you?"

"Poor bitches."

"What a waste."

Murphy stared at the pale softness under Mrs Holman's chin where it creased and spread silkily round her slender neck. Inspector Holman rode up on a horse, flanked by Fraser and Sergeant Dirlsky.

Holman split the crowd like the prow of a boat as he barged his way to where the women lay in the dust and grass of the carriageway's turning circle. He walked to where Murphy knelt guarding the dead bodies like a dog. Holman wasted no time. Murphy heard the boot-heels coming toward him, crunching the gravel pebbles. Holman strode straight to where Murphy knelt, and he looked down at his wife.

Holman shook his head. He thought the two servant girls would have escaped with their mistress, Mrs Gill. But then, he had also thought his own wife had gone. He could not guess why she had returned.

"Why didn't she go, like I told her to?" he asked helplessly, turning to Dirlsky. "I said goodbye to her."

But then he saw something that made him stop cold. Dirlsky was speaking, but Holman did not hear a word. He turned his head slowly back to the body beside his wife's.

He knew the dress and the shoes... She had worn them the last time he had seen her, sitting in the sulky with his wife. He knew her hands... He froze at the sight of her unrecognisable face. He knew...it was her, but it could not be...he knew that body...but it was dead. He knew that beautiful hair, but now it was tangled in the dirt, trodden on, singed and still smouldering.

"Oh, no!" Holman gasped, clutching his face and crying out without any hope of redemption. "Oh God! It's Rebecca!"

He ran away. Everyone in the crowd turned and followed him with their eyes. Their mouths fell open.

Murphy still knelt staring at the golden glimmer on Mrs Holman's neck as it caught in the brightness of the dying fire.

The Inspector ran out of sight — and wherever he went he was followed by the dead girl's bulging, blistered, unblinking, accusing eyes.

XXX

EVEN BEYOND THE fire's furthest advance, where the flames themselves had not reached, the heat of the furious, uncontained furnace had discoloured the leaves to the colour of scorched copper. Whole tree crowns were singed, and the sap was boiled out of branches, trunks and saplings. Then the wildfire retreated upon its own tracks and diminished, leaving behind the smouldering, scorched damage.

What secret fires were left behind, burning in people's souls, was not yet known. Secret fires can burn deep inside many an outwardly cool log or under many shallow layers of cooled ash.

There was nothing visibly alive left in the fire's tracks. Everything was charred or glowing. Black ash clung like pitch to the burned shapes, white ash lay about like a layer of snow, thin whispers of smoke rising like mist. All had been consumed.

At the fringe between life and death, animals lay burnt or wandering blind, their fur melted into their eyes, their sight ruined by heat, their last instincts flickering in hopeless travels. Logs lay sparkling with embers. Hollow tree trunks still roasted with flame.

Signs of civilisation lay obliterated. Signs of lives of labour lay in ruins: the mill, the huts, the fences. The hanging tree was burnt jagged and more sinister than ever. It was leafless, twigless and smouldering. Bared branches had been burned to stumps.

Suddenly, the hanging tree roared like a mortally wounded beast; and with a deafening, tearing wrench the largest branch separated from what remained of its trunk, crashing down in a scattering of sparks bursting from inside its long-concealed hollow. The earth shook with the whack; and a blue flame, like fire from the muzzle of a cannon, burst from the opened hole in the side of the tree trunk. The tree was a furnace burning out its own insides.

The giant branch lay smouldering out of existence in Main Street. The sparks drifted across the street where life flowed aimlessly, passively and casually, each fate indistinguishable from the fate of all, the souls and faces all submerged within a soulless and faceless tide. The sparks fell into the wheel-ruts and hoofprints, they fell into the dust and soot and ash where trod the good and bad, the best and the worst, the losers and the lost.

After the fire, Dancer Hughes sat a long time in the wide part of the street, telling everybody all about it...

"Didn't I say there was nothing to worry about?" he cried happily. "You've got to reason with the forces of nature. Keep away from the fire and you don't get burned. That's my opinion."

The blond blacksmith's boy came by, dragging his boots as if he had never had a night's sleep in his life. His face was a pouting baby's. He was covered all over in dust and soot.

"Hey, Paul," Dancer called out. "Paul...hey, boy... it's me..."

Dancer got no answer. The boy's ears were dead and his eyes blind. Christ almighty, Dancer wondered. What happened to him?

In the distance the fire continued to feed upon its own ashes, deep in the hills, down ravines surrounded at last by its own self-wrought devastation, with nowhere to go now but down in memory.

"If ever a man died of shame, that wildfire did," said Dancer. "I told it. I said, You should be ashamed, I told it, You should be ashamed."

In bare dirt and pebble patches, among the ashes, ants crawled gingerly from deep in the cool ground and tasted the air and the warm stones; later they would spread their domain and resume their anonymous frenzy of mindless toil, no doubt happy, in their own way, in their miserable, swarming existence. Such was life. Such was death.

These things greeted the morning, just as they would greet the following night. The time had come to regard the future. Red eyes stared from pale faces, to the ungreen hills, to the hills without cedar, to the gutted mill, grotesquely resplendent in its bleakness, now a haunting spectre in its twisted wreckage.

Tom Shannon waited for his wife to return to town with their wagon.

"That fool woman has took my pipe with her," Shannon snarled to his eldest son.

"I'd have thought you'd had enough smoke for a little while by now," said the son.

Shannon ignored the remark. In the heat of disaster boys had become men.

Up the hill, up at the cemetery, the men with shovels found a woman alone, asleep on a tiny grave. Her mouth was all foamed up, but she was breathing even though she did not look alive.

Murphy found his newly purchased horse mad with fright and half-dead with thirst. He led her back to Main Street and left her there strapped to a post. Then he walked in the street, among the people of Blood Gully. They moved along, inside invisible walls as thick as stone.

Huley Colquoon's body was found under the camphor laurel, among the dead, between a child crushed by a wagon and a man with blood clotted in his ears.

Constables Jones and Taylor marked Huley's name down at the bottom of their long list.

"Well, at least he went with his old woman," Constable Jones quipped.

Constable Taylor stared at Huley's corpse. Huley sat up, opening his eyes and blinking blindly.

Taylor's mouth fell open.

Murphy tipped his hat to Mrs Donaldson, whose eyes stared at the dirt.

"Good morning, Murphy," she said, going by without a glance.

Constable Taylor gaped at Huley.

"He...he...he isn't...he isn't dead..." Taylor stammered.

Constable Jones turned back and stared at Huley sitting up, rubbing his eyes among the dead.

"Mr Murphy, you look as if you're going somewhere," Huley drawled as Murphy set his blanket roll down at his feet.

"Yeah," Murphy said, glancing up at the burnt ruins on the hill.

The helpers were loading another wagon. Murphy turned away at the sight of Mrs Holman's bare feet sticking out of her torn skirts. Huley looked down at the faces around him. They all looked dead. The coverings had been taken off them for constables Taylor and Jones to compile their death toll. The flies swarmed round the breathless noses and mouths, round the ears and the often-open eyes.

"Poor old One-eye," sighed Huley.

One face remained covered. Huley raised the flap and recoiled in horror. Murphy gestured toward the corpse in uniform.

"Holman?" he asked.

Constable Jones nodded.

"He blew his brains out last night," said Doctor Morrison gruffly, bustling into their midst, with no shirt on, his braces over his singlet, his flab glistening with sweat.

"Get those faces covered up again before the flies blow the lot of them," the doctor snapped at the two policemen.

He shoved Constable Taylor and pushed Constable Jones into motion.

"Come on, come on," he muttered. "They won't bite you."

Then he looked at Murphy.

"Dirlsky is in charge," he said, raising his eyebrows and jerking his thumb in the direction of the Havelock Hotel.

The hotel stood like an impregnable bastion, sprinkled with ash-dust and soot. The shutters on one side had been torn off to be used as stretchers. The hotel guard had returned to his post outside the hotel entrance. Murphy saw Sergeant Dirlsky's thin face peering over the balcony, surveying his domain.

Doctor Morrison looked at the blanket roll beside Murphy's feet.

"You're leaving us, man?" he asked. "A nice time to get away."

"I was on my way when the fire started," said Murphy defensively; but the doctor had turned away.

"Can I come with you, Murphy?" Huley pleaded.

"No. You've got to look after your mother, son."

"You mean look after her grave," said Constable Jones, as he covered up a dead face just before the helpers carried it to the wagon.

Murphy glared at Constable Jones, then he looked at Huley, then he held out his hand. Huley put his hand in Murphy's and Murphy shook it. Huley's arm flopped in response to Murphy's shake, and his shoulder jerked and his head wobbled.

"I'm proud to have met you, Huley. You're a remarkable man."

Huley beamed a big grin at the sweet sound of Murphy's words.

"Hey!" he yelled out. "Everybody! Mr Murphy said I'm remarkable...he's proud of me...eh...did you hear that...he called me a man...me a *man*!"

Murphy blushed. He smiled as he walked back to his horse, staring at the ground. He could hear the constables giggling. He looked dull and sick. His ears were red. He thought of travelling...of anything but her...maybe catching up to Danny and Price along the way...anything but think of her...

His muscles ached dreadfully as he raised his weary leg to put his foot in the stirrup, and he thought of her face the last time he saw it fleetingly alive, and the last time he looked away...

He sat still on horseback, his own back aching as he heard her laughter again. He thought of the reins in his hand, and felt the blanket roll behind him for the hardness of the pistol. He thought of anything...of anything but her, and he breathed deeply riding out into the sunlight.

His shoulders hunched and his head ducked and he sat like that, stone still, glaring ahead, his eyes downcast, when he heard the blood-chilling scream behind him. It was Huley Colquoon. This time no-one was giggling.

"Mumma!" Huley screamed hysterically, throwing his body about in the dust and crying. "Mumma! Oh, Mumma!"

Without turning, Murphy rode on.

EPILOGUE

SERGEANT DIRLSKY looked down from the balcony of the Havelock Hotel as Young Mr Callow joined him. The men below were subduing Huley Colquoon.

"Look at that bloody half-wit," laughed Dirlsky.

Sam Sodge sat staring at nothing, at the door of the parlour, his head drooping drunkenly. He held a bottle of brandy in one hand and a glass of the same in the other hand, both clutched close to his chest.

"Which one? That's the big question," laughed Sodge sardonically. "They're all as bad as each other. Not one of them stuck by me. They're *all* half-wits."

Sodge shook his head, his flaccid mouth silent for a moment. Next to him Major Stumic shrugged his shoulders helplessly and continued to fan himself.

"We could have saved the mill," Sodge blubbered. "If only we had ten men! We could have saved the mill. I didn't have even one."

He sat silently, staring at nothing, moving his lips, clutching his glass and his bottle. Dirlsky looked away, back down into the street. The hotel guard stood watching at the door, with half a smile on his face.

A dull whimper occasionally arose from the midst of the town's eerie quietness. Callow rested on the balcony rail. Even the sound of an empty dray passing in the street seemed muffled.

Callow could still smell the soap from when he had washed his dirty hands and then scraped the blood, dirt and grease from under his nails. He noted the busy lines below, beginning already to salvage, repair, establish and heal. He shook his head slowly with amazement at the resilience of the common horde, at their drive, their stamina...and that herd-like, undisciplined instinct.

He shook his head again, amazed now that he had been part of it. Now he could only look down. He saw the women share their children — those that were left — so that there would be more hands free to slave in the open, communal kitchen. He watched the teams of workers knuckle down to hopeless tasks. The plainest folk began to shine with a new-found beauty. The meek grew bold and the lazy grew willing. The strange indomitable will to survive and combine began to amuse him, for it had a funny side to it.

Callow turned back and looked across at Sam Sodge, and he smiled. That was the funny part. That was the truly amazing thing...that things could ever have been the way they were before. Callow wondered if they could ever be the same again.

He turned away from Sodge and again admired the strength of the common folk below — their genius to improvise, to make sense, hope and desire out of nothing. He raised his eyebrows and breathed the dry, acrid tang of air.

"Things will be back to normal before very long," said Dirlsky as Huley Colquoon was led away down the street by two men dragging one arm each.

"You've done a very good job, Sergeant," said Major Stumic, speaking for the first time. "Although I am sure it won't be *Sergeant* Dirlsky for very much longer."

"I expect not," said Dirlsky, grinning.

"A pity about Holman," continued Stumic. "He was a damned good chap."

"The finest," said Dirlsky, adding after a respectful pause, "I sent Constable Fraser with a detailed report of the disaster and a request for assistance."

"An excellent move," said Stumic. "Don't you think so, Mr Callow?"

"Yes, very good," said Young Mr Callow.

"Isn't it a bit late to send for help?" Sodge sneered.

OVER THE TOWN *hung an air of abjection. All about lay only desolation. No animal moved in the burnt-black fields and no bird flew except, far and high above, the eagle, beating its wings slowly, its bones aching with age as it soared above the devastation.*

Far below, as the eagle looked down, upon the dirt of lost days and the ashes of ancient fires and the dust of bones, another layer of ash was spread on the ground. In the new-born ashes lay a large blackened blade of iron with its wooden handle burned away, leaving only the melted rivets that once held it; and across the gully, part-way up the other side, lay the bone-ash of the black dancer, the dancer who sang and burned the most ancient truth out of the air — the distilled essence of time itself.

The eagle looked down under its broad wing, down on the half-dead town of pale faces, down among the incinerated dreams...down where the wind spoke of all things, and the people only heard what they already knew.